D1522265

THE MEEK SHALL INHERIT

Certain names and identifying characteristics may have been changed and adjusted for varying degrees, for various purposes.

All content by authors Cynthia Siira and Julia White
Cover design by Laura Myers
Edits by Rebecca Chedester Dussault & Sandy Theile
Art by Cynthia Siira and Julia White
Published in the United States of America

ISBN: 9798567209202 (paperback)

Any reference to historical events, real people, or real places are used fictitiously. Names, characters, and places are products of the authors' imaginations.

Facebook https://www.facebook.com/The-Meek-Shall-Inherit-117286506853251

Years ago while waiting for students in a small office next to a humming computer mainframe and over the whirring sound of the window air conditioner, Cindy and Julia wondered what would *really* happen if there were a pandemic and what the aftermath would be. Being writers, both women knew there was a story in it somewhere. Soon, these discussions morphed into delicious and creative meetings with Quiche Lorraine, muffins, and tea...and a novel was slowly nurtured to life.

Imagine our surprise when the calendar flipped to 2020...

To our families with love.

DANGER

VIRUS OUTBREAK

KEEP OUT!

February 26

Dear Dandelion,

    I can't believe so many people were absent from school today! I really didn't mind that Lily and Zoe were out. They are so obnoxious! They make everybody else feel like crap just because they think they are better than EVERYONE, but they are SO not!

    I did miss Jerimiah though. He always makes me laugh in Driver's Ed and he's a total babe! Too bad he's dating Emma. I see them together in the hallway and find myself staring. When will I get a boyfriend who looks at me like that? You know they're not married...and nobody really stays together from high school right? So...you never know!

    Mom and Dad have been crazy worried lately. It's this K-Pox thing. I get it I guess, but seriously people freak out over everything nowadays. I think that's why some kids are not at school. Yeah, I know we see it on the news every night but our country is SO dramatic! It's mostly in other countries anyway, but I guess they did say that some people are getting sick over here like in the big cities where the major airports are. I don't know, I wasn't really paying attention. I was texting Mandy.

    Some people say it's God's judgment coming. It's Revelations...talk about drama! It's all probably a ploy from some covert company to sell cough medicine. I mean look around! It's not like fire is raining down or darkness or whatever. Those people are just crazy. There's always someone spouting off about it being the end of the world. Crazy cults everywhere. My pastor always says the world is an unreliable source of information when we are deciding how to act. I would say he is definitely right in this case.

    I did hear today though that they have started to restrict entry into the United States. I don't know how they are going to do that! What about US citizens? Who does the government think they are? They can't just start kicking people

1

out or not letting people come back to their families!! We are Americans...not freakin Nazi Germany! People are so obtuse sometimes.

Watch. Tomorrow it will be the Chicken flu or the Manatee flu...ha ha. I'm going to text Mandy that. She loves Manatees. But anyways, whatever this "serious care of the sniffles" is, I'm sure we'll wake up tomorrow and it will all be gone.

Partly sunny, but Optimistic
Ashleigh

To: Theresa.schultz@zahoo.nop
From: Meg.schultz@zahoo.nop
Date: February 27 at 4:31 pm
Subject: Coming home?

Hey Mom,

I'm sure you've heard about this K-Pox thing. You said you had one more meeting in LA and then you were coming home. I sure hope you got your ticket cuz I hear that some flights are being canceled. So...keep that in mind and get home soon!

Life is going on here as usual, but there are rumors that school is going to be closed soon. Probably just for a few weeks til all the disease is gone. I hope it is only for a few weeks. It's my senior year and I don't want it to mess up all my senior year stuff!! Prom and graduation I definitely don't want to miss. Can you imagine!

Anyway...Jen and Rachel and I drove around town yesterday and ended up at Albee's Diner for some hot chocolate. Not too many people there, but they still had chocolate! Which is important. Can't run out of chocolate! We are all totally upset about losing our senior year if school is closed. I mean for how long? How do we make up our work? Do we graduate? When? Will colleges count credits if we are missing days? Lots of questions that no one is answering!! But we want to KNOW! NOW! Of course there are a bunch of kids that are totally excited about no school. But they aren't thinking about the future!! I mean what do we do if there is no school! I know! I'm a nerd. But...oh well...

Anyway we're doing okay here. Just let us know when you are coming home. AND Mitchell is driving me crazy as usual. And Dad is letting me handle the Mitchell babysitting situation, as usual. Not good!! Another reason to get home!!! You'd think that since Mitchell is 11 he wouldn't need babysitting, BUT he is always into something and needing something—mostly food. I don't know how you put up with it! I really don't.

Gotta run. Homework to do...assuming we'll be in school tomorrow.

Your favorite daughter! 😊
Meg

PS: To be honest I don't think there will be school tomorrow. Teachers were acting like we'd not be back soon and the administration made an announcement at the end of the day that we should take home any books we needed in case we'd be out for a while. The kids all cheered. But I'm just trying to be optimistic...

March 1

Dear Dandelion,

    I am SSSOOOOO freakin frustrated! They cancelled school! They cancelled music concerts, they cancelled travel, they cancelled EVERYTHING! People are completely freaking out and we don't even have anyone sick here! The bigger cities have people getting sick and all the news can talk about is this stupid virus. The stores are basically being overrun by people trying to hoard food and supplies and hospitals are getting swamped with people. It's crazy!!!

    Mandy and I have been texting and I think I am going to sneak over and see her later before my parents lock me in the house. I can see they are getting worried and THAT freaks me out. If THEY are scared, then something is REALLY wrong. But I can't stay in this house with Mom and Dad worrying and the world going CRAZY! It's like the whole world is screeching to a sickening halt and I don't understand. I am so confused and scared and angry and frustrated and terrified. WHAT IS HAPPENING?????

Wind gusts and astonished,
Ashleigh

To: Theresa.schultz@zahoo.nop
From: Meg.schultz@zahoo.nop
Date: March 7 at 4:31 pm
Subject: Coming home?

Mom, they closed school and your flight was canceled and you aren't home and Mitchell is a mess and Dad is working from home and we haven't heard from you in days!!! Please get in touch! This is driving me crazy. We're all stuck at home and can't go out.

People are dying like crazy. It's so scary!! We're all hiding in our houses...hiding from death. You need to be here. If we're going to die we should be together!

You said you got a car and are heading east. You said that you'd be in Arizona 2 days ago when we last heard from you. You said you'd keep in touch! You're not answering your texts or emails or phone or anything. ANSWER!! Please!!!

I love you Mom, Please come home.

Your favorite daughter
Meg

March 8

Dandelion, it's here! People are getting sick and dying!!!!! They are DYING!!! Kids from my school, people from church, EVERYONE! I know that I haven't talked to you since I was little. You were just my toy doll then, but Dandelion, I wish I could go back to when everything felt safe and death wasn't an ugly rain pouring its poison out everywhere. Churches are having funerals and they ring the bells at the end of each service. It feels like they just keep ringing and ringing...like a noisy blur of clanging death and despair!!!! I sometimes wish whoever's ringing them would just die too...Uggggh! You KNOW I don't mean that, but it's just so horrible!!! We stopped going to funerals b/c everyone's too scared of getting sick. There's a few priests and ministers staying at the churches so they can give funeral blessings.... I just imagine them standing there alone praying...surrounded by all those dead bodies. They're not even putting people in caskets b/c they ran out! They said they're just going to start cremating people and maybe that'd help stop the infection. I don't know. I can't imagine just burning everyone. Just piles of ashes... Do you think it's all going into the air...like PEOPLE-ash??? And we're breathing it in?! Oh I'm going to be sick!

What if we're next? What if I lose Mom and Dad? It's just me! Why didn't they have more kids??? At least then I'd have a brother or sister to be scared with. Mandy says it'll all be okay, but I don't know what to do. Mom says we should stay secluded because it's safer, but now the radio says we should all go to central meeting places to conserve and share resources and have access to medical care. But I agree with Mom!! I don't want to go out there! But Dad says we're going if that's what they tell us to do and no arguing! He's sooo obnoxious sometimes! We don't always HAVE to follow the rules DAD!!!

Dandelion, I'm so scared. I feel like that little girl again that used to hide under the covers. Do you remember? You were

7

my favorite toy and I just knew you had magical powers to make everything ok. I held you so tight and prayed for the closet demons to go away. I used to imagine that when I closed my eyes you had real wings and they were so powerful they covered my whole room and the demons with their ugly faces just bounced off them. Then I would laugh and I wouldn't be scared anymore. Do you remember?

But it's not like that now. This demon is real and every time I close my eyes I can't make it go away. If you have any magical powers left or if you turned into a real angel, please help me not be scared. I wish God would come and rescue us! It's like He's turned his back on us! Why would He do this to us? I feel like I'm going to die from fear. I don't want to die.

Cloudy skies and stormy heart,
Ashleigh

To: Theresa.schultz@zahoo.nop
From: Meg.schultz@zahoo.nop
Date: March 9 at 5:34 am
Subject: Where are you?

Hey Mom,

They're putting skull signs on people's doors where people have KPox!! They just have to die there by themselves cuz there's no help for them!! There are signs on our block!!! Where are you?????? I haven't heard from you in days!!!!! I tried leaving texts and voice messages. Are you getting my emails????? If you are, please respond!! I'm scared. The news is talking about riots and looting all over and transportation's messed up. And you aren't here and I'm afraid you won't be coming home soon. Your last email said you'd be home soon. When is soon? Arizona isn't that far away. We haven't heard from you since your car broke down. Did you get another car???

Please respond!! If you don't then I'll know your email isn't working or your phone's messed up or something. Please let me know where you are! I'm telling Mitchell you hope to be here soon, but I don't want to lie to him. I really don't. Dad says things will be okay--we just have to be patient! PATIENT!? Come on.

So many people dying!!!! I'm scared!! It really makes me think about death and what I'd want at my funeral. I don't want to think about death!! But if I do--which I won't--but just in case—I want to be cremated and have my ashes sprinkled in the backyard. I know that sounds silly, but I want to stay close to home. But that's just morbid. We'll be okay!! Dad keeps us at home so we won't get sick. I hope.

Your favorite daughter
Meg

PS: Please come home!! I'm scared!!

9

US Highway 54, New Mexico. Newspaper after newspaper blowing in the wind from the back of a truck. Driver still at the wheel. Dead.

The Boston Times
March 9

Jason Williams

It has been a nightmare scenario. Kongla Pox. The virus everyone has nicknamed K-Pox or the "Red Death" is responsible for the plague that is ravaging our homes and destroying our world faster than even nuclear war. A viral mutation that mimics the deadly symptoms of Smallpox and Ebola, has not responded to traditional treatments or medicines and has left doctors and healers confused, aghast, and most likely dead from contact. The few cases that started out as anomalies have blossomed into a full-blown epidemic, raging through cities and towns, tearing families apart, and leaving a sickening carnage of bodies in its wake. Dr. Herman Fitzgerald, leading virologist at Hayden College of Medicine reported that he believed "K-Pox, the deadly airborne virus, is now known to be the most lethal virus ever to strike mankind." K-Pox has spread around the world at an unfathomable speed showing no signs of stopping.

The first victim is unknown; the first village, Zambulu, will not be forgotten. A village of 87 souls--but within two weeks, not one survivor. One after another, neighboring villages fell. The largest medical teams ever assembled tried desperately to find ways to stop the disease. No cure has been found.

After inhaling the virus, K-Pox immediately attacks the respiratory system and lymph nodes. The virus does not incubate, but explodes through the body. Painful lesions quickly form on the skin, in the mouth and on the scalp, spewing putrification into the air, to be inhaled by the next victim. High fever follows, then fatigue, nausea, vomiting, pain, and disorientation. The once flawless collaboration of the body's organs ceases to exist. Then the bloodshed begins.

Blood begins to permeate the body cavities and seeps out of the eyes, nose, ears, and gums. The skin is mottled with contusions and congealed pools of blood; limbs swell and contort and bodies blacken as death draws near. For the lucky ones, they lose consciousness and are spared the final hours of torture; for others,

10

an excruciatingly painful death before the heart collapses.

We have all been witness to friends and family succumbing to this vicious disease, and billions of unrecognizable corpses tell our stories of sorrow. K-Pox has shed more blood than all wars combined. It has barely been three months since the scourge began in Zambulu, but as of this date it is estimated that 90% of the world's population has been lost, with reports that it will be higher.

Before emergency alert systems failed, city officials ordered everyone to take supplies and head to central locations for food, shelter, and medical care. People arrived in droves seeking hope and sanctuary in large cities, but many died in that vain journey. Others chose to take profit from loss—fighting, vandalizing, killing, stealing supplies they would never use. These riches did not spare lives. Lifeless bodies of vandals clutching useless treasures lie next to the innocent dead. There is no one to support technology, no one to operate electrical plants, no one to provide medical care. Reports are scattered. Communication broken.

But deep within the carnage, there is a glimmer of hope. The last radio message received from Dr. Judith Web, Director of Infectious Disease Control, reported, "Surprisingly, there appear to be some human survivors, those that have encountered the disease and not gotten sick. It could be that people from the same bloodline may be genetically immune. We don't know for sure. There are too many questions, but hopefully the answers are still out there."

This is the last printing of the Boston Times. I have printed 100 thousand copies of this editorial to stand as a testimony for a future that is unknown. I am taking a truck and driving west to distribute this to as many locations as possible. Hopefully this testament will find its way to the living for history's sake.

May God quickly gather those of us infected, and have mercy on the souls left behind.

March 10

Dear Dandelion,

   Dad found two little kids hiding in the barn at the farm...Adam and Ava. They were both carrying little kid backpacks...the kind with their names embroidered on the front. The backpacks were stuffed with food and survival stuff and they had emergency cards with their full names, birth dates, and last address. They were from a different town. They had little toys and pictures in there too...their parents must've packed them up...but we have no idea where their parents are, it's so horrible! Dad said they must've wandered from the interstate. Poor little kids. They were so hungry and terrified. Adam's only four. He's not talking much. I can't believe he was watching over his sister too. She's so little, just three! What would've happened to them if Dad hadn't been going out there?? What if there's more children out there with no parents?? What if there's just tons of people wandering around lost and hungry and desperate???? God HELP US!!!

March 11

Dear Mom,

I hate that email is down! And I can't contact you at all! But I'm going to write anyway cuz I like writing to you. It gives me something to do, as the days are sooo long and boring since we can't go anywhere. Dad says we have to stay away from everyone since we don't know who's sick or who isn't. Or worse yet—who we can trust. Before we lost tv and the internet all the news talked about was looting and riots. It's scary how people freak out when life gets messed up. Like what gives you the right to trash stores and steal stuff in people's houses when it isn't yours. Really!? You just take stuff? Like kicking people when they're already down. And what's weird is people are taking everything. The news filmed people hauling off furniture and jewelry and food. What do you do with jewelry when you're dead? Now food I can understand. You actually <u>need</u> food so I think that is different. And toilet paper. Can you believe that people were totally freaking out about toilet paper. The news said that some people who died had tons of toilet paper they were hoarding. And now it can't be used cuz it is all covered with KPox germs. Dumb! Come on. You shoulda shared!

So many people have left town or maybe they died but you just don't see people anywhere. At all! Not even any cars driving anymore. But Dad says we aren't leaving our house. He says if KPox is spread through the air, it's stupid to be in contact with people and then maybe die. So we stay inside and see no one. I understand, but it's <u>so boring</u>!!! I mean Mitchell's absolutely going nuts. Trying to keep him in the yard is crazy hard.

It's weird how many people on the block are gone. Partly cuz we were told to go to central meeting places for food and

13

shelter. But apparently tons of people died due to all that closeness—so they closed all the Centers. Oops! Bad initial decision! But Dad totally refused to go. I was glad, but Mitchell had a fit when he first found out we weren't going. He sulked and carried on and said he wanted friends. I didn't have the heart to tell him some of his friends were probably dead. But he got over it fairly quickly when Dad said "That's enough!!" in his very stern father voice. Which we don't hear very often to tell the truth.

btw I stopped carrying my cell phone as no one is texting. I guess the system is down or friends are all dead. Don't want to think about that!! Do you know how weird it is not carrying that little rectangle in my left hand everywhere I go? When I first stopped carrying it, I kept wondering what was wrong, that something was missing! But now I'm getting used to not having it. But it's still kinda weird. And I really miss not having my friends there with me in seconds.

You know I told you that Jen and Rachel's families left when everyone went to the Centers, and I haven't gotten a text or call from Jen in ages. And I'm pretty sure that Rachel didn't go because…well…I don't even want to say she's not with us anymore. It's too hard. And I want her to be with her family and laughing her silly giggly laugh and picking on her little sister. And we'll all get together soon and drink diet cokes and eat chips on her back porch and plan for our graduation beach weekend. So I keep pretending that she's at a Center, but Mom, I really don't think she is. And I've cried and cried about it. I really miss not having my friends around. We could've all talked about this whole horrible situation. We had so many plans for graduation and prom and everything. This was our senior year.

We had so many things planned!! And now we can't do any of them!! It is SO NOT FAIR!!! IT IS NOT FAIR!! I really hope they both made it. I hate not knowing! <u>I really hate this</u>! But I will assume the best. I don't think I can live with my thoughts if I don't. At least I know that Dad and Mitchell are alive. And you are too! We just don't know where.

Speaking of Dad, he's totally depressed! When the internet started messing up he sat at the computer for several days trying to get things going—hoping it was just our connection. I don't think he knows what to do without his computer—which is pathetic. He actually went into other people's homes hoping to get a connection at their houses! He finally gave up, but he still sits at his desk. Mom—I think he's a bit nuts. He barely talks to us. He expects me to cook and clean and take care of Mitchell like I'm some kind of live-in nanny. I'm his <u>daughter</u>! Not a nanny! Besides, Mitchell's almost 12, NOT 2. He needs his Dad more than his sister. And even though I'm almost 18, I still need to be taken care of too! I need him to be there for me—and Mitchell. Not just <u>me</u> being there for Mitchell. When Mitchell tries to talk to Dad, he's "busy". He says "Go talk to Meg." Go talk to Meg??? Who put me in charge?? He's not my kid. He's Dad's kid—and <u>your</u> kid. So Mom--I really need you to come home. NOW!!!!!!!! Your very last email said you were on the way home and driving through Arizona. You were concerned about getting gas. Well, even if you have to steal cars with gas...get back NOW!!! We need you! Just steal cars!!!

You should've been here already. I'm totally mad at you and Dad! I'm so MAD!!! You should be here! Dad should be doing his part of the chores. Mitchell should stop expecting me to entertain him. K-Pox should stop and go away so life can get back to normal. I want to go back to school. I want to graduate this year. I _am_ graduating this year! I better graduate this year! I better!!

I have to go now. Mitchell's whining that he's hungry and Dad's yelling for me to feed him. AAAAAAAAAAAAAA!!!!!

Your favorite daughter
Meg

PS: It's really scary—this KPox. Really really scary. I'm trying to pretend that I'm not totally freaked out, but I am. I really am. I want to be strong for Dad and Mitchell, but I'm not strong. I'm scared to death...actually not "to death".... Too much death around here to say that when you don't really mean it. Only there's no one around to talk to. I really want you home. Please? Please come home. I cry every night wishing you were here to take care of us. I love you Mom.

March 13

Dear Dandelion,
    Grrrr!!!! I can't believe I can't talk to my best friend! My parents are so unfair!!! My cell phone stopped working and they won't let me go over to see Mandy b/c her brother started coughing. That was like 2 days ago! Maybe they're better! But Mr. and Mrs. Worrywarts said absolutely not! She's my best friend! I want to just run over there and tell her it'll be okay. I know Mandy's scared even if she says she's not. I may just go anyway...no one's gonna catch me. There has to be something I can do for her!
    AANNNND MOOOOOM won't let me go with Dad out to the farm right now to help milk the cows and feed the other animals. I know he's going to other farms that have been abandoned to gather supplies and save other animals if he can, so I'm sure he needs my help! But SHE says she doesn't think it's smart for a young girl to be anywhere alone right now. I would only be alone for short periods of time I'm sure...Ugggh! So annoying! I can take care of MYSELF! And of course Dad agrees with her! I think THEY are just scared and afraid to be around other people and don't know what to do, but it's RUINING my LIFE!
    Weeks ago, we went to the central meeting place like they told us to. Mom and I didn't want to go, but Dad said the radio said we should so you know him and his rule-following! It was so weird sleeping on cots and sharing space, but it was nice to have other people to talk to. We were only there part of a day and overnight though.
    At breakfast that last day, Mrs. Fox (she was cashier at our grocery store) started coughing and everyone around her started jumping up and covering their mouths and noses. I just knew she was a goner! But when two staff ran over and grabbed her arms, she yelled, "I choked on my water! I just swallowed wrong! I'm not sick!" You should've seen the looks on everyone's

faces. And then everyone just cracked up! It was hysterical! we were all laughing for like 20 minutes. I don't think we'd laughed in ages. :) But then Mr. Westford (he's dead now :(ran in and said that meeting places were closing down due to high rates of infection and no medical staff. Everyone needed to leave NOW! Mom started crying and Dad just started throwing our stuff back in the bags and yelling for me to grab Adam and Ava and get moving. Everyone was wild and just trying to get out as soon as possible. We came right back home and locked all the doors!

I'm sure Mrs. Fox is dead now too. She was always snotty to us at the grocery store, but she didn't deserve to die. It doesn't seem to matter if people are snotty or nice. They just die. And so many people left town too. It's mostly quiet during the day, but we hear trucks driving around at night and hear gunshots. Not in our neighborhood, but close enough! Mom covered our windows with black out curtains so people couldn't see in the house, or the lights at night.

I know I wanted to stay secluded at first, but now I keep thinking we should be looking for other people...allies you know? But how could we feed everybody? Dad's been getting bottled water from the grocery stores (the stores' doors have been broken open) because we're afraid the water system's going to shut off, but how long will that last? And he's only taking a little at a time b/c he doesn't want somebody dangerous to find out and follow him home. We have the stream nearby too...bottled water is not worth getting killed over!

We've been going to our neighbors' houses to get food. Not the ones with the skull signs...we only go to the ones where we know healthy neighbors left town. We have a stockpile, but Dad keeps saying we don't know what winter will be like. How do we plan for months...or YEARS from now? Are we going to survive this disease only to starve to death?? What if Mom is right and people try to rob us???!! I know Mom can shoot Dad's rifle, but what am I going to do?? Hit them with a bat??? I don't want to knock anyone out! What if it's a gang of men and they....I don't even want to think about anything worse! Isn't this all bad enough??!! Ugggh! I don't know what to think! I just want to go see Mandy!!!!

AND Dad was talking to mom about judgment day and I get so confused! I wish he'd shut up about that. I mean, this isn't how it goes, right? Didn't Pastor Ben say when the world ends Jesus will come down and take us back with him? And look! Nobody's been swept up by a heavenly wind or anything! Pastor and his wife left in a plain ol' car just like everyone else. They could be dead now for all I know. Christian or not, lots and lots of people are dying. I don't get it, I never understood that stupid judgment day thing anyway. But if it's not that, then why are we getting wiped out? How will we live? Like thieves and animals that scrounge for food? Is that all we are now? Just mindless animals left to fend for themselves?

My heart aches for all that's been lost. Not just the people, but EVERYTHING. All the knowledge in the world. All the history, all the memories. K-Pox ate it all. Like a filthy gluttonous pig. All that we've done to make the earth a better place...and now it's ravaged. It's a barren wasteland of hopelessness. What will ever make us whole again now?

Moonless night and aching heart,
Ashleigh

March 16

Dear Mom,

Damn damn damn damn damn damn damn!!!!!!!!!!!!!!!!!! We lost power. Apparently for good. Electricity hasn't been that great for several weeks--flickering on and off. So when it went down again, we weren't too worried. But it hasn't come back on so.... I guess we're stuck now with no power until the utilities get back up and running. Assuming they will get back up and running. They always have before. But it's so frustrating not to be able to call and get someone--even a stupid recording would be nice--saying that the power company knows the power's out in such and such an area and they're working on it--expect power back in an hour or so. But no, nothing. Just nothing. So here we are with no power. Thank goodness Dad got us heaters, lanterns and flashlights and stuff so we aren't totally in the dark. But my goodness, is it dark outside! But no power means no frig or real stove (just a stupid camp stove) no washing machine--I hate not having a washing machine--or lights or phone or tv or music or anything...It's the total pits!!! I'm really hating this whole KPox thing. It's ruining my life! I was supposed to graduate this year. I don't guess that's happening anymore. I should be planning for the prom and shopping with Jennifer and Rachel for prom dresses and sending out graduation invitations--and I don't suppose you'll be here--as you haven't shown up yet. I hate not having my friends! I really miss them. It's really lonely. I hate it!

Oh, and no power means no water!!! Do you know what that means?! NO WATER!! No flushing toilets. No tap water. No washing anything. No water. How do we live without running water? Dad and Mitchell took the car (yes the car, even when

20

Dad said we shouldn't do that or people might find us) and filled up the whole car with bottled water from the grocery store. He said he took half of what was there cuz we know other people are hiding around town and he didn't want to be a water hog. And he and Mitchell are going to bring back water from the river, or is it a creek? How do you know the difference? Anyway, we'll be getting skunky water that we have to boil and filter and yuck! I am <u>so done</u> with this stupid KPox! It can be over <u>right now</u> and it wouldn't be too soon!

AND I was thinking...since gas stations need power for their gas pumps, and if you don't have power where you are, I guess you won't be able to get gas for your car anymore. And the credit card companies won't be able to okay your card. So now what will you do? I guess you'll have to keep stealing cars to get home and hope that people were stupid enough to leave keys in their cars--and have full tanks of gas. Or siphon gas out of other people's cars. Can you do that with new cars? I asked Dad. He said that he didn't know. He said, "I'd tell you to google it, but the internet is down." Brilliant comment. Duh! So I'm worried about you even more now. Well, I'm worried about you a lot all the time. I wish you were home with us. We really need you.

Your favorite daughter
Meg

btw—I totally appreciate things more now that they're gone. I never thought about trash pickup before. It just happened. Once a week all trash just magically disappeared! And now we have to reduce reuse recycle all the stuff we can and Dad either burns or buries our garbage. But to be honest, we don't have much garbage anymore. Since trash is all over, in some places the smell is <u>not</u> good. I think the only thing saving us is that it's been cold, and the animals have eaten most of the food garbage, but there's still a lot of mess around. Dad's making Mitchell and me clean up around our street so it isn't too bad, but when we walk to the grocery store there's still some really stinky messy places. And I tell myself the stinky houses with the skull signs just have a lot of trash in them, but I think it's more than that. Totally sad (and a little creepy).

March 17

Dear Dandelion,

    Mandy's sick! Dear God don't take her! I don't care if Mom and Dad say I just need to pray, that doesn't seem like enough! I want YOU and God to save her RIGHT NOW!! Do You hear me??!!!

    I snuck out to see her. I know I wasn't supposed to, but she's all I have left. I waited until everyone was asleep and I ran down the back trail to her house. The moon was full so I didn't use my flashlight, but I was running and tripped and fell. My hands were all bloody and gross, but I didn't care, I just needed to see her and I had to get back before my parents knew I was gone. I brought her some food and candy that I snuck from a neighbor's house. I wanted her to have something and I don't know if they've been getting supplies like us.

    When I got there...they had the sign in the window. The stupid creepy crossbones signs that the ignorant, worthless health department made everyone put up when they knew people had K-Pox. It's supposed to warn others of contamination, but it just seems like once people put those stupid, horrible revolting signs up, no one ever leaves those houses again. I wanted to tear it down. Tear it down and just burn it to ashes!!

    I climbed the tree outside her window and pulled the cord that jingles the bell in her room like we always did. I just kept praying and praying that she was in there and not downstairs. But then saw a match spark and there she was...standing with a lit candle at the window. She struggled as she opened the window, and I could finally see her face...she looked bad...pale and...even when she smiled...she looked so gray. She held up a walkie-talkie and pointed to a bag hanging by where I was sitting. She said she'd left it out there when her family got sick. She even put the walkie-talkie in a plastic bag so it wouldn't get wet when it rained. She's so smart. Not like me. She's always the one that made sense of things...

23

I told her that we're okay and we're not sick and I told her about finding little Adam and his sister Ava. She said I finally got the siblings I always wanted. I smiled at that, but I told her she was the only sister I ever really wanted. I told her I don't know if K-Pox is coming for us, but we feel like we'd have it by now if we were going to get sick. I told her we were trying to prepare for the future and we both laughed a little because that's what Dad always says...You gotta be prepared! With little sticky note reminders everywhere!

She was quiet for a minute then she told me her brother will probably die tomorrow. She said they've been praying for him to go because he's been so sick and it's horrible to watch. He'd been crying and screaming b/c he hurt so bad and there's nothing they can do...but now the fever's so high he just lies there and he's started to bleed out his nose and eyes. She said they just want him to die quickly...so he won't be in pain anymore.

He's only 8!! He shouldn't have to know all that suffering!!! Her Dad is sick too and the fever has started...and her mom just started coughing today. Mandy said her mom says it's only a matter of time now...so all they could do is wait for God to bring them home...

And...And...then Mandy started coughing... Just this awful, sickening sound. Like her lungs were wet sponges filled with glass and syrup. It sounded like her lungs were ripping apart but collapsing all at the same time...She had to sit down and I couldn't see her below the window. I just wanted to scream and scream...just yell her name and go to her...but I was scared...God help me I was so scared and I just froze in that tree and I waited and I sobbed because my heart was dying in my chest.

Finally she stopped coughing and I was terrified I'd lost her already. She grabbed onto the window sill...her hand and arm was covered with bleeding sores...then I saw her face again and she said I was her best friend and she'd miss me when she was eating all her favorite foods and running around on the clouds in

Heaven. She even smiled and said it was too bad we didn't have that double wedding like we planned. I just cried and cried and I told her I loved her and she was my best friend too and I didn't want to leave her here to die. But she said I had to...there was nothing to be done.

She said her mom told her there's nothing to be afraid of in death. They know where they're going and Heaven is a beautiful place with no sickness and no pain. God is with them...with all of us, even if we couldn't see each other. I couldn't stop crying.

And I kept my head down so I wouldn't see her eyes dying in front of me. But then she said "Remember this?" and I looked up. She was holding a picture of us at Camp Levande when we were ten years old. I remembered. That was the year we pierced my ears and my parents had a cow and we went canoeing in the moonlight and she ate nine s'mores all in one night and we laughed so hard the counselors threatened to move us to different bunks. She smiled. It was our favorite summer. I smiled back.

And then she looked at me the way she always does...with that no sass allowed look. She made me promise if I lived through all this, I'd protect my family and I'd fall in love like we have always talked about.......only if a hot guy survived though! We laughed at that. And I had to promise to take her with me...I told her that she'd be awfully heavy in my backpack! But we laughed and cried at the same time and I told her I'd always carry her with me in my heart. I told her she better watch over me real good in Heaven too and not get distracted by all the angels singing and chocolate and cute boys that have died from our high school! And she smiled that sad smile again and said she promised.

Then she told me to go. We didn't want my parents to come out looking for me and something bad happening to them. I wished the walkie-talkie signal reached to my house, but it doesn't. I left it behind. I told her I'd be back and be praying for her...I didn't want to leave. I don't even remember how I

25

made it back in the dark. I was crying so hard I had to stop a couple times, but I kept going.

I snuck in the house and just went right into my room and locked the door. I didn't want anyone coming in and seeing me crying. I feel sick in my very soul.

Maybe Mandy will be okay, right? God, maybe you can work a miracle through her? She's all I have...the only true heart sister I have...please, please help her! She's such a good person! Remember she volunteers at the nursing home? Remember she's the one who offered to tutor those terrible Smith boys when they got expelled? Remember?? You don't need her. You've taken enough!!! If she dies God, I will hate you forever! FOREVER!! YOU HEAR ME??? FOR-EV-ER!!!

March 24

Dear Mom,

    Last night was horrible!! I was so scared! Two guys tried to break in our house! I told you our neighbors are gone. So that means lights are out—except for solar powered ones. Some houses were broken into already but Dad cleaned yards near us so houses look like someone might be home. Anyway...we had our lanterns on in the living room with curtains closed and were playing cards and you can't see the light from the front door. All of a sudden we heard a car outside. Actually what we heard were car doors slamming and guys laughing. So Dad says to Mitchell, "Turn off the light!" And Dad looked out the front door window. He waved for us to move back, but me and Mitchell went to the front window and peeked out. Two guys walked to the house across the street. They broke the windows by throwing the yard gnomes through them and laughed like crazy. I think they were drunk cuz I don't think people laugh like that when they're sober. They climbed into the house through the windows. We could hear them trashing the place. It sounded awful. Glass breaking, chairs (or something wood) crashing, loud ugly laughs. I was so focused on watching to make sure when they came out that I didn't notice that Dad had slipped away and had gotten his guns out. You know Dad--he's not a gun guy, but since all the looting, he's gotten a gun for each of us. We haven't had to shoot them yet, but he showed us how--just in case. Yuck! I don't like guns! He quietly slid up the window where we were crouching, cut the screen, and pushed the rifle barrel out. My heart was beating like crazy. I could hear us breathing. It's weird when you can hear people breathing--though we were trying to breathe quietly. Dad whispers...If they come this way I want you

27

to get away from the window. Mitchell asked. "What do I do? Will they come in our house?

Dad said "Don't be scared--but we do need to be careful. Just do as I say. You hear me!"

We both nodded. The only reason we could see was cuz the moonlight was so bright. (Doesn't it seem odd that you can see at night by moonlight?) Anyway after a while--seemed like ages--those guys finally came out carrying tvs and big black plastic trash bags with stuff in them. They must've made at least 3 trips each. We could see them trying to decide what to do next. They looked at our house and started to walk up the sidewalk. I was totally freaking out in my mind. Dad told us to get away from the window and told Mitchell to get behind him and to do what he was told NOW! He handed me a rifle. "You too, Meg. Use the gun if you have to. Protect yourself. Take the safety off now. Get behind me!"

Mitchell and I went behind him, kinda going into the living room, but where we could still see him. We heard Dad yell out. "Stop where you are or I'll shoot!"

The laughing stopped and the guys yelled back, "Hey man, don't shoot. We're not interested in your house--just bring us your jewelry and cash and we'll move on."

"No! Get out of my yard now or I shoot!" Apparently they didn't move away so Dad put his rifle out the window and shot. BLAM!! OMG it was so loud! Mitchell jumped and I almost screamed.

The guys yelled "Whoa Dude! There's only one of you and two of us. Just give us your stuff and you don't have to shoot. And we won't have to shoot you." They started laughing again.

Dad whispered to me, "Meg, go upstairs and open the

28

window and shoot high right after you hear me shoot again. Mitchell, get ready to take over in case I get hit." Mitchell looked scared but stood behind Dad with rifle ready.

I ran up to the master bedroom and opened the window, making as little noise as possible. After a minute or so and giving me time to get upstairs, Dad responded. "I'm not here alone. Get off my lawn!" He shot again. BLAM! I saw grass fly up in front of their feet. I shot then through the screen--way up in the air above their heads. I heard the bullet hit the neighbor's house. Gosh the gun kicked my shoulder so hard I almost dropped the gun! OW! But it worked! One of the guys said, "Okay, okay, you made your point. We don't need your stuff. Plenty in these other houses." They laughed again, climbed back in their car, and drove further down the street. We heard them for hours. Trashing houses, yelling, occasionally shooting guns. We stayed up all night to make sure they didn't sneak back. By morning the car was out of sight. Dad went out and was gone for ages to make sure they were gone. And it was quiet again. It's kinda weird we found out through them that we're definitely the only ones left for at least three blocks down. The only ones left! How weird is that!? But we're going to stay put. Dad wants to stay here and so do I. You have to be able to find us when you get home.

Well I'm tired and I'm going to get some sleep. Last night was awful. Glad it's over! And my shoulder's sore from that stupid gun!

Your favorite daughter
Meg

PS: What if I'd had to shoot one of those guys? I guess I could, to protect Mitchell—but could I? I don't know. I hope I don't ever have to find out. And if I did have to shoot someone...I'd have to learn how to actually shoot the gun! Would I even be any good at it???

March 27

Dear Mom,

Since the break-in a few nights ago things have changed! Actually <u>Dad</u> changed things! Dad's actually becoming involved with us!! Very cool! So anyway...Dad said we need to make our house look deserted and ransacked so we won't be targeted again. We smashed our front windows, taped a KPox sign on the front door (which we stole from a dead neighbor's door), and knocked over our garden ornaments. Sorry Mom--I know you like the little stone bunny by the door. Well, he's still there--he's just lying on his side like he's dead—like most of the population around here. I'm glad it isn't winter anymore cuz our front windows are broken now. Dad had us move a bunch of stuff upstairs. We made yours and Dad's big bedroom into the living room. He took the guest bedroom to sleep in. We don't have much to cook anymore but we do go downstairs to warm up our soup on the camp stove and eat our pbj crackers. Powdered milk tastes gross by the way. So we're now living upstairs and can't go outside--which totally freaks Mitchell out--cuz he's inside too much as it is.

But Dad even fixed that too! :) I know! Dad fixed it--not ME! Mitchell was running up and down the halls bouncing a basketball, throwing the ball into a trash can, and making loud cheering crowd noises. Dad was reading a book--about computers of course--and he said "Mitchell! Be quiet for about the 100th time. Find something quiet to do!"

Mitchell said "I'm trying to find something to do! I'm tired of being quiet! But there's <u>nothing to do</u>!! Can't <u>you</u> spend time with me? You never spend time with me! Ever! I hate this! I have to be quiet and I can't play with friends and I can't do anything!

You and Meg like to read. I hate reading. There's nothing for me to do. I hate KPox and I hate you!" He ran to his room and slammed the door! Wow, that was surprising! He's been so good and patient (for Mitchell) all this time. But I'm not surprised at what he said.

Well, Dad just sat there about two minutes--looking into space--thinking. Then he sighed, put down his book, and went to Mitchell's room. I followed him--yeah, I'm nosey.

"Mitchell, may I come in?" Mitchell said something but he was talking into his pillow so he could've said no. Dad went in anyway, and sat on the bed.

So Dad said he was sorry and he's been so focused on the overwhelming problems we're going through that he's been ignoring us kids. But he was going to change that and do more with us. He asked Mitchell what he wanted him to do.

You should've seen Mitchell. He sat up and his face just lit up. "Will you let me go on exploring expeditions with you?"

"Sure we'll hang out more, go exploring. And Meg"--he knew I was in the hall—"what do you want from me?"

Well, if Dad was going to spend time with Mitchell then apparently he was taking over part of the "babysitting" which was great. But I still had stuff I wanted to tell him. I started out quiet and nice, but kinda got carried away. "Yeah, I don't want to be the cook all the time. Just because I'm a girl doesn't mean I should have to do all the housework. That's not fair! It's just not fair!" And Mom--I started to cry. Seriously--I really truly cried. So embarrassing. I was going to be all grown up and say what I had to say. And then I burst into tears. I just bawled like a baby, big old sobs--crying on Dad's shoulder. But I was so relieved that he was there for us, acting like he cared, like he loved us. He's been so uncaring for so long--even before KPox. He went to work, came home and went to the computer. That's it. I've been doing your job and his. I'm so tired and scared. And Dad said he was sorry, that he shouldn't have been so blind. He called me his little angel. He hasn't called me his little angel in ages and ages. It was so nice to have him hold me and I felt so much better knowing he was there for us again. And then I cried and cried some more. Anyway in the middle of all my boo hooing and nose blowing--Dad said he'd help more and we'd work it all out so things were fair. He said he'd be there for us now and to let him know when he wasn't doing what he should be. Mitchell got tired of all the talking and crying and slapped Dad's arm and yelled, "Tag! You're it! You're too old to catch me!" Dad raced after Mitchell and they ran out the back door.

So I ran after them. We played tag and hide n seek and kickball. Little kid games, but it was so much fun. And for supper we made tuna salad on crackers and ate outside on the picnic table. We didn't go in until it got dark and cold. Then we went up to our new living room and Dad started to read us Peter Pan. Mitchell fell asleep in the middle of the first chapter and Dad carried him to bed. I went to bed early too. It was a VERY GOOD DAY! First one in a very long time! All we needed was you, Mom.

Your favorite daughter
Meg

April 8

Dear Mandy,

I haven't written in a while, but it's been too hard. After I went back to your house and you didn't answer the walkie-talkie...I knew you were gone. I feel like there's a huge hole in my chest...like I'm walking through muck and I can't shake it off. I feel pulled down by the weight of my sorrow. Chained in a cavernous pit of anguish and misery...

I'm writing to you now cuz I know you're listening up there. Writing to Dandelion used to be fun, but she wasn't real...just a childhood toy...a memory of something that used to be...like this town. Some days I just feel so lost. I want to run and run and run...but where would I go? There's nowhere. There's nothing! My whole life is a mess! Helping with the little kids is the only thing that gets me out of bed in the morning...that and my parents nagging me to help out. Can't they see the boulder of despair I carry on my shoulders??? Can't they see my eyes are dead to the light?! Can't they see that I'm broken into pieces...

The kids help a little. Adam always comes in and yells "Af-lee, Af-lee! The sun is up!" He looks so much healthier now. I'll never forget the fear and confusion and shock on their tiny faces when we brought them home. It's almost like they were proof of the horror that really happened out there. Dad says we're alive and we should be thankful...God blessed us...but I sure as heck don't feel blessed. I feel cursed.

You know when people started dying, I got out our yearbook and marked off the people that died but then I couldn't keep track anymore. Yesterday I counted two hundred and twenty-three classmates of ours that are probably dead. A lot of people left town too.. It's so eerie quiet... But then there's these other sounds...Dogs howling at night, birds chirping during the day. Stupid animals have no idea what's happened to us.

I remember the first couple of kids that died from our

class. Jamie and then Sarah, then Hailey and Luke and the Hill twins. That was the first time we saw those damn skull and crossbones signs, remember? The health officials said it would be easier if people knew which houses were K-Pox houses so we could stay away from the infection. I don't know...it sure didn't seem to stop people from dying. Man, even that kid Jobe died. Remember we used to dare him to eat bugs and snort fun dip? I thought nothing made him sick. I was wrong. Then all the bells ringing for the funerals until the one day they just stopped.

It's been over a month since my family went on lockdown. Well, not really lock down but it feels like it. Hiding I guess. "Underground" Dad says. I don't really think that makes sense since we're still ABOVE ground. Sometimes I think about making those little lines on the wall like they do in old prison movies. Little lines to mark every day we've been hidden. Lots of little lines. Slash. Slash. Slash... But then what's the point? How depressing! Besides we still know what day it is. We have the calendar and the days keep moving along, starting and stopping just like before. Even though the power's out and no running water, we have batteries to run things and propane tanks to cook things. It's like a big camp-out. I'm growing a couple pots of violets in my room. I know you always liked those. Hopefully they'll live. It's nice that the weather's getting warmer. We can open the windows a bit and have a little breeze blow through this cage of a house.

So I guess it's not the end of the world after all, but why did all this happen? I know we are supposed to be brave and feel blessed that we are alive, but what good is all that when it doesn't bring anyone back to life?

Mandy, I know you saw me, but I snuck out the other night so I could put up your cross. I painted you one of those nice wooden crosses with curly scrolls around the edge. It says "We'll always have Camp Levande. Love you." Now there's only blank space in my heart where all our jokes and talks used to be.

There are tons of crosses everywhere around town. When

they couldn't bury people, families first put crosses in the cemetery or in the open field behind church, but then they started putting crosses everywhere. Splotches of white...Under the willow trees by the school, by Jim's Automotive, next to the transformer box where the skaters used to hang out. Honestly, everywhere! So I put your cross by the stream where we used to cut through when we walked to school. We talked once about how nice it would be to float away down that stream in a giant orange boat...away from all the rules and just fill our day with laughter, string cheese, and pretzels.

And I dyed my hair for you...purple, your favorite. Mom had a cow over the water I used, but she can get over it. I put my key chains on your cross too. All the ones we collected together. And I put a jar of your favorite pickles next to it. I will miss you forever.

Torrential rain and weeping heart,
Ashleigh

April 16

Dear Mom,

It's Mitchell's birthday! We're celebrating quietly, no big party of course. But we tried to make it fun by playing board games all day and having a nice meal. He was disappointed with his 12th birthday and I don't blame him. I'd be disappointed too. But it is what it is.

In general things are about the same here. We don't know what happened to people who left cuz no one's ever come back. You know how we can kinda see the interstate from our second floor? Back when people were driving to find safe places, Mitchell watched the traffic with binoculars. We used to see buses with bunches of people heading east or west or wherever, or military vehicles, some with guns on them, or big tanker trucks and food trucks. Now there's nothing. Except for those thieves that showed up that night.

You can't believe how quiet life is. It's kinda funny— remember that clock we gave you with the bird calls that chirp on the hour? Well, every hour we hear bird calls. I never remembered what bird went with what hour, but now I know each call. Sometimes the only noise in the house is the sound of that clock ticking. I'm glad we have the clock. It reminds me of you. I can hardly wait for you to get back. Please hurry but be very careful. You don't know what kind of bad people are out there.

Well, let me tell you about Dad and Mitchell. Dad's much better. He was so depressed (and depressing!), but since our big break-through, he's more into life. You know how he spent <u>all</u> his time at the computer—and I can't blame you for getting mad at that! Well, he <u>has</u> to do other things now and figure out

37

what to do with all his spare time. And since he's taking charge now, we feel <u>so</u> much better. Actually he decided we'd better go to the grocery store to get more food before it's all gone—cuz people are taking things—which means there's people around. (I hope it isn't those bad guys! Just good people here.) Anyway, he made an initial scouting trip and said he was surprised that so many things are still left on the shelves. He came back with several grocery bags of canned goods. He said that the store smelled pretty bad with all the rotten meat and vegetables. Phew! He was right. Mitchell and I went with him and it <u>stinks</u>! Gross and barfingly wretchedly stinky! Now trips to Sav-More will be a part of our routine.

I imagine you know Mitchell is absolutely loving this. No school. No daily bath (water conservation). Just one big camping party. We go out in the day, sneak into stores (mostly Sav-More cuz it's close) and bring back supplies. Mitchell thinks it's all one big fun game and pretends there's bad guys in the houses and behind trees. It gives me the creeps thinking about people watching us. Mitchell runs sneakily along the walls of houses and peeks around holding his fingers like a pretend pistol. But he's not as brave as he'd like to be. I've heard him cry out at night and Dad had to wake him and comfort him from nightmares.

I wonder if there are people watching us. We know people are taking food n stuff cuz things are missing from one time to the next. Like there's these crackers I like and there were only 5 boxes left last time we went. When we went back, <u>all</u> the boxes were gone! I was so ticked off! <u>I</u> should've grabbed all the crackers when I had the chance. So we know other people are around, but have no idea who. Which makes me really nervous. But Mitchell and I are very quiet when we go in and out and make sure the coast is clear before we do anything. Creepy. I really don't like this. btw...Dad is making me carry a gun now whenever I go outside. He wanted me to carry this stupid pistol in a holster. A holster?? Really!? I totally refused. I understand carrying a gun—especially since the break-in awhile back, but I'm not going to walk around packing heat—looking like a stupid cowboy. So I took one of my leather purses and I carry the gun in my purse. I may not be able to draw my pistol out too fast, but since I've never shot it before anyway, I don't guess speed is going to be an issue!

Anyway...I'd love to have someone to talk to. I wish it could be Jennifer and Rachel, but it isn't. I can't even think about them without crying. I just can't. I hate that they're gone and I miss them so much it hurts. And I miss you more than I can say. I wish grief didn't hurt so bad. My chest just aches and aches.

Perhaps we'll meet those other hidden people soon. More people means more protection. Safety in numbers. It's bound to happen. I just hope they're nice and not scary. And not those thieves. I hope they're long gone. And what do we do if they're not? Dad said we'll cross that bridge when we come to it. I don't know. It makes me really nervous.

And, the fixing meals thing is better too. We all take turns—even Mitchell—though his meals of crackers and pbj and canned green beans is getting a little old. But I guess it's okay since he's only 12. I'm working on extending his menu options! :)

I have to go now. Mom, I love you and hope you come back soon. Perhaps by July 4?

Your favorite daughter
Meg

PS: I know Dad misses you and he talks about you and what you would want us to do. We all miss you.

April 21

Hey Mandy!

 I can't believe it! Dad met someone else!! It was so random! The weather's warmer, so Dad said he'd try fishing. We've been dying for some fresh food...and when he got there, there was ANOTHER man fishing! Someone who wasn't a sociopath or a zombie or whatever else we've been afraid of. A real person! With a FAMILY!!! And you know who it is??? The Kinseys!!! Remember Jason played on the basketball team? He always thought he was pretty hot stuff...and he was :-) Can you believe it? A hot guy survived!!! Hey Mandy! You hear me up there??!!

 I'm pretty sure he has a brother too. Caleb, I think, in the class below ours. What a wondrous discovery of immense proportions!!!

 Dad and Mr. Kinsey are getting together in a couple days and then maybe we'll all meet together. Yes! I just knew it! I KNEW everything couldn't be so terrible.

 Waaa-hooo!

Partly Sunny but ECSTATIC,
Ashleigh

April 25

Dear Mom,

I have really exciting news! There are more good people left!! <u>There are other people</u>!! And apparently they're normal regular people, just like I'd hoped! So let me tell you...

Dad was walking to the store to get supplies and he saw this other man. So they talked a little—both pretending they were alone. Then after talking awhile, they realized they were okay and not bad guys. The other guy, who we found out was Mr. Kinsey, had met another family as well (the Graces), and he's organizing a meeting with all three families. So we're gonna meet more people!! Oh I'm so glad. I am soooooo tired of being around just Dad and Mitchell since for ages. I have soooooo missed my friends. I am soooooo tired of being alone. I am soooooo tired of being scared. And now there are more people!!!

There was a Jason Kinsey in my class at school. I bet it's him. He was a bit of a jerk—people said he was a real partier and totally into being a basketball star. Gag! I hope it isn't him.

Just to be safe, Dad didn't tell Mr. Kinsey where we live. We're gonna make sure everything's okay before we totally share where we live and everything. But we'll be meeting tomorrow!!!!! I can hardly wait!!!!! I'll write more tomorrow and let you know how it goes.

Your favorite daughter
Meg

REMEMBER THE LID
FOR THE COMPOST PAIL
NO ONE LIKES FLIES
AS ROOMMATES.

— DAD

April 26

Dear Mandy,

Dad met with the other dad<u>SSS</u> this morning. That's right! There are TWO families! Can you believe it! Mom seems a little nervous...I mean, I know they are strangers and all and yes, they could be totally weird, but still!! We aren't really worried about any of us getting sick any more. Mom was saying something about we have all been exposed already, so if we were going to get sick we would have gotten it already, blah, blah, blah. I'm just so excited we're not alone!!!!

It was Mr. Kinsey who Dad met first and then Mr. Kinsey met Mr. Shultz too. I don't really know the Shultzes, but when I looked in the yearbook, I recognized Meg. She always hung out with the science nerdy kids and some other girls I recognized as being ok. Whatever! Who CARES!! I'm just excited there's other people my age!

Dad said we're all going to meet today and the dads talked about writing down what we talk about at our meetings so we won't forget. I asked if I could keep notes, since I always wanted to be a writer and he said that was fine. Awesome!! So I am the "Official Historian." Dad had an old typewriter in the attic from grandpa that I am going to use too. Type, type, type, DING! Pretty amazing right?

I'm just glad to have other people I can hang out with instead of Mom and Dad and the little kids all the time. We're meeting for lunch at Martha's Café. Mom suggested that we all bring food...Like a picnic! I'm going to bring those tasty crackers Adam wanted last time we were at the store...and maybe make a bean dip. We eat LOTS of canned beans now. I'm so excited to actually do my hair and put on makeup for a change and get ready! I'll let you know how it goes!

Blue Skies and THRILLED,
Ashleigh

April 26

Dear Mom!

I have seen the new people! I can't believe how exciting this is!! Oh gosh! Where to start. Okay...I told you Dad met Mr. Kinsey yesterday and they planned a meeting. Well, the dads met first in the morning and then we all met at Martha's Café, you know that little restaurant downtown on the corner? And there were actually three families there (including us)! So exciting. We're not the last 3 people living in the world! There are more living people in town!! I almost cried seeing all the people sitting in the restaurant. Ashleigh's mom cried—I think from happiness or relief seeing other people. Knowing we aren't the only people left in the world is <u>such a wonderful feeling that I could just scream for sheer joy</u>! I don't think I knew how scared and lonely I was. And all ages of people were there! The adults were talking about survival stuff but us kids were hanging out at another booth and talking about our kind of stuff.

So...this is who's here. First the Kinseys. The dad is Donald and mom is Janet. They have 3 kids: Jason, Caleb, and Tricia. Mr. Kinsey's totally into this whole survival thing. I wasn't at the same table as the grownups, but I could hear him talking all excitedly about water n supplies n stuff. Mrs. Kinsey's really sad. She smiled only at the Grace's little kids—who aren't their real kids, but I'll get to that later. When the Graces came in with the little kids, she left her seat and sat with Mrs. Grace so she could be next to them. Mrs. Kinsey used to be an elementary teacher.

Jason's the oldest son. Yeah, he's the jerk I told you about. He used to be this big basketball star and he's tall and good-looking and sooo into himself. Still. I mean, there's no basketball team anymore. Get over yourself! He and his friends used to post

45

pictures on twitter and Facebook showing them drunk at parties. Apparently he got suspended one time for being drunk at school and we heard he got a DUI, but I don't know if that's true. So, while I'm excited about new people, I wish it was Jen and Rach instead. I'd rather hang out with them way more than with Jason. But I suppose he's better than nothing. I guess.

The younger brother's Caleb. He's 15. He seems nice enough. Nice looking and not stuck-up like Jason. He's the middle kid and kinda blends in between Jason and Tricia—who also stands out in an unpleasant manner. Caleb didn't say much at the meeting, mostly letting Tricia and Jason do the talking.

Tricia is 13 and omg does she whiiiine. "I haaaaate this. I haaaaate that. There's noooo one my age around here." (Apparently Mitchell who's 12 is so totally not the same age!) She's a cute girl, but her scowl makes her seem really bitchy. I was tired of her before the end of the meeting, and the meeting didn't even last that long. Hopefully she'll improve with age. She better!

The other family is the Grace family—Jackson, Caroline, Ashleigh, and the two little kids, Adam and Ava. I'll start with Adam and Ava. Apparently, Mr. Grace found them hiding in the barn and brought them home, and they've been living with the Graces ever since. Running and laughing and they're awfully cute. And talking like crazy! Adam is 4 and Ava's 3. Mr. Grace seems a little uptight. Very concerned about weird petty stuff, like making sure we share everything exactly correctly. Like he's too fussy about the small stuff. I mean first we need to be worried about survival—we can worry about how to divide the paperclips later. Okay, slight exaggeration, but not too far off! Mrs. Grace is really nice. She's so sweet about the little kids and sat down and spoke to us at the "kids" table. She also brought candy and that was cool. Can't go wrong with chocolate!

Ashleigh's their daughter. She's 16 and used to have different color hair every month or so. It's a funny color purple right now. It doesn't look bad actually, but I'm not crazy about all the eye makeup. I wonder if she wears it every day or just for the meeting today. To be honest, I put on makeup today too. Just not <u>that</u> much. Tricia had on makeup as well—and like most middle school girls do—too much color. I think I'll get along with Ashleigh okay. She's the closest in age to me so I hope we'll be friends. She and her parents talk too much about God though. They wanted to start the meeting with a prayer! I'm not sold on all this religion stuff. I'll be polite if they insist on group prayer and lower my head, but I'm not praying. It's like that stupid moment of silence at the beginning of every school day. What a crock! If I want to pray, I don't need a specific moment of the day to do that. I can pray anytime—and would—if I prayed—which I don't. If prayer worked, KPox wouldn't have happened!

Back to the meeting. We're all gonna meet again tomorrow and talk about the committees we'll be on. I think we kinda get a choice, but the parents may decide for us. We'll see. Part of me wants to be a kid still and have them decide everything, but more of me wants to decide things for myself. After all, I was supposed to be graduating in a few months and going to college. So was Jason. We both had a good time complaining about not graduating. We said that we <u>were going</u> to have a graduation ceremony on May 31—just like it was scheduled! We weren't the ones to shut down the school, so we should be able to graduate! That made me laugh and I felt so much better just talking about it with a fellow senior (even if he is totally self-involved). So we made plans for our graduation. We'll find robes and silly flat hats and have the audience hum the graduation song. Dum dum dum dedum dum dum....

I hope we get to be friends with the new people. It is sooo nice to have other people to talk to. It really is!!!

Your favorite daughter
Meg

The Beginning
April 26

I, Ashleigh Grace, record keeper and official historian of the surviving townspeople of Laurel (previous population 10,860 according to the town sign), will be keeping record of all decisions made in this new society.

We officially met as a whole group today:
> Donald, Janet, Jason (18), Caleb (15), and Tricia (13) Kinsey
> Jackson, Caroline, and Ashleigh (16) Grace; Adam (4) and Ava (3) Parker
> Sam, Meg (17), and Mitchell (12) Shultz

Mr. Kinsey suggested we take care of Maslow's Hierarchy of Needs: shelter, warmth, food, water, and safety. The group agreed. Committees will be formed.

Shelter: Moving closer together was discussed even though some were reluctant to leave their homes. However, it was agreed a more central location would be better for safety and for sharing resources.

Warmth: Now that it is spring, we'll soon stop using our propane heaters. We talked about moving into homes with working fireplaces for next year, but security was discussed because of smoke coming from the chimneys. Mr. Shultz said we did not want to alert others to our area until we know how we'll deal with new (potentially dangerous) people (if/when they show up).

Food: Everyone said they have been gathering food from the stores and from neighbors' houses. We will continue to do this. The group decided to take these steps:
* Keep all surplus food and supplies in the Sav-More Food Store in the established aisles.

* Rotten food will be buried, so animals or bugs won't contaminate the good food. Sav-More doors will be closed to keep out stray animals.
* Certain foods like crackers or items with easy to chew through packaging will be kept in plastic tubs.

Mr. Kinsey, Mr. Grace, Caleb Kinsey, and Mitchell Shultz said they would put out bait and traps for pests inside and outside Sav-More. Everyone agreed we would start working on clearing out rotten food, cleaning, and preparing the store for food storage.

Water: We have all been using the limited supply of water in bottles from local stores. There is a stream that runs near the Grace's subdivision. It was discussed that we use and boil water from the stream. Mr. Grace also said there was a working windmill and well at a farm a few miles from town we could use.

Safety: We decided to stay in our town and not look for other survivors. The last reports we heard on the radio were that people were rioting, stealing and killing so we want to protect ourselves. We talked about rules for weapons and what to do if new people come to our town, but made no decisions yet.

People will choose which committees they want to be on the next time we meet. Committees will be:
* Shelter and Warmth
* Food and Water
* Safety/Security and Health

Our next meeting will be tomorrow (April 27th). A committee sign-up sheet will be posted at Martha's Café.

Minutes Recorded by Ashleigh Grace

April 26

Dear Mandy,

    I was so exhausted after the meeting, that I just ate dinner and went to bed. But it was so exciting! I'm glad I got to be the historian! It's finally my chance to be an author and that makes life a little better. I know my audience will be a very tiny group, but hey! At least I'll have a 100% following! It's pretty cool to think that maybe years from now people will be reading my words to find out how the new world began again!

    So... the meeting! I'm grateful to have people my age to talk to. We split into a 'kids' table and adults table even though Meg and Jason are practically adults and I'm certainly not a kid! But we got to hang out while the adults were talking. That was amazing! We introduced ourselves and said a little bit about who we were...well who we were <u>before</u>. Jason went on and on about how he was a starter on the basketball team and then we were asking each other if we knew so-and-so or whoever...but then it hit us...those people are gone...probably dead and we just stopped for a minute. Awkward! And TOO sad...so we changed the subject.

    We talked about how weird quiet it is now. There's no humming from appliances in the house or dinging and buzzing from our phones. Even the sky is quiet with no planes or any flashing lights or...anything! And remember how you could see neighboring town lights glow against the night sky, even from a distance? Now it's so crazy dark, the only light is from the moon and stars. The nights when the moon lights everything up is really pretty...the world draped in a blue glow....And we all talked about the stars! You can see so many since there isn't all the light from street lamps...even though some houses still have those solar lights that lead up their front walks and backyards...which is a little comforting imagining everything's still the same...but a little creepy too.... Anyway, we talked about the stars and how we understood why people ages and ages ago used to study them. We agreed it's a WHOLE new world now.

So anyway, eventually I had to go b/c Mom signaled me they were going to start the official part of the meeting and I was taking notes (I am AWESOME!). Meg and Jason came too, since they're almost grown up.

Oh, and Mom said I need to watch what I put in the official notes...just in case... Just in case of WHAT? I really don't think the squirrels and birds are gonna be interested in my notes and start reading them to find out where we're stashing the candy bars!!! Like Mom's a professional editor or something! Whatever. But I will tell YOU the real story Mandy-girl and just keep the meeting notes short and basic.

So Mr. Kinsey already had notes and a list of things to talk about. He started with 'Maslow's needs.' Seriously? Who would even know about that? I mean, I remember it from one of my science classes and it makes sense, but we don't need to get all technical about it. THERE ARE ONLY THIRTEEN PEOPLE LEFT DUDE! Regardless...that discussion led to making committees to help with different parts of our NEW community, which everybody could help with...even younger teens, like Mitchell and Tricia (even though I can't see Tricia helping with ANYTHING!).

So now I have to decide what committee I want to be on. Maybe the food committee? I like to organize stuff and I could help make sure everything is equal. I guess I'm like Dad in that way...He said a few times he wanted everything to be fair and split equally. I agree! So yeah, maybe the food committee would be bearable.

BUT...I hope it won't be depressing! Counting all the cans and all the 'things' left from our old life...then watching them disappear...just like everything else has. Sometimes I don't want to think about survival stuff. It feels like that's all we talk about at home...Do we have enough water? How do we make sure we have enough to eat? How are we gonna keep the farm going? How are we gonna keep our lives going for 50 more years? It's like we live in this fear-of-how-we're-going-to-make-it mode all the time and I want a break! The problem is though, if I'm not doing something 'to survive' then all I think about is everything we lost and THAT'S freakin depressing...so maybe counting cans to occupy my mind would be better. Maybe then I could at least come home and get lost in a book like I used to without my mind wandering...

which is SOOOO what I'm doing right now!! Okay, back on track! The people! Let me tell you who everyone is. I have to hurry b/c the sun is going down soon and I don't want to write by the lantern b/c it's next to Mom and Dad and the kids. A girl needs some privacy!

First, the Kinsey family. Mr. Donald Kinsey—he's okay. He has all kinds of lists and notes and has thought this whole thing out like we're on a permanent camping trip. Honestly, I think he LIKES life this way...getting by with only what we have and all. AND he's totally into planning ahead—you know, with that whole Maslow thing.

Mrs. Janet Kinsey—she didn't say much, but she seemed to like the little kids and smiled when Ava sang her Twinkle Twinkle song.

Jason—he's 18 and was a big basketball star at my high school. I think he was almost expelled from school? But I don't know why. I think he used to be a partier. AND he's HOT!

Caleb—He's okay for a 10th grader. Whoops! We don't have grades anymore. He's 15. I don't know much about him. He was drawing stuff at the council meeting but wouldn't show me his drawings. It's kinda fun he's an artist. He can illustrate my books someday! HE'S kinda cute too...

Tricia—Well, to be nice, she is VERY cute and can be charming...WHEN she wants to. She was acting nice and trying to talk Jason out of his last peanut butter cup, but he told her no and to knock it off...and then as soon as she didn't get her way...POUT, POUT, WHINE, WHINE, WHINE! Geeez. After that I totally remembered her from football games with her snotty group of friends. Apparently she still has MAJOR attitude. I mean SERIOUSLY! Get. Over. Yourself!

Next is the Shultz family! Mr. Sam Shultz—Meg said he used to work with computers and was like totally lost and depressed when the power went off for good. (Weren't we all!) But he's better now. He seemed helpful.

Meg—She seems okay other than maybe a little uptight, but that could be b/c we haven't talked to other people...outside our families...in FOREVER! She watched over Mitchell real close and shushed him when he was getting too loud (which he didn't like). Maybe she'll have some tips for me and the little kids.

Mitchell—'Busy' is a good for word for him! He could become REAL annoying real fast! Thank goodness he listens to his dad. I was kinda wondering where Meg's mom was, but then she said that her mom was on a business trip in California when K-Pox hit and she's on her way home. Meg didn't really say much more after that, so I don't know if her mom is dead or just not here...I can't imagine either way though. I know Mom and I don't always get along, but I can't even stand the thought of her being gone.

Then the only family left is mine...which you know of course.

Jackson- Dad. Sometimes he gets pretty grouchy about having to start over. He's used to working hard, but I think he's just mad all the work he's done no longer matters...like his business and stuff. I could see him trying to hang on to "normal" after all this happened...He was ACTUALLY out in our yard pulling weeds and trying to keep everything tidy after K-Pox wiped out the town...I mean, really? Come on Dad...Nothing is normal anymore.

Caroline—Mom. Her parents were rich, but died before I was born so I never knew them. Mom didn't work after she had me, but did a lot of volunteering. She was an event planner when she met Dad. There's lots of planning to do now, so maybe that's why she's doing okay. She's always liked to cook and now she's trying out new recipes using our limited supplies. I've seen her out scrounging for roots and wild herbs to use. She made a really awesome soup with the fish Dad caught a couple of days ago. The kids even ate it!

Then our adopted kids are:

Adam – He's 4 years old. He likes trucks and trains and his favorite food is canned green beans. Go figure right?! We don't know much about the kids except their parents must've died or been killed somehow. Or maybe a car accident or they hid the kids from something terrible and meant to come back and didn't make it? We'll probably never know.

Ava – She's 3. She likes princess books and her favorite toy is a stuffed rabbit. She barely talked when they first came. Mom and Dad said both kids were probably in shock and terrified from all they'd seen.

Both kids seem pretty happy now. They still wake up with nightmares sometimes and Ava yells out for her Mommy. I guess she thinks Mom is her mom now and Adam is Dad's little buddy. Dad finally has a son! I like them most of the time.

Then there's me. Ashleigh Marie Grace. I'm 16 years old and was trying to finish 10th grade with honors. I was in the creative writing class and on the yearbook and literary magazine, but so much for that. Dad reminds us every day that we are ALIVE and that's a blessing. I know he's right, but sometimes...it's just so hard to feel grateful JUST for being alive, you know?

So that's the whole overview. And can I just say again how totally THRILLED I am to have more people to talk to b/c it can get REALLY REALLY boring being around your parents and two little kids all the time (even though the kids make me laugh). AND thank goodness Mom is busy worrying about them and she leaves me alone—well, sort of. My parents still feel they need to have rules for me. Hello! World destroyed! Ease up would ya??!! Well, it's getting dark. I'll write again after our next meeting.

Dusk and sleepy,
Ashleigh

PS--Did you see the extra facts I put in the meeting notes about our town's population before and now we're only 13?? I thought that was pretty fantastic journalism work. Go me!
PPS - - You know it's great to be around people and all...but I still really miss you, Mandy. I guess I was hoping that meeting other people would make me *feel* different, you know? But I don't yet. We'll just have to see how it all goes.

April 27 Meeting Minutes

The second meeting of survivors met this afternoon at Martha's Cafe.

Those attending were:
    Donald, Janet, Jason, Caleb, and Tricia Kinsey
    Jackson, Caroline, and Ashleigh Grace; Adam and
        Ava Parker
    Sam, Meg, and Mitchell Shultz

The meeting started. Committees were discussed and decided upon, and Donald read aloud the final decision on committees and their members.

<u>Shelter and Warmth</u>: Jackson, Jason, and Tricia.
<u>Food/Water and Power</u>: Caroline, Ashleigh, Caleb, Mitchell, and Sam.
<u>Safety/Security/and Health</u>: Donald, Janet, and Meg.
Everyone met in committees for thirty minutes then rejoined the main group.

SHELTER/WARMTH (SW)

<u>Shelter</u>: The SW committee expressed concern over conserving resources and suggested living closer together so we could help each other. Jackson spoke for the team and said his neighborhood, Legacy Estates, was the safest and most stable in town. (He designed and built it himself.) He listed the benefits as follows:

* All houses have wood fireplaces, if needed.
* There is a clear stream that runs nearby to make water easier to get.
* Houses have yards large enough for compost bins and storage units for recycled items.

One concern about us all living close together was possible discovery by 'unsafe outsiders.' If someone was careless and led them to one house, the intruders would find us all. However, Donald and Caroline said there was safety in numbers and this should be considered, especially if we want to get a message to each other quickly. Also, it would be easier to divide work if it didn't take so long to get to a central location.

After discussion, the parents took the first official vote. The vote was unanimous for moving to Legacy Estates. The system for moving is:

* Families will take over abandoned houses (or ones that have no dead people in them).
* The community decided lawns would be mown at occupied houses to keep away rats and other pests.
* One house was chosen for the clubhouse where we would meet for our meetings and other events.

Winter Warmth: Even though winter is in the future, the SW committee brought up heating issues. Possible solutions were:

* Kerosene, propane, and other heating sources
* Fireplaces will not be used until we have gone through alternate heating sources as smoke could draw attention to our homes

Sanitation: Since all the toilets still run on gravity we just have to keep filling up the tanks to keep using them. Eventually, we will need to consider outhouses. Only toilet paper must be used in the toilets as other papers do not decompose quickly and will block the system.

I, Ashleigh, suggested we start looking for information at the library since I have read several books on Medieval times and am pretty sure there was something about water and primitive plumbing. Caleb brought up the idea of researching Eskimos and how they keep their homes warm. All were in favor and a research team will be sent to the library.

FOOD/WATER/POWER (FWP)

The FWP committee recommended the following:

Water

* Everyone needs to conserve water.
* Boiling and filtering were discussed as the best way to purify water for drinking.
* Well water from the farm will be distributed to each family every morning. They will be responsible for boiling and conserving their own rations.

Food

* Need to research how to grow and preserve our food supplies.
* We will plant a community garden.
* We will consider way of providing meat (hunting and animals at farm)

Storage: Many ideas were raised about how to keep food supplies safe and secure. Input was given from the Safety/Security/Health Committee. Recommendations were:

* Inventory at the store will be kept so we know if food or supplies are missing.
* Searches of neighboring houses will continue with supplies being kept at Sav-More and divided among all families.
* We voted on and agreed to this system. The library team will address the research questions presented regarding primitive plumbing and alternative heat sources.

SAFETY/SECURITY/HEALTH (SSH)

Health: Following the discussion of food and supplies, the SSH committee brought up issues of health.

* Soap and water are the most effective ways to kill germs and should be used first. However, hand sanitizer and wipes are also acceptable.

* We need to keep our teeth clean and flossed so we don't get cavities.
* We need to stay as clean as possible to prevent infection and disease.
* Meg said we should make sure we know how to treat illnesses just in case.
* Research is needed on natural remedies and to gather all medicines.

Security: Additional discussion was given to the houses we'd be looking through. The SSH committee recommended:
* Marking houses we have already gathered supplies from.
  - Donald suggested spray painting a 3 – 4 inch splotch on the lower left side of the front door on each house checked.
  - Jackson suggested avoiding houses with skull signs posted as there were likely decaying bodies inside. This was agreed on by all.

Also, it was recommended that families should move by the end of the week.

Minutes recorded by Ashleigh Grace.

April 27

Dear Mandy,

Today we met for lunch and it was SOOO much easier having more hands to prepare the food...and waaaaay more fun! Even the little kids helped.

Donald had LOTS of ideas. I swear you'd think he was one of his kids the way he sat up all straight and grinned like that cat from Alice in Wonderland! And then there was his wife Janet, sitting beside him like she was in a trance or something. Man, she seems super depressed! Thank goodness Ava colored her a picture and she perked up a little.

I know we have to survive, but doesn't anyone else think it sucks that we have to work harder than ever for a whole lot less? Seriously, the parents try to act all calm and civil like, but I looked at Meg a couple times when we were talking about having enough food and from the way she looked back at me...let me tell you, they're not fooling anybody. Everybody's nervous. I guess grown-ups don't have a world they can control any more so they're like us kids, just trying to figure it out.

Housing...Geez! We spent like a whole <u>hour</u> on that, just trying to get people's opinions and then working out details. It started with Donald talking about location so we can figure out all the other issues of how things are gonna work. We have to know what we're close to so we know where we're going to get our food. We have to know how big an area is that we're going to live in so we know how we're gonna protect ourselves. The dude even drew a chart with colored markers! He said we need to be close to water, food sources, and other stuff so we can manage "logistics" easier.

But then Dad! He started in with all his "I worked hard my whole life and I built this house with my own hands to keep it safe and strong." He even swore! Well, kinda..."hell" isn't really swearing, but it is for Dad. He said how all the houses in our neighborhood were built to make them run smoothly for a long time and we'd already lost enough...too much to move away. Oooohhhh, and then Mom, the perpetual cheerleader, suggested since all that was true, everyone should move here! I'm not sure that's what Dad meant...but that's what's happening! Then, the conversation about protecting ourselves from desperate people stealing or...worse than stealing... At the end of the K-Pox thing, people WERE acting pretty crazy and who knows if all those crazy people died or not.

At first I didn't see what the big deal was, not letting other people know we're around.... I didn't really think it'd be dangerous to look for survivors. Don't we want to find others so we can help each other? I mean what if there's other nice people out there?? None of us decided to turn to cannibalism or tried to kill each other over their canned goods...yet :-) But then Meg told us about some guys who tried to break into their house and basically ransacked and terrorized their whole neighborhood.... I guess Mom was right and there are still scary people out there. We have to be careful. It's probably good that we'll have a system for bringing other NON-CRIMINAL people into our community...IF there are any. BUT what'll we do with the criminal people if they do come here? I don't know.... We didn't decide on anything yet and just said we'll talk about it later.

I liked Donald's point about us getting messages back and forth faster if we live closer together. We can always signal each other if there's a threat. We can't just call anymore. Maybe we could send up smoke signals! LOL! Of course, I'm sure that would violate the whole 'don't let others know we're here' rule.

At some point, Mitchell went on a tangent about making booby traps and forts. Meg shushed him pretty quick, but at least this whole thing hasn't ruined his imagination. Maybe forts and booby traps aren't such a bad idea!

After that BIG housing discussion, the parents voted and of course, everyone's moving over here now. The Kinseys didn't seem like they cared much, but Meg seemed kinda upset about it. I don't know...she said something to her dad about her mom finding them...I feel bad for them. It must be awful not knowing if she's out there somewhere or maybe dead....

Sanitation was next. Grooossss!! Can I just tell you how happy I am that the toilets still miraculously work??!! Dad explained it to me. Something about gravity and water pressure so all we have to do is fill up the tank and voila! Indoor plumbing!! We're still going to research to make sure it's a good idea, but I think I'd die if I had to walk back and forth outside to pee! Double Yuck! And now there's people around, no thank you!! With the stream and the farm well at least we have water...But we have to haul it inside. What a drag!!! (har har)

Speaking of water...Mom is still complaining that I've dyed my hair a couple of times. "Using too much water and you're going to contaminate the water supply, blah blah blah." Just let me be myself you know?! I feel better doing the same things I did when life was NORMAL. And besides...purple was your favorite color Mandy. And it's MY freakin hair!

Back to the meeting...then we talked FOREVER about food and water and supplies. Jason asked what happens when our supplies run out, but everyone said we'd discuss that issue later. It's a good question though! I guess we can go to stores further out for more supplies when we need them.

Did you see the research team?! Awesome! Finally! Something to do! Caleb volunteered to go with me to the library this week and Meg's going and maybe Jason, even though I'm not sure how much actual help he'll be when we get there. He's always rolling his eyes or has this "are you stupid?" look on his face...but he'll be cute to look at!

Well, I'm gonna read before the light is gone and go to bed. Big research trip tomorrow!

Clear skies and sleepy,
Ashleigh

April 27

Dear Mom,

Guess what! Since we met the new people we've divided into committees and everything! Guess what committee Dad chose—Power! Isn't that funny? But not surprising. If he could build the internet again, he'd do it! He's definitely checking into generators and how to restore power with wind and solar and other alternatives. I haven't seen him so happy in ages! He said he loves having a job again—he hated being unemployed. He didn't think of it as a nice long summer vacation. I wonder how he'll handle retirement? But I guess that isn't an issue anymore. Oh! I guess we don't have to worry about Social Security anymore! We'll just work til we die. Great! (Can you hear the sarcasm, Mom?)

I am on the Safety and Security committee. We'll be helping to figure out what to do with all the guns. Don't freak out Mom. This is being handled pretty well and <u>very</u> safely. I think we'll start storing them at the farmhouse. But we may change that. Besides, I'm on the committee so will help make decisions. And I always think of you and what you'd want. Mitchell n Caleb are on the Food and Power committee and they have already started searching for and gathering up food and water in deserted homes and shops.

We're also thinking of ways to stay safe from intruders. We haven't had any since those guys awhile back, but we're planning ahead. There could be good people wandering through or totally bad ones like we already had. So we want to be ready. We're also in charge of cleanliness issues. Like continuing to brush and floss our teeth cuz ...no dentists! And no one wants to have rotten teeth! Or cavities! Ouch! And washing hands is totally important so we don't spread germs. As you can imagine—Mitchell <u>doesn't</u> like that part.

He's hooked up with Caleb Kinsey who's 15. I'm not crazy about the age difference, but there's no one else and Caleb seems okay. They're planning on spending hours out exploring, to bring back supplies—especially food and water. They're very excited about being the supply guys...making plans to ride bikes all around town finding food, water, and all kinds of survival stuff, then load it all in grocery carts and bring it back to the committee's storage areas. We're going to store water at Sav-More as they're closest to everyone.

I have to go now. Mom, love you and hope you come back soon. Perhaps by July 4th?

Your favorite daughter
Meg

Red Death Victorious
by janet kinsey

Red Death comes smashing through gates of dark hell,
Sweeping sweet child and grown evil alike.
Potions of man or the church holy bells,
Stops not the Red Death from breaching the dike.
Children with bright colored eyes used to shine,
Those innocent eyes now covered in red
Stare at Red Death through lens crimsoned like wine,
But it's not enough; Red Death must be fed.
Skin soft as velvet, now crusted red sores
Beg you to help. Make Red Death go away.
Young arms plead for life; there are no safe shores
And life has slipped earth at end of the day.
Life did depend on the young to live on.
Red Death has charged forth and trumpets he's won.

May 1

Dear Mandy,

So everyone's in the process of moving into our neighborhood. I'll definitely feel safer knowing people are actually around if we need anything. And we can go 'next door' to ask for a cup of sugar or something. :) We'll be moving a LOT of boxes in the next couple of days! We've been working on the house we're gonna use as our meeting house..."clubhouse." It was the Peterson's old house. They didn't have kids and were both specialty surgeons or something...so they were LOADED. But the house has lots of open space on the main level so will be great for get-togethers. I already feel tired and worn out from helping though. I wish I could bottle up the little kids' energy and drink it! They never seem to stop running...until they crash at night of course. I can't believe I was just a kid a couple months ago...

It'll be nice to see other people out gardening and working too. Bring some LIFE back to this town. Dad's just happy we can mow our lawn and tidy up again. I swear...he must think God's going to give him an award for having neat grass. Ha! Maybe He will!

Going to bed. Ni-night.

Foggy night and sleepy,
Ashleigh

May 3

Dear Mom,

We're moving to a McMansion in the rich area of town! To Ashleigh's neighborhood! That's so we'll all be in the same area for safety reasons. I'll like being near more people cuz I still worry about those two guys who almost broke into our house a while back, and I'd rather be around other people in case they come back. Safety in numbers. Makes me less stressed knowing I can relax more. And I won't be so scared of weird noises at night. Noises can be really loud at night!

It's kinda weird moving to the new house—besides the fact that it's bigger and nicer than our house. We've been packing only our personal stuff into boxes and piling them into the back of our car, as the new house has furniture and all kinds of kitchen stuff (but the refrigerator <u>stinks</u> and needs to be thrown out!) and bedding and everything. We're bringing clothes and I want our books, and Mitchell's making sure we have <u>all</u> his junk, and Dad's packing up his tools. And I'm bringing some of your things and of course all our photos. I'm glad we had some old-fashioned photos because all of my online ones are gone. So we spent a couple of days boxing up the former residents' personal items and putting them into the basement storage area so if they come back they'll have all their stuff. Which was weird!! Moving other people's things—especially their medicines and private stuff like underwear! Clean underwear, but still! (We did throw out the dirty clothes. I hope they don't mind.) Then we moved our stuff in. Moving is making me think of you all the time--packing your things and moving away from our home. We put up several notes in the house about where we've moved so when you get home, you'll be able to find us. But it's weird and kinda creepy moving into someone else's house specially since their stuff is still there. I wonder who they were and where they are now. Hope they're okay.

We're all helping each other move boxes from old houses to new and it's a nice way to get to know each other better. Of course the Grace's aren't moving. He seems very excited we'll be taking care of the yards. The lawns were getting totally ridiculous--really tall grass and those baby trees that start growing so quickly. (How do those trees grow so fast!?) But the Safety committee decided that to keep away the rats (shudder, gross gross gross!), we need to keep lawns mown around the houses we're living in. So Mitchell and Caleb were set to mowing everyone's yards. They asked how much money they'd make per lawn! Everyone laughed! Back in the old days, perhaps...but now you don't earn money to make the community work. And if we gave them money, where would they spend it?? Which they realized very quickly. So instead, they turned it into a game and raced to see who could mow faster. I wish I could take this whole thing like a game. I'd be a lot happier. But I just don't feel like trying to make it fun. At this point it's just hard work.

I was hoping Ashleigh and I'd get along better, but she doesn't seem to be as interested as I am in being friends. For instance when we were at our new house, I asked if she wanted to walk to the clubhouse together and she did go for the walk, but was hard to talk to. Maybe she's just shy. Kinda awkward though, so I'll back off and try later. To be honest, I don't have a lot of patience right now for anything. Maybe I coulda tried harder. I don't know. We're both going through a lot and it's not like I'm trying to be best friends or anything. I just miss having a girl to talk to. I miss Jen and Rach so much!

69

Well, it's my turn to make dinner this evening. First night in the new house! I should make something nice to celebrate. Hmmm...what to make? Which reminds me...another good thing about the Dads and Moms all working together—they know a lot about what used to be boring stuff—like how to hook up gas to appliances and generators for electricity and stuff—which they're doing!! When they get our stoves to work, that will be FANTASTIC! Having a working gas stove will be the most fascinating and luxurious thing in the world! But as we don't have that right now, I'm off to make dinner on the camp stove. :(Funny how one's interests change with the situation!

Your favorite daughter

Meg

PS: The clubhouse is the biggest house on our new street—used to be owned by some rich people and is really awesome! Even w/o electricity! Big rooms with really fancy furniture and curtains and rugs. You'd love it! Makes our old house look like a shack!

May 5 Meeting Minutes

Present:

Donald, Janet, Jason, Caleb and Tricia Kinsey

Jackson, Caroline, and Ashleigh Grace; Adam and Ava Parker

Sam, Meg, and Mitchell Shultz

Meeting called to order at the clubhouse.

Housing: All families have moved closer together. There was a discussion about using generators for cooking and some appliances for a restricted amount of time. Plans to install generators will start tomorrow.

Research showed water and sewage could start to back up in the drainage pipes as the sewage and water plant don't work. Toilets are still being used, but outhouses WILL have to be built. Possibly later spring/summer.

Water:

* Water will be hauled to our houses daily by truck, either from the farm or from the remaining supplies in the stores. Families will boil and filter in their own homes.
* More wells may need to be dug at some point.

Food: Many books were found at the library regarding vegetable gardens, fruit trees, finding edible plants in nature, as well as curing and smoking meat. Also, books on canning food so we can preserve produce for upcoming winters.

Animals:

* Current livestock at the farm include chickens (15), pigs (4), cows (2 dairy cows), and horses (3). Farm animals will supplement our community diet with eggs and eventually meat.
* Limited hunting for food will be allowed in the woods. Silencers will be used with guns.
* All adult community members will learn to hunt with guns and bows/crossbows.

<u>Sanitation</u>: Everyone is responsible!
* Trash and chemicals must be kept away from food and drinking supplies, and put in the assigned areas.
* All violations must be reported immediately.

<u>Recycling</u>:
* Vegetable scraps will be disposed of in compost bins. Bins have been provided to each family.
* No meat will be disposed of in the compost bins in order to avoid bugs and wild animals. Meat scraps will be buried or fed to community dogs and pigs.
* Large plastic containers will be recycled for water and food storage, fuel storage, etc. Rain barrels will be set up to capture rain water at each house.
* We will stop using items that cannot be recycled, such as spray cans (when possible).

<u>Hygiene</u>:
* Clothes will be washed regularly and kept in good shape.
   - We're still working out the best way to handle washing clothes, but everyone is using a washboard and tub or the bucket and toilet plunger (clean--of course!).
   - Wash water and bath water will be used to flush toilets or recycled in gardens so biodegradable soaps must be used.
* Houses and yards will be kept clean and well maintained.
* Cuts, scratches, and wounds will be taken care of immediately.

Jobs: Since all adult members of the community are required to have a job, they are listed below. They will delegate duties as needed.

Jackson – Farm duties

Caroline – Gardening, canning, etc.

Donald – Town Security and Protection

Janet – Medical and teaching duties. It was decided all children will continue to be educated at the clubhouse. Textbooks will be gathered from the schools.

Sam – Energy, fuel conservation, and alternative power (wind, solar, hydro, etc.)

Valuables: Jewelry, guns, and other valuables from searched houses will be labeled and stored securely.

Additionally, teenagers aged 16 and above will be considered adult voting members of this community and will have jobs as well. Younger teenagers and children will also have chores and duties as delegated by their parents. Meg volunteered to take on responsibility for gathering medicines and supplies from doctor's offices and pharmacies. Jason was assigned to lead scouting missions for food and supplies. Ashleigh will keep track of food/supply inventory and coordinate storage.

Notes taken by Ashleigh Grace

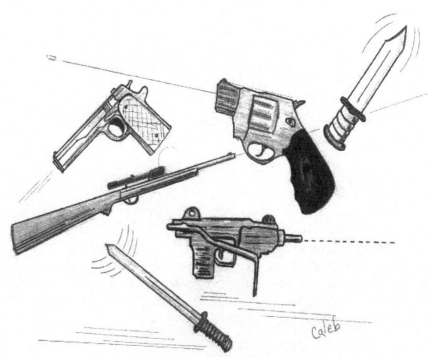

Caleb

me and Mitchell have picked up so many guns and other
weapons. Hard to believe there are/were so many people around
who would be able to blow us away! And now they're
gone and we have all the weapons. Too weird to think
about much.

May 6

Dear Mandy,

     I had this really weird dream the other night. I was sitting at Albee's (our favorite!!) having a banana split and waiting for you to get there. I was irritated because you were late, but then I got a gigantic nosebleed! Gross right? And I've never even had a nosebleed! But it was disgusting, it was all in my banana split and then it was leaking on the counter and I was yelling for napkins but everyone was just looking at me like I was crazy. Then this airplane crashed outside and everything started to catch on fire and people were still just sitting there. I'm screaming and screaming at them to get up and run, but no one was moving. They just sat there. They didn't even know they were on fire. I woke up and was still screaming and Mom came in. I told her I was fine but I couldn't sleep the rest of the night. At dawn I finally got up and went on a walk to see you. I know, I know. I'm not supposed to be going out by myself without letting someone know...danger of outsiders, risk of injury, blah, blah, blah. I get it, but I just had a dream about bloody ice cream and people on fire!

     I was coming back from your cross and you'll never believe who I saw by the stream. Jason! I totally hid behind the first tree I saw! I know, coward!, but I wasn't expecting to see anyone, especially him and there I was in my pajamas with crazy hair and dragon breath. AND he's just wearing his basketball jersey and shorts.... you could totally see the muscles in his arms and the sun all reflecting off his blond hair. It was almost angelic...lol! So there I am trying not to breathe for fear he'd get a whiff of my breath and see me hiding and he starts to walk towards the houses where no one lives. So I followed him. I wasn't stalking him or anything, but why was he going over there? Thank goodness I know all the cut-thru's we used when we were playing zombie tag during the summers. We were getting really close to the main highway and all of a sudden he stops in front of the Garcia's' house and whips out this can of spray paint! He starts looking around and I ducked down behind the fence, but then I heard a spray can and I peeked out. He was spray painting ANYONE OUT THERE? on their garage door! We are NOT supposed to be using aerosol cans and we're REALLY NOT supposed to be letting outsiders know anyone is here. And the Garcia's house totally faces the main road on the way into town. Maybe I'll go back and paint over it...that could be dangerous right? And I don't want him to get in trouble. He always has that sour look on his face...what did Ms. Armand call it when we read that old book Wuthering Heights about Heathcliff who was always in a bad mood???...Brooding! Yeah, that's what Jason always looks like. Kinda sexy though. Maybe I could cheer him up....

Of course, right when I'm thinking about all this and not paying attention, Jason's done painting, he tosses the can and starts jogging back towards home. My heart starts beating like it's gonna pound right out of my chest. I wait til he's gone and then I walked back too. What a way to start the day! I think Jason's cute and all, but I don't want him to think I have a huge crush on him...we just met! And I'm not trying to be a dork!...but he smiles at me sometimes. He's all mysterious and all. I can't help it. I just wonder what's going on behind those big blue *brooding* eyes.

So that was my crazy morning! Now let me tell you about the past few weeks. Talk about craziness! The parents decided we need to continue on with school so Janet's going to teach us. I'm glad no one has a problem with me calling the adults by their first names. My parents were never big on using formal last names. We always just said Mr and Ms and then their first names. So this is easier for me to remember. Anyways!!! The school thing is more for the younger kids...can't have ignorant people running around! But the grown-ups will get old one day and we young people will have to manage all this so we need to be educated too. Ugggh, how depressing to think this is our life...for the rest of my life...I don't know, maybe we'll wake up one morning and it'll all change back. I wish!

The trips to the library have been really fun. Having a project and working on something together makes us feel more normal I think. There's finally a purpose to our days instead of just waiting for the hours to tick by until we can go to bed again. Caleb's actually coming with Meg and me to the library. Jason and Tricia come sometimes, but only when their parents force them to. Caleb's pretty nice. But wow, he can be a talker! I guess I don't *really* mind. He's pretty funny and it fills in the quiet. He's not bad to look at either. LOL. I know I sound boy crazy, but I'm just sayin. It's not a bad thing to have something nice to look at when the world's disappeared. That's what I miss about everything before. I just miss people being around...To look at, to talk about with you...even some of the drama to laugh at would be okay. Not to say Tricia doesn't bring enough drama! Good grief! If complaining was an Olympic sport she'd be a twenty-time gold medalist by now! Uggggh. She comes with us to the library but grumbles about having to walk ALLLLLL the way there. And ALLLLLL the way back! Geez. Suck it up or stay home!!

Anyways, we've found some really cool books. Like some medical books Meg was excited about. It felt kinda weird not checking books out and just taking them instead. Ms. Oswald was always so organized and knew exactly where everything was. I'm sure she wouldn't mind us taking the books as long as we're taking care of them. So Meg's taking the medical books to her house. She even said something about making a clinic in the basement of the clubhouse. Sounds cool. Then we wouldn't have to keep ALL the medical supplies in our houses. We took a lot of the gardening and food books to Mom, and the water, power, and sanitation books to the dads. We went through a lot of books on disaster preparedness...too bad we didn't read those before all this happened! There seems to be a lot of those missing too...maybe the scouts will find more in people's houses or other buildings. Ten cents a day late charge! I guess debts really don't matter now. A clean slate.... if you're alive.

I'm calling the scouting trio 'The Scouts' now. Jason, Caleb, and Mitchell. It seems to be more Caleb and Mitchell, since Jason is brooooooding all the time, but he does get the boys moving or keeps them in line. Not always in a nice way. I thought Jason would like having a job to do, leading and coordinating all the poking around, but he'd rather just play basketball by himself or avoid everybody. Now Caleb and Mitchell on the other hand are loving it! Mitchell really just follows what Caleb says, but they're totally into setting up strategies and missions to different places. Caleb's pretty handy too. He's fixed a couple things at the houses when people moved in. He seems to take after his dad...and said something about being a Boy Scout. I don't know...Jason was walking in front of me...and I was distracted a little by his cute butt. :-) BUT (haha) it's nice Caleb actually wants to be a part of the community and is DOING things. AND he's letting Mitchell tag along. I'm sure Meg appreciates that. I know the little kids drive me nuts sometimes, but at least Mom takes care of them most of the time. I wouldn't really know what Meg thinks though cause we haven't talked much. It's hard for me...she's totally different than you...and I just miss you more sometimes when I think about hanging out with the other girls...like I'm being unfaithful or something. And I don't know what happened to Meg's mom, but I'm not ready for a conversation about how someone else lost somebody...I don't think I could handle the sadness. I feel like my chest will cave in...

But anyway, it's nice Caleb has adopted Mitchell for some of the time...oh! and a bunch of dogs too! So there was like a dozen dogs running around and Caleb started taking them out to the farm. Mom and Dad said NO WAY when I asked about having a dog, but the Kinseys had dogs before and they've adopted a few to have around the community. The nice ones! There's more that Caleb keeps together as a pack out at the farm. He's

78

keeping them in pens and large fenced in areas now, but he said he was going to start training. He totally raided the pet store to get leashes and lead ropes and all that stuff. I recognize some of the dogs from neighbors. It's sad to think of all the pets that died when their owners died...Maybe they refused to leave their owners and died right next to them. Oh, that breaks my heart! Caleb and Mitchell started feeding the pack (that's what he calls them, but it's really only a few so far...) and are getting them to obey commands. Caleb said he's been reading a lot about training them. He said we can't just love and feed the pack, we have to teach them how we want them to live WITH us in our community. We can love them, but he has to show them that HE is their pack leader. Then we can teach them how to protect us. Cool right? It's like all of us working together.

AND here's the deal with the jewelry and the weapons. Caleb walks into the meeting the other day with a crossbow. We're like...Dude, what's up with the heavy artillery?? He says he found it in one of the houses and that's not all the weapons they've found. OMG, they were so excited you'd think he'd found a pit full of human heads! Ewww, that could probably happen. Gross! Anyway, I guess there's some talk about all of us carrying a weapon of some sort, like knives or a crossbow. Yes, that's what I said! Carrying. Weapons. Use them for hunting or protection or fighting off wild boars...who knows! Only a few of us will have guns. I think I'll just carry a pocket knife...can you imagine us all carrying bows and arrows...like Robin Hood. Come ON!

Mr. Kinsey...Donald, has extensive hunting knowledge and all this crazy info about weaponry and battle-ness. So his job is going to be training everyone. We'll learn how to use bows and guns and be required to have target practice. Donald is going to inventory what weapons we find. I think he said Jason, Meg, and Caleb would help. Then they'll make dummy weapons piles in a few locations so if outsiders come in and start demanding weapons we can give them the dummy ones...like guns with firing pins removed and crossbows with broken triggers, things like that. That'll give us time to get a plan together and kablam! Out with the outsiders! So that's the scoop on that.

Oh! Then there's the valuables too! So while we're all talking about these fabulous weapons and stuff, we start talking about the other things we should take out of houses, like valuables and jewelry. Basically we decided to do the same thing as with the weapons. Mom knows all about jewelry, so the scouts will gather, me and mom will inventory everything, and then we'll set up some dummy stashes to give to hoodlums who wander through town. It's very mission-impossible-ish. We'll keep track of where it all comes from so if someone does return, then we'll be able to give them their stuff back. I found some of those polaroid cameras we can use to take pictures of things and notes where they came from. The dummy stashes of jewelry will be stuff from people who we know for sure have died. I really hated the thought we could be taking live people's stuff, I'd feel kinda like the Nazis who stole everything from the Jews and 'mysteriously lost' the records of who it all belonged to. SO I am keeping good track of whose jewlery we found and keeping ALL the records in a safe place.

And what else, oh yeah, the new jobs....I guess all the 'grown-ups' had to have a trade, a main job they're gonna do. Like in the olden days you know? One blacksmith, one butcher, one saloon owner, ha-ha. The farm's not far....4 or 5 miles I guess...not really far, but I'm sure it'll be like walking cross country to Tricia!!! I can just hear her now, complaining about her feet being sore. Thank goodness her dad went to the store and got her a pair of sneakers. Good grief, the girl was walking everywhere in fancy sandals. Ridiculous!

Whew! My brain is tired. Lots of info to process now that we're out of hiding...well, kinda. Hiding...but with others. Totally more fun. I was helping Adam and Ava make little cards and beaded bracelets for Mom for Mother's day. It IS kinda fun to have a little brother and sister now. I keep wondering about the future and how this will all turn out. Today I was remembering when Dad got the call from Mr. Flint to take over the farm. He and his wife were already sick and they decided to drive to Niagara Falls before they died...they went there on their honeymoon. He said they'd go as far as God would take them. It was the first time I'd ever heard Dad cry. I guess I keep thinking about it b/c it sounds like what we're going to do here...we'll go as far as God takes us I suppose. Night girl!

Dark and cloudy but hopeful,
Ashleigh

ANYONE OUT THERE?

YOU ARE NOT ALONE

NEW COMMUNITY HERE!

May 9

Dear Mom,

So we have a stove <u>and</u> washer <u>and</u> dryer!!!! What a treat!! The dads set up generator electricity (one generator/house) and gas tanks for the stoves! We're only allowed to use the power from 5 – 8 every evening for cooking and washing and stuff. OMG!! A washing machine and dryer!! Mom, I thought I'd died and gone to heaven the first time I washed clothes with the new washer! They felt and smelled so good! Not smelling like stream water and all stiff and gross. I hated doing laundry without a machine. It's <u>so much harder</u>! We're not supposed to use the dryer til winter so we'll still use the clothes line, but that's okay (sort of). The dads had to get water to the washers with buckets but it still worked! Absolutely absolutely <u>wonderful</u>!! And Dad and Mitchell and I are taking turns washing clothes. Sharing the boring chores.

We've been gathering up guns, bows and arrows, knives, and whatever. But I don't like it. I don't like the idea of weapons. Using weapons. Gathering weapons. Anything about weapons. Too depressing. Dad doesn't make me carry a gun everywhere I go anymore, but I still do. I'm still scared those guys might come back. We're going to start target practicing soon. The guys found guns and ammo and silencers so we can practice outside without making a lot of noise. I'll let you know how it goes! I'm a bit nervous, but I want to know how to shoot. Just in case!

Janet said I could help her with her medical practitioner duties. I'd like that a lot better than weapons, so I'm gonna do that. So I'll be in charge of gathering and recording all medications and will have to learn first aid and all kinds of stuff. Which will be pretty interesting. We've been to the library and I found a bunch of books on first aid and herbal cures. Me and Mitchell and Caleb are gonna search doctor's offices for medical books and meds and bring them back to Janet. Not that I could understand the books but maybe there'd be some way of telling what medications are for--just in case. What do you think, Mom? You always said I'm a nurturing person. I'd rather be on the healing side of the weapons. Wouldn't that be weird? Me, being a medical person?! Your daughter—a doctor! Well, sort of. I have a <u>lot</u> to learn!!!

We're all doing so much to make things better. If planning made a difference, the world would be back to normal—as we plan a LOT. At least we found people who want to make positive changes so that's good. Actually that's more than good—it's making me feel so much less alone and hopeless.

Mom, I'm not sure if writing to you makes me miss you more or if it helps me by making you closer. I just miss you so much! Everything here would be so much better if you were here. I always think of you making your way home. I just can't think that you aren't. You have to be coming. I'm waiting.
I love you Mom,

Your favorite daughter
Meg

PS: I thought of you on Mother's Day. The other families celebrated with their families but we didn't have a community get-together—as you aren't here. That would have been tacky. I got mad thinking about how the other families have moms and I don't. And I can just hear the Grace family praying about how good the Lord is and how He was with them and saved their whole family and they're all grateful. Like we aren't <u>good</u> enough for God to save <u>you</u> or that the rest of the whole world was so pathetic they died, and <u>their</u> little family is so wonderful that <u>they</u> got saved over all the rest of the world. That is such a <u>conceited idea</u>. And what kind of god would kill everyone off except a few random people? It makes <u>no sense</u>. But whatever. Let them believe in their false prophets and gods and ideas and feel smug in their superiority. I just can't believe that and I won't buy in. Ever.

Jason and I went to the car dealer. All those cars to drive! All those cars to drive!! Took us awhile to find the keys, we only drove in the neighborhood though. Strict rules by Dad. And I don't even need a driver's license!!

May 10

Dear Mandy,

    I'm SOOOOOO friggin tired!!!! Mom had me working out in the garden for like 3 1/2 hours this morning! We did take a little time off yesterday to celebrate Mother's Day for her...we made her breakfast in bed and put wildflowers all around the house. The kids TOTALLY loved that. I think they know Mom isn't their real mom, but they don't talk about their real parents much anymore. I heard Adam tell Mom once that his parents were trying to drive away, but there was a big crash...and he cried about riots and soldiers and fires. Poor little kids :(

    This afternoon I walked over to the library to get more books on building outhouses...Oh yeah, I don't even want to TALK about that project we have to do now...uggggh... And then I had to walk back and help Mom with dinner b/c we're like freaking pioneers and everything's hard and dirty and stupid. Oh and we had target practice today because now we all have to be master marksman! Even though I wasn't doing too bad, I'm tired. And grouchy! I bet the settlers argued all the time with each other. Uggggh.

Partly Sunny, but Disgruntled,
Ashleigh

May 11

Dear Mom,

 I thought I'd share some of my studies with you. It's becoming more interesting now that I'm getting into it. Still scary if I'm expected to use it, but I'm getting to where I like studying. When I first got the book, Anatomica, I just sat there with it on my lap. I was sitting in the living room on the couch with the sunshine coming in—and the sun was making those little dust sparkles dance. Did you know when I was a little girl I used to think tiny people rode those dusts? Kinda like an amusement ride. I'd wave my hand and make the dusts move faster, and listen closely to see if I could hear the tiny screams of kids having a good time. I never heard anything—which is probably a good thing!

 Anyway, I was sitting there thinking about the past and the normal good-ol-days, with this huge book lying across my lap and I just couldn't open it at first. I didn't want to begin to learn medicine or anything to do with it—the task seemed so gigantic I couldn't even fathom how I'd ever get anywhere—learn anything. So why begin?! But I knew Janet and the community are counting on me, and Dad and Mitchell are proud I'll be one of the local "doctors". And I knew you'd be proud of me too. So I opened the cover. When I read the first part, it said it'd explain all about the body, provide listings of diseases and injuries, cover stages of life, and include a wide range of alternative therapies. It also has a first aid section and a symptoms guide. When I read that, I felt better. I like the idea of the charts and stuff to help me figure things out. That I won't be alone and that the doctors who wrote the book were helping me. Which made it easier for me to start.

 So I sat there for hours just paging through the book,

stopping and reading the interesting parts, looking at the pictures, just generally checking it out. Medicine really is fascinating. Sitting there looking and reading, got me to thinking about K-Pox. Why did some of us survive and others not? I wonder if some of us have a specific recessive gene that when both parents have the gene, their children have it also. Like red hair. Both parents have to have the gene for red hair for a child to have red hair. I learned that in science class one year. So this would explain why some families survived K-Pox and others did not. And if this is true, this means there's other people out there like us—way fewer than 1% perhaps, but more people out there! Isn't that exciting! And that means you'd be coming back to us cuz you'd be alive also! Cuz all of us have that recessive gene! That'd be so cool for you to be back soon.

Another reason I'd like to have some other people on the earth is that I really want to get married someday and have children. And if we don't get more people around here, I'd be stuck with Jason (a sulky jerk) or Caleb (too young). Not thrilled about those options! But what if the other people we find (if we find anyone else) are even worse—too old or too young or too stupid or seriously ugly!! I don't want a stupid ugly husband or stupid, ugly children! I'd rather be a lonely old lady. sigh

Well, I guess I shouldn't complain about this yet. We haven't been in the community that long and who knows what will happen. And I'm young. Well, sorta young. Lots of time to find someone—I guess. I try not to think about it too much.

I love you Mom. Thanks for listening and I'll write again soon.

Your favorite daughter
Meg

PS: Don't worry! I'm not wanting to get married any time soon. You know me...I like to plan for the future and hopefully marriage will be in the future someday. But a REALLY long time from now. Things are way too weird to be any time soon!

May 12

Dear Mom,

I can't believe it! So much work and now it's gone! All the food we stored was torn apart by stupid dogs and other animals and they trashed the place.

We had all our groceries like cereal and rice and boxed foods in sealed plastic containers in the grocery store so animals couldn't get them. Someone left a door open (no one will admit to it) and the stupid dogs got in and tore stuff up—knocked over the containers and tore the lids off. So much food just tossed around—after they ate what they liked. Of course, it wasn't just the dog or cat food. It was stuff like sweet cereal and mac n cheese. The store aisles looked like an explosion hit. Food all over—rice and pasta bags spilled open, boxes of food torn open—all sorts and shapes of trashed mess. Toilet paper and Kleenex looked like snow all down the paper aisle. Walking down the pet food aisle was like walking down a gravel road—kibbles of all shapes and sizes scattered everywhere.

If we'd checked the food storage every day this wouldn't have happened—we'd have noticed the door was open and stopped at least some of the damage. As it is we've probably lost a quarter of our food! We were already concerned about not having enough. At this point we have no way of easily replenishing what we have.

First everyone dies!—then we lose our food. It's just too much. I hate this. Something's always going wrong. No proper bathrooms, no running water, no phones, no friends, no school, no heat or air conditioning (and summer is already hot and sticky with no ac or showers and we haven't even gotten to August!), no cars, no movies, no takeout pizza, no tv, did I mention no hot baths or showers, no lights that we can switch on all day—only 5-8, and have to drag flashlights and lanterns with you everywhere, no hair dryer, no school busses, no video games.

So what do we have? We have cold running water—in a stream with dirt and fish and creepy crawlies in it; tons of cool clothing in the shops but nowhere to wear them or someone to wear them for; schools and books but only one teacher, movie theater with no movies, electricity but only for 3 hours a day, roads but nowhere to go, people but no friends, houses but dead stinky dead people in them, a dad but no mom.

The things we don't have far outweighs the things we do have. I know I used to complain about life—wah wah wah, but I <u>swear</u> I wouldn't complain one bit about <u>anything</u> if life could go back to normal. I WANT MY LIFE BACK!!! I WANT MY MOTHER BACK NOW!!! I WANT MY LIFE BACK NOW!!! I can't stand this. I really can't. I hate everything about this life—<u>everything</u>! I hate all the things I have now that replaces my old stuff. I hate having no friends. I hate how dark it is at night. I used to like looking at the stars—they made me feel like I was a part of something bigger than me. Now the stars make me feel intensely small and cold and alone—emphasizes how we're all tiny specks in a vast cold unending universe—that our lives are small and meaningless. That we are <u>nothing</u>. And yet we have to go on—survive—and for what?! Are we starting the human race again? I'm just not up to it. I'm really not. I find nothing exciting in the challenge before us. Nothing. I want no challenges other than what I had last year. I want to be preparing for college, thinking about prom, and graduation and a part time job and friends and whether I should cut and color my hair, what outfits are cute, what boys are cute (boys my age, not kids, and NOT grouchy boys like

Jason), what my first car will be, what shoes are on sale. I want to go to parties that have more people at them than are living in this town. I want to have secrets with friends. I want my normal, boring everyday life back—that same wonderful life I used to complain about.

I know I could make this whole new stupid life into a fun challenge but I just don't have the energy. I just want to sleep. I want Mitchell to be an older brother so he can do more, and sometimes take care of me—instead of me taking care of him. I want Dad to be Superman and make everything okay again. I want my tears to stop making splotches on my paper and my nose to stop running. Crying is so messy. I want messy crying to be gone as well—since I'm wishing for all these other impossible things. At least the dogs didn't eat ALL the tissues. We have years of that, if we don't cry too much—only some of it's now stashed in bags cause the dogs tore the boxes up, some of which I'm using now. At least we've not been asked to recycle used tissues. The adults are so fussy about our trash. Trash we can use again goes here, burning trash goes there. Here there whatever. It's just all trash, trash, trash! <u>I don't care. I just don't care!</u>

I think I'll hide so I don't have to feed Mitchell tonight. He can eat peanut butter and crackers and raisins. At least tuna is in cans and the mayo and pickles and good old peanut butter in tough plastic or glass jars. We should have several years of peanut butter or tuna sandwiches on hand. I'm already sick of tuna. SICK SICK SICK OF TUNA!!!!!

Meg

PS: I just had a thought...with our luck all the expiration dates for canned tuna and salmon and jars of mayo and peanut butter

93

are probably for next month or something. That would be about right!

May 12

Dear Mandy,

   It's all destroyed. It's hopeless. I was SURE I'd shut all the doors, but I don't know...somehow one got left open...Is this all my fault??? I'm not the only one who goes in there and I was in there only in the morning like THREE days ago...I don't know, I'm driving myself CRAZY thinking about it. And Caleb says it wasn't his dogs b/c he keeps their pen secure out at the farm.

   And NOW we're all going to starve to death or start eating each other and then we'll all die anyway. I don't know even know how to start to fix the damage done by the animals. AND I'm NOT scrounging around at stores further away! Somebody else can freakin go! I'm too freakin tired and I'm too freakin upset!

   Mom said we'll have to work harder to make sure our crops grow. But I don't want to work harder...I just want to give up. Why couldn't you and I have died together? I hate it here all alone.

Thunderheads and dying inside,
Ashleigh

May 13

Dear Mom,

Sorry about my rant yesterday. But sometimes I just get so overwhelmed and lonely. And I miss you so much. And even though we're alive, it's just so discouraging I can barely stand it. So we all picked up at the store and reorganized everything and the damage isn't as bad as it could've been. We repacked the food in big plastic tubs and put the tubs on higher shelves to keep them away from animals. I hope it works.

So Dad found me in my room crying and tried to make me feel better. He sat on the bed and gave me a hug and said he understands and he feels like that too sometimes. But we just have to get on with life--like it or not. And he knows none of this is easy but complaining doesn't help. And that made me feel better, knowing he understands and gets down sometimes too. I'm glad he's here—makes me feel less alone and like he's there for me. Maybe he isn't Superman, and can't turn life back to what it was, but he is here and that helps so much. So...I'll try to move on...but it won't be easy!

Speaking of Dad, he's obsessed with getting more power going. It makes me tired just thinking about everything he wants to do. If I knew about meds, I'd put him on something for OCD! Seriously! He reads everything he can about power and is working on alternative energy sources as well as using what we already have. And the parents are all talking about putting solar water heaters and panels on the roofs—which means hot showers!! But this will all be a long time coming yet as we have to get the crops in the field and vegetables in the garden. It's a good thing Mr. Grace knows so much about the farm or we'd be sunk! Since we want to keep animals we have to raise crops like corn and oats for them. We're thinking about wheat and corn for us to make bread and stuff next year. The moms are working mostly in the gardens with vegetables. About a month ago Mrs. Grace was out with a small tractor plowing up the backyard of the clubhouse for the local garden. Looked like she was having a blast!

You know, come to think of it, most of the parents seem like they're really enjoying the challenge of this new world. Well, maybe except for Janet Kinsey. She used to be really really sad most of the time. Now she's just sorta sad most of the time. I think having her as our teacher makes her feel better. Sometimes she laughs at the silly things that Caleb and Mitchell do. And she gets so frustrated with her daughter who still sulks about almost everything, especially about learning algebra! It's kinda funny (but mostly aggravating) to listen to her whine--"Why do I have to learn stupid Algebra!! I'll never need it! We're just going to be here in this pit of the world with no use for any education so why bother!!" Her mom just says, "Because I said so. Now do it!" That's the advantage of being both Mom and teacher. "Because I said so" is the ultimate reason. No other reason needed, at least according to parents. :) But she seems to be doing better and that's good. AND Mrs. Kinsey is working with me and Jason so we can graduate in early June! I'm so excited!!!! I'll actually be able to graduate! I didn't think that would be possible when the world fell apart, but now I'm actually going to graduate! Since Mrs. Kinsey's a real teacher, she can make sure we complete our courses and get the credits we need to graduate appropriately--not just some pretend, you turned 18 graduation. But a real, number of credits completed, graduation. Jason doesn't care about the credits but he wants to graduate. I want the real thing.

I worked so hard all through school to get good grades and do well. It just seemed like such a horrible waste to have lost all that work. And now I get to see it all pay off!!!!! I want my black robe and silly flat hat! I can hardly wait! But I have to finish my finals and one more term paper for US Government. US Government--I wonder if there's anyone left at the Capitol? I hope so.

Oh btw...we had our first target shooting session! I actually liked it way better than I thought I would. I shot a 22 pistol and a 22 rifle with a scope and a 30 30 rifle with a scope! We shot at cans and I did better than Mitchell and Caleb and I never shot before! I think I did better cuz I squeezed the trigger carefully and the boys jerked the trigger. Using the scope is fun and I really like how you have to be really really still and careful and then crack! The can falls over or flies in the air! The 30 30 wasn't as much fun. It's way louder and slams into your shoulder. I held the gun tight against my shoulder and was wearing a padded vest so it wasn't as bad as I thought it'd be, but I like the 22s better. I'm looking forward to shooting again! It was fun!

Still miss you and still waiting. Hurry home!

I love you Mom,

Your favorite daughter
Meg

PS: I've been reading books about herbs and plants in the wild we can eat and use for medicines. Did you know the blue flowered plant you find all over in weedy areas is chicory? The name comes from the Arab word *chicouryeh* and the Romans called it *cihchorium*--which also was used by the Greeks. The plant we find in the ditches was used by the ancient people? Isn't that weird? You can use the leaves in the spring for salad or tea. The root in the fall can be used for tea as well. The ancient Romans used it for jaundice, anemia, infertility, and liver problems. I wonder if we'll end up using it for medicine? I'll have to come up with a system for remembering/finding what herbs can be used for various illnesses—to get my medical library set up so I remember where everything is. And just a random thought—since chicory was used in the ancient world, is it an invasive species here in the Americas? I'd look it up online...but...

May 16

Dear Mandy,

　　Sometimes I just don't know what I'm supposed to be doing around here. I'm exhausted...and that's making me depressed. Sometimes I just can't stop thinking about you and everybody...and I get so sad...and honestly sometimes...I feel pretty jealous of those who are gone. We've started to work SO hard now. Like REAL physical labor camp stuff and I'm just...sooooo tiiiired.

　　I mean I like my jobs I guess. The gardening is fine. Mom and I did that a little before...but this is WAY more and WAY harder. And I like keeping all the inventory organized. We're still moving food from the other grocery stores, so there's lots to keep track of, but...THIS is my job?? Forever? And we haven't even had a group meeting b/c everyone's working and we really don't have anything to report.

　　Janet and I were talking the other day while we were planting pumpkin seeds. She was telling me all about the lessons she's planning and that led to her talking about where she went to college and how she and Donald met. It was nice to see her perky about something. It's funny to think about Janet and Donald when they were my age. Do they still feel the same now as they did when they were younger? I can't imagine not feeling like me. Feeling older...what's that feel like? Will I not be fun? I can't imagine wanting to work all the time like my parents do. Mom LOVES planning out what we are growing and how we will preserve and can everything for the future. I don't know how she keeps track of everything and organizes who is supposed to do what and when...It's pretty amazing actually. And Dad is still excited about drawing up plans and building things, even if it's outhouses or small additions here and there for storage. He even started asking my thoughts about hand washing stations and heaters in the outhouses. I remember visiting his office and seeing the plans for foundations, walls, ventilation systems, bathrooms...It was like a giant puzzle. It was interesting...But he worked ALL the time.

   It's hard for me to see how all the pieces of this new life fit together. I'm blind to imagining the future. What will help me see again?

Partly cloudy and uncertain,
Ashleigh

IF YOU HAVE TIME
TO COMPLAIN, YOU HAVE
TIME TO BRUSH YOUR
TEETH AND WASH
YOUR OWN SOCKS.

-DAD

May 16

Dear Mom,

It's official!!! We're going to have a prom!! It's going to be the night before graduation so we can use the set up/stage/dance floor/ etc. for both events. This is going to be soooo cool! We won't have dates--obviously, but we'll all get dressed up and we'll all be there--even our parents. I know. Kinda weird having your parents at the prom. But it gives us more people to dance with. Tricia's so excited about having something to get dressed up for she can hardly stand it! She's been to all the shops in town and tried on every outfit she likes. I know this because she decided that I'm the person she needs to tell--I guess because I'm the only senior girl. She's also taken it upon herself to help me find a dress. And, I must admit, it's more fun shopping <u>with</u> someone than looking for a dress by myself. So we've spent the last few afternoons talking about fashion and our flattering colors (mine is red; hers is blue) and make up and the advantages of fake nails for parties etc. Which I might use, as all this work has NOT been good for my nails — pretty sad looking hands actually. It's been fun. Tricia's not so irritating now especially when she's talking about stuff she likes. And we're both totally psyched about being about to get all the clothes we want for <u>free</u>!! As underclassmen, Ashleigh and Caleb shoulda put the prom together, but as they're only 2 people (and one a boy!), the moms decided they'd be the prom committee. So...we'll see what they come up with. It's exciting to have something to look forward to. I wonder how Jason and Caleb will look all dressed up and what music the parents will find — hopefully a variety of music. And we'll get to dance! I love dancing! I don't even mind if all my dances are with Mitchell. It would've been nice to have a boyfriend to go with. No sense thinking about that.

But will I ever have a boyfriend? Jason's the only boy my age and I really don't like him. He's too self-absorbed and "all about me". He complains about working, about his responsibilities, and likes to boss the boys around. He can be a total jerk. Besides even if I was interested, Ashleigh really has a crush on him. Which he pretends not to notice, but it's hard to miss! She's always sneaking looks at him. So I may never have a boyfriend or get married or have children. A part of me wants to run screaming from here—wants to leave and find more people—wants more options than what I have. Maybe things will get better and more people will come by, or maybe the government survived and will be sending out search parties for the survivors and we'll all go back to normal. Well, maybe not, but I can dream can't I? wah wah wah...I feel like I'm always complaining to you. I'll try to be more positive for the next few minutes.

Mitchell n Caleb n I found a ton of medical books so I'm trying to sort them by type and difficulty. Some books are waaaay beyond me. But the books on meds, first aid, and alternative meds are going to be where Mrs. Kinsey and I can find them. And, of course, there's tons of words I can barely pronounce, much less understand. But I have to start somewhere, and First Aid is at least a start.

So far, I'm the chief dispenser of aspirin and band-aids. Hope that's all I ever have to do. Mrs. Kinsey will do the tougher stuff. But I've read about what to do if someone breaks a bone or gashes a leg or something. I don't think I'll faint or throw up in an emergency, but I don't know how I'll react. Sometimes I imagine something serious does happen and think about what I'll say and do. I want to be ready and not run around screaming my head off. But we'll see. You know, the way Mitchell and Caleb run about, won't surprise me if our first real patients will be one of them.

We've decided all medicines and supplies will be kept in two separate places. We don't want all our medical things in one place in case something happens. I always think about those guys who broke into the house across the street. They or someone else could come back. So our supplies with the addictive medicines are in a locked storeroom at the local elementary school and Mrs. Kinsey's supplies with the extra cold and flu meds and stuff are in the locked storeroom at the Like-New Consignment Shoppe. We tried to come up with places that wouldn't be high on the list of places to be looted—just in case. And if we have to tell about a medicine stash, we'll tell about Mrs. Kinsey's stash.

btw Mitchell really hates that we all have to go to school. At first he argued every day about it and doesn't see the purpose in learning more than he already knows—which isn't much! But he doesn't have a choice. The Committee decided all children have to go to school until 18 or they complete the high school curriculum. And all adults are required to be trained in some skill. But Mitchell only wants to be trained in a skill. I tried to tell him he needs math and reading and writing before he can be good at anything or do research in his chosen field, but he wouldn't listen. Dad sorta got through to him—said we don't have the luxury of being ignorant. Actually the person who made the biggest difference in getting Mitchell to shut up was Jason. We were sitting around the clubhouse and Mitchell started on about school again. Jason looked totally ticked off and snapped,

"Stop being an idiot and just go to school. Do you want to be keep on being an ignorant kid?" Mitchell got angry and stormed off. But he's gone to school every day since then without too much fuss. And school will let out for the summer soon. And Jason and I will graduate!! <u>Very cool!</u>

Anyway I decided to use school time to work on my medical books, as it forces me to study, cuz sometimes it's hard to do on my own. And I'm almost done with US Government and I've completed English 12 so I don't have much left. So far my plan's working and I'm getting through chapters of the medical book. I forget a lot, but when I finish the book, I'll go through it again to help me remember the important stuff. Then I'll start on another book. Not sure which one. I'll decide later— whatever seems most important at the time. Mrs. Kinsey and I are going to use Dr. Embrey's office to store equipment—like we know what to do with it!! NOT! And we're going to bring stuff to our clinic (We have a clinic!) in the clubhouse. I liked Dr. Embrey and we went to him for years. I hope he's okay out there somewhere.

Dad really enjoys working with the energy committee. He loves reading about solar energy and water and wind. I'm glad he's happier. It makes it so much easier for me n Mitchell. The energy group is still working on solar water heaters—which is a fantastic idea—and we might get hot water sooner than I thought! I'd give a year's supply of chocolate for a long hot shower! So far we take tub baths--bring water up from the farm well, and heat it. Luke-warm and shallow. After the bath, we use the water to flush toilets. I never knew how much I'd appreciate having a plain old bathroom with a toilet that flushes, and a shower and sink with hot and cold water. I guess that may never happen again. You know, not having something as simple as a working bathroom makes me so depressed.

I'm doing okay mostly. Still get depressed sometimes and wish we could go back in time, but that isn't an option. I miss you so much and wish you could be here. I want to talk to you about so many things. Like what am I going to do when I grow up? I mean I know I'm almost an adult—legally—but I don't feel like it. Things as simple as I don't feel like I should call adults by their first names. Ashleigh likes calling adults by their first names and jumped right on board with it. Maybe part of my not wanting to is, if I call them by first names, that will make me an adult. I <u>don't want</u> to be an adult yet. All the responsibility. I guess I have the responsibility now—whether I like it or not, but it's scary. I just want to be a little girl again and go back in time. This new life is scary. I want someone to tell me everything will be alright.

I really wonder what my future's gonna be. Will I be a "doctor" for the rest of my life? How am I supposed to do that? What if I make mistakes and someone dies? At first I thought it'd be fun to be a doctor, now I'm just scared. At least Janet is head "doctor". I couldn't be in total charge of medicine!

Please come home soon. I need to talk to you. I'm lost without you. I need you Mom.
So much love,

Your favorite daughter
Meg

PS: I was supposed to be positive and I wasn't, so I'll end with something useful. Did you know you could eat those rose hips that are on rose plants after the petals fall off? They're apparently full of vitamin C and the British and north Europeans used them during WWII when they couldn't get fresh fruits and vegetables. The book said they could be a bit bitter, but were healthy. If we have to eat them, I'll let you know what they taste like. And they're supposed to make a good jelly—when you add lots of sugar!

May 17

Dear Mandy,

It was your birthday today. I mean, I know you know that...but I was thinking it's only your birthday down here b/c up in heaven you never get older anymore. I got up super early (you owe me! you KNOW I like to sleep in!) to plant some violets around your cross. Remember I started a few in my room? They'll be really pretty and have a good spot there by the wet and sandy stream. I had to hurry back and I didn't want to explain why my eyes were red and blotchy...but I made sure the leaves were raked away and your pickle jar was safe. I buried it a little and put the leaves around it to protect it from any predators. I hit your keychains with my hand and it sounded like a mini wind chime. Maybe you're singing to me.....Miss you....

After breakfast Adam worked with me in the garden. He's so crazed about how everything grows. It was super cute ;-) He kept asking all these questions about how seeds can change into plants and how we get food and how God knows what food we need. I think I'll get him a kids book on plants from the library. Too bad he can't be a scientist one day...but maybe he'll be a farmer. Made me kinda sad for him...but I guess he'll only ever know this world. He won't remember how it was before or the choices he won't have.

That got me thinking you know? Adam and Ava will barely remember how things were before now...before K-Pox. They won't remember what we're missing. Sure, they'll hear the stories from before...but they'll only know this world.

I suppose that's something right? This is their world and how wondrous it must be to them. I can't even imagine what that must be like. I guess maybe if I could learn to see through their eyes, I wouldn't feel sad sometimes. I would just see all the new stuff to learn, even when I'm dead tired. Like now...like always... bone tired! But still...it'd be like seeing a rainbow for the first time. And that would really be amazing!

I talked to Mom a little after dinner. I think she remembered today was your birthday too. Last year you and I ordered pizza and watched like the worst scary movies we could find. Remember? I don't want Mom to know how much I feel inside and how much it all hurts...I just don't think she'd understand. I mean, I hear what her and Dad say...about God not MAKING any of this happen...and I know they're right...but it doesn't make it hurt any less to know that, you know? I think Mom knows something's going on with me. We were sitting in the living room and I was trying to read my book, but kept spacing out so finally she asked what was wrong. I told her I was just sad and tired and just...didn't want this to be our life.

She came and sat next to me and gave me a big hug. Then she said this isn't the life she'd have chosen for me, but it's what we have. We're lucky. I told her I don't feel lucky. She reminded me God has bigger plans for us, even though we don't know what they are. I wish I knew what they were!!! Then I started crying like a stupid baby. I didn't want to...but I felt better crying with her there.

I guess I never thought about Mom and Dad being sad for me too...all their dreams for my life and their lives are gone, not just my dreams. Everyone's hurting and scared and uncertain, even when they don't show it. I know Mandy, you told me to live too. Live for the both of us...and I've been pretty caught up lately in my pity party. You'd have told me to snap out of it by now! Is this your way of sending me a cosmic message? That can be my gift to you...no more pity party!!

We do have to try and make new dreams...just like little Adam. Maybe the prom will cheer me up. Meg and Janet decided we're going to do prom and graduation. No dates or anything, but we'll go all dressed up and blare the stereo. It'll be in the clubhouse family room—which is pretty big. Mom wants me to go decorate with her. I just wish I felt more...festive.

And then they're going to do a graduation for Meg and Jason the next day. I guess they're both Valedictorians. You survived! You graduate at the top of your class!! Too bad they won't get to go to college. I suppose they're missing their dreams too. But maybe it's not so bad that we don't have to go to college anymore. We can have the job we want and have it now. We'll have to figure out who we are in the midst of this new world. Well, I better go...gonna read, then I'm dress 'shopping' tomorrow with Mom and the little kids. Hopefully I'll find something you'd have liked. This will be our first prom.

Dusk settling in and weepy,
Ashleigh

May 19

Dear Mom,

Such a strange life. I wonder if I'll ever get used to it. It wasn't too many months ago I was driving around and buying useless stuff for no particular reason, and planning on college and whatever. Today I spent my morning in the garden, planting tomatoes and other vegetables, weeding the lettuce and peas, and fixing holes in the fence where the bunnies got through and nibbled away a bunch of our food. Dang rabbits! They're so cute but they sure can eat a lot! And the deer! We need to get rid of the deer...perhaps eat more venison? I've more muscle now than I ever had and I don't even have to go to the gym! I am fit and tan and can lift more weight than I ever thought I could. Pretty soon I'll be throwing those 50 pound bags of fertilizer and mulch with ease! I almost can now!

I've been trying on prom dresses with Trish and it's kinda cool to see how good my body looks now that I'm in good shape. And nobody but Jason and Caleb to even care. Though I wouldn't <u>mind</u> if they thought I looked good! I'm looking forward to dressing up for the prom and I'm really looking forward to graduating!!!

Tricia and I found the dresses we want to wear—I think. We shopped only in expensive stores and tried on so many beautiful dresses! We took turns being the sales lady and helping choose the outfits—shoes, accessories, jewelry, everything! And no one else there to get in our way...which was a little creepy at first, but is actually quite convenient! :) So after hours of shopping, I chose this beautiful deep red full-length dress with a sweetheart neckline, a natural waist, which flows in an A-line to the floor. Trish said I look wonderful in it and the color makes my eyes really shine. We're working on makeup and what colors we want for eye shadow and liner and everything makeup and hair! It's been fun--especially fun to do girly stuff after spending days in the garden getting all sweaty and muscle-y. And Trish and I are getting along pretty well--considering she's so young. But none of us is too fussy about who our friends are these days or cares about ages. If we're fussy, we'd not have anyone to talk to! We asked Ashleigh if she wanted to go with us. She said she's going with her mom. I understand, but it would've been fun to have her with us. She's a bit moody so perhaps it was best she went with her mom. Trish is having such a good time shopping that it makes me have a good time too. Ashleigh may have brought the mood down if she'd gone with us. I hope she becomes friendlier or it'll be really hard to like her. And we're too small a group to be "not friends".

Well, I'm heading to bed. I'm tired and the garden will be there again tomorrow.

Your favorite daughter
Meg

May 23

Dear Mandy,

    I can't imagine thinking about only one thing at a time. I feel like I've so many thoughts running through my head that I'm just going to explode. And liking only one thing at a time...is that what we learn to do when we get older? How <u>not</u> to get bored so easily? Honestly, I don't know what I feel most of the time or what I want or where I'm going. It's all so confusing and exhausting.

    I mean take Jason for example. There are times when I just get so excited and nervous to be around him...Like just the other day I was walking home from the farm and Jason came up behind me and threw his arm around my shoulders. I guess he was wandering around and saw me walking...I hope he wasn't painting on any more houses!! But he smiled at me then started walking backwards into the woods. He said "Come on" and then turned and walked off. I was totally nervous, but I followed anyway. We walked for a little bit and then we came to the stream. Jason started picking up rocks and throwing them across the water. I didn't really know what to do, but I felt disgusting and sweaty from working so I sat down and took my shoes off to put my feet in the water. It was a warm day and I was dirty anyway so it was nice to sit and lean back with the spring breeze and sun whispering across my face. All of a sudden Jason starts talking about how his dad and him and Caleb used to go fishing and camping there. He said they had a big trip planned for the summer before the disease wrecked everything. He kept talking while he was throwing rocks. Plunk, plunk. I've never heard him talk so much before! He even laughed about when his friend Ben came camping with them and they threw a firecracker in the fire just to see what it'd do. His dad knocked over the tent trying to get out and see what was happening! I laughed too and told him the story about when Mandy and I covered the inside of our friend Hailey's car with sticky notes and watched her come outside and totally freak out and blame her brother Dylan. That was hysterical! He smiled this really cute grin and said "Bad girl, eh?" I didn't know what to say so I just laughed and looked back at the water. He got real quiet then and said Ben was one of the first ones who died. I said Hailey and Dylan were too and then you, Mandy, died a couple months later. Jason sat down next to me then and we just sat quietly watching the stream.

Of course then I totally freaked out. Because I'm a dork. I looked up at him and he was looking at me and all of a sudden I realized it was getting late and I jumped up and said I had to go b/c it was getting dark. He probably thinks I sleep with a night light or something! Hahaha...yeah right, like a night candle! Honestly though...us alone was making me nervous and I didn't want Dad to come looking for me. It would be totally embarrassing if he found us at the stream...gazing into each other eyes...or more!

So Jason got up too and flashed this fantastic smile and said "K. See ya!" and then he was gone. How weird! I mean I've always wanted a boyfriend. Remember how we used to talk about it?...rate all the boys in our class and talk about how our kids would look if we married certain boys. We even had a 'who would you choose' game! It all seems so silly now, but how was I to know I wouldn't have anyone left to pick from just six months later! But this is what I mean...right there at the stream I felt like I could totally go for Jason... but when everyone's together, he doesn't even look at me, which drives me crazy! It makes me think I've just imagined him being nice to me.

And I'll tell you someone else who drives me a little crazy. Meg. It's not like she's ever said anything mean or done anything...but she keeps trying to talk to me and invite me places to hang out...but I'm just not ready you know? So BACK OFF! I won't be rushed into another friendship that's going to break my heart.

I'm just... so frustrated sometimes. Are these really the

people we're going to live with forever??? Moody Jason and ANNOYING Tricia!!! Complain, complain!!! At least she's been helping Dad with the animals on the farm. Dad says she's pretty good too...but all her fashion stuff. Uuuggh. Don't get her started on what trends might be in the future...she has this whole theory about style and what we'll wear in our new society. On and on. Caleb's really nice sometimes...I've seen him drawing pictures for her of her new outfits just to make her laugh. Better than her grumpy other brother!

I should probably take it easy on Meg and Tricia. Dad always says you don't know someone else's story or what goes on in their homes. Maybe Meg is lonely too and her asking me to do stuff is her being nice. I don't know.....I think that prom will be the last time I dye my hair. I hate to give it up, but I'm so tired all the time and what's the point anyway? I used to do it to stand out and say that I didn't have to fit in with anyone else because I knew who I was. Then I did it for you...but now, I don't really know WHO I am anymore...who does after all this???

Better go help Mom with dinner. Maybe I'll find some answers in the beans. Like tea leaves right? Bean reading...yeah, I'll become the town fortune teller. It's like living in a circus anyway.

Sunny and confused,
Ashleigh

May 25

Dear Mom,

Prom and Graduation! are almost here!! Tricia and I have been talking about doing our nails and hair a day early so if we don't like what we choose then we can do it over again. But OMG my hands and nails look horrible with all the hard work we've been doing. So Tricia and are planning on using some hand treatments (lotions and creams and stuff) and then use gardening gloves for the next few days. Actually Tricia has been using gloves already. I've never really bothered before, but I think I'm going to use them from now on. I can't believe how quickly soil dries out your skin and stains your nails. So annnyway... we plan on having beautiful hands and nails and hair. We asked Ashleigh if she'd like to join us, but she turned us down (again). Oh well. We'll keep asking...

Gotta run.

Your favorite daughter (and almost graduate!!!!!!!!!)
Meg

May 26

Dear Mandy,

    I was working in the community garden today, and it's really looking good! I know I was totally freaking out about us having to eat each other when the animals got into our food at the store, but I'm really impressed with how much food we're growing. Granted, we planted tons of seeds in hopes of a good season.

    I guess it's b/c we always had food...well, actually all sorts of stuff...before. If we ran out of peanut butter...just go to the store! We didn't have to think about it. And there wasn't this constant worry in the back of your head about what happens if things don't grow...if the crops get destroyed...if the wind takes down the corn...or there's too much rain...or not enough! You know all that stuff we think about now b/c this is all we have. There's no stores to back us up. Life's not a hobby anymore. It's an active sport!

    Dad always says God will provide...but I've never really seen it happen you know? I never really saw Him grow things and I think about all the simple things He must do all around to keep us going.

    Caleb came by today when I was working. That was fun. I took a break and went with him to see his 'dog pack.' He has a whole obstacle course out in one of the fields for his dogs. It's pretty fantastic! Bars for them to jump over, a field set up for them to find things (mostly tennis balls under different boxes)....He said he's even started to take a few of them on patrol. He was saying how awesome it would be if the dogs would alert us about outsiders, but then only attack on his signal. I said that really wouldn't help if armed bandits were attacking us and he was taking a nap!!! We cracked up! He said he thought about making whistle signals we could use in an emergency too. It's pretty amazing the way he's thought about all of this. It would be really cool to train one, but I KNOW Mom and Dad won't let me have one. Buut...There's a super cute fuzzy girl puppy that just wants to be mine! :) Oh well, easier for Caleb to keep them all together I guess. Ok. Gotta run!

Sunny and sore,
Ashleigh

May 29

Dear Mom!!!

Can you believe it!? Tomorrow is prom and then graduation!!! I don't think I can stand the excitement. No one is as excited about this as I am, but I'm so excited, I almost feel sick. But a good kind of sick!

Tricia and I have been doing our nails every evening and trying on different nail polishes and nail accessories. I love putting little jewels on my nails! We have the best finger and toe nails in the whole community. Janet is letting us play with her nails as well and that is fun. She likes to be included in things that Tricia is doing, as Tricia is at that age where doing things with your mom is so totally uncool! I'm glad I'm past that age. What I wouldn't give to do your nails right now!! So we play with hair and make up and clothes and we are having the best time ever! I never thought I could get along so well with someone so young. It's almost as good as having my old friends again. Almost. But not quite. Some things I don't feel like talking about to someone that much younger...but, hey, this is working out and I'm not going to fuss. I'm just happy that things are going so well!

I love you Mom!

Your favorite daughter (with lovely nails)
Meg

May 30

Dear Mandy,

So the big day is here! PROM! I'm actually feeling pretty good about it! Mom and I are going this morning to the clubhouse to set up decorations. Caleb's helping too. And Dad said something about having to get the archway in place? He has something up his sleeve :) It's nice working together for something fun...not just working so hard to survive.

We have sparkly lights and streamers and lacey tablecloths and chair covers with bows. It's probably even nicer than prom at the high school would've been! Janet's making corsages and bootonears (sp?), boutinears?, I miss spell check...flowers for the boys. The kids are dressing up in fancy clothes too. Adam says he's my date and I love it! Dad is Mom and Ava's date...he keeps saying he'll be a thorn between two roses...lol. They're going to be so cute.

We have a photo backdrop and we have the Polaroid camera we can take pictures with.

Whew! Okay! Lots to do! I'll write more later! I'm off to the clubhouse with Mom and the kids!

Clear skies and upbeat,
Ashleigh

PS — I found a flower keychain at the store the other day and hooked it on your cross. Now you have a corsage too! We can still share our first prom. Miss you.

Cool sunlight fades gray
One dull day to another
And sleep is preferred
Children and laughter
Coax the sun to brighter heights
And make life worthwhile

janet kinsey

May 30

Dear Mandy,

OMG!!! I cannot believe how wonderful it all was. And a little sad too, but that's ok. I really started missing you at the end of the dance. SOOOO much. I think it was just all the dancing and I was exhausted and I'm just sloppy from so much activity today. But it really was amazing!

Before we went to the dance, Mom cooked this awesome veggie pasta dish. YUM! We had candles, which is nothing new...but they were the elegant stick candles with crystal candle holders and she let us eat on the good china that we used to only use at holidays. Then Ava and Mom and I got ready upstairs and Adam and Dad were downstairs. I could hear Dad telling Adam how to 'kiss a lady's hand' and pull out chairs for them. Ava couldn't stop giggling about being a princess while she got dressed. She looked so beautiful! Mom and her had picked out this incredibly poofy dress in a soft yellow, which goes great with her big brown eyes and light brown hair. It had little flowers on the top and she wore a matching flower in her hair. Mom pulled her hair up, but let a few curls dangle around her face. Sooo cute! We kept telling her what a big girl she was.

Mom found her dream dress too...it was one she said she'd looked at it in the specialty boutique, but it was too expensive to get before. How awesome is it that money doesn't matter anymore! SHE even giggled a little and did a twirl in the mirror when she was ready.

I found a gorgeous purple dress...a real deep purple, not that tacky fuchsia color or lavender. The dark like-royalty color...for you girl! You should've seen how amazing I looked... floor length dress with one crystal shoulder strap that went all the way down to my waist and wrapped around the back. It had a small slit on the side...not too scandalous :-) Speaking of...I heard Caleb say something about Tricia bringing home a crazy skimpy black dress that his mom flipped out about and made her take

123

back. So I wondered what she'd wear....

But back to my dress :-)...it had a small train on it so I had to lift it up a little when I was walking, which was great b/c I could show off my crystal shoes! I'm pretty sure my dress was supposed to be a bridesmaid dress, but who cares! I looked FANTASTIC in it! :-) Even Dad got all teary when I came down the stairs and Adam started clapping. He kissed the back of my hand after I had my corsage on. It made me feel so good after how down I've been feeling lately. Oh!! And I put purple streaks in my hair since my other purple had faded. It looked awesome! Mom and I pulled my hair up on the sides and curled it all down the back. It was so great! We took a few pictures at home and then off we went to the clubhouse. The solar lights along the path were amazing! Like little stars to light our way. I'm glad Mom thought of them.

When we got to the dance, it was like heaven on earth. Adam opened the door for me and immediately I saw this big balloon arch Dad made. I said 'Thanks Dad!' and then almost started to cry b/c Mom and him were looking at me with tears in their eyes too. But I didn't want to mess up my make-up!

The Kinseys were already there (well, except for Tricia, she came later with Meg) and boy did Jason and Caleb look hot in their tuxes!!!! Wow!!!! I couldn't wait for them to show me their moves!! lol. We got some punch while we waited for everyone and I'd just started to talk to Jason when the Shultzes walked in. Mitchell looked really grown-up in his tux.

And I gotta say...Meg and Tricia clean up really nice too. They got ready together...which kinda made me sad because I miss girl time...but I just can't seem to open up yet...It's too hard. Meg was wearing this really pretty red dress and Tricia was wearing blue. I guess her mom made her take the black one back! Everyone just looked beautiful. It was like we were on another planet--one that didn't involve working in the garden and feeding animals or worrying about clean water. It was great! Oh AND hysterical!! Sam yelled out, "Let's get this party started!" and I about died laughing. The guy who always seems so brainy was getting ready to boogie. It was sooooo funny!

So Jason and I danced :) Boy did he look hot in his tux!!! Did I mention that already?? :-) I danced with Adam first of course b/c you have to dance with your date! And then Dad cut in and Adam danced with Mom. Donald asked Ava to dance too...it was so sweet! She was just twirling and twirling. Then I danced with Donald and Sam. Jason and I danced a couple of times...on slow songs I could feel his warm hands on my back...The songs were definitely over too soon! Mom and Dad showed off their ballroom dance steps. Oh, and I danced with Caleb too. He had some pretty fantastic moves on the fast songs! The slow songs he seemed shy, but that was kinda sweet too. The little kids crashed out at some point during the night. (Mom and I made a bed in the corner for them to sleep til the dance finished. We figured they wouldn't last the whole time.) We danced until 11 or so! Then you could tell everyone was getting sleepy so it was time to call it a night.

Aaaaahhhhhh. What a night! And tomorrow's graduation. Mom and I are going over early to reset everything...but tonight it's nice to think that our sparkly world is still over there even if we're at home in bed. Like some little piece of heaven on earth that we could share for just a moment. Something that let us forget hard reality...and let us remember that we are still people who need joy in our lives.

I hoped you liked my stellar moves Mandy....and that you were rocking out with the angels up there. Night Night my friend.

Starlight and content,
Ashleigh

May 31

Dear Mom,

What a wonderful weekend!! We had the prom last night and graduation today. It's almost midnight and I should be sleeping, but I just can't sleep. I wore my black graduation gown and my red beautiful glamorous evening gown--all within 24 hours! I am a graduate!!! OMG! That's soooo exciting. I finally made it!! I'm not going to think about all the kids who didn't make it. I'm just going to focus on us here. Us now! And ME who graduated!!!

Dad and Mitchell treated me to a really nice dinner. They heated up a canned ham and got new potatoes from the garden with spinach (which I kinda actually like now). Dad found a really nice bottle of champagne (and expensive--$125!) from the wine shop. It was really good, not chilled, but still yummy! I could get used to drinking champagne! And we used the good china and crystal...very fancy and beautiful. Mitchell picked a bunch of flowers for the table and we ate by candlelight. And for dessert Mitchell made a chocolate cake and Dad made whipped cream and they picked strawberries from the garden. Everything was so delicious! Amazing what having a cow and chickens will add to our diet!!!

Then Tricia came over with her dress and we got totally glammed up. We were allowed to use normal lights from the generator to get ready. Thank goodness! I helped Tricia tone down her make-up choices (what is it about middle school girls and their love of bright colored makeup?) and she pushed me past my more "tasteful" selections of color. We made a good pair. Tricia did my hair. She left most of it down, pulled some of the front hair away from my face, and settled a small tiara across my hair style to finish my ensemble. Gorgeous! Then it was my turn to grab the brushes and style hers. She wanted her hair down with a rhinestone flower barrette for the back. Her hair is long now and a really pretty honey blonde. She was beautiful in her royal blue dress. When we were finished we stood in front of the tall brass-framed mirror and in its reflection saw Trish, her hair gathered by the glittering barrette tumbling down her back, looking pretty and young and sweet. I was tall and regal in my red gown and we sparkled with jewelry. We were beautiful! As glamorous as movie stars on the red carpet!

We walked downstairs and Dad and Mitchell met us at the bottom of the stairs with corsages. Mrs. Kinsey made them with artificial and real flowers. Dad pinned them on us as Mitchell would've probably stuck us with the pins. Oh btw...Mitchell looked at Tricia totally different--like she was a real girl and not a noisy brat. I think he might be growing up! I don't know if that's a good thing or a bad thing! ;)

We walked to the clubhouse as the sun dipped below the horizon and the sky was that deep blue that can make your heart ache from its beauty. Solar lights lit the path to the dance as though the stars had fallen from the heavens to light our way. We entered the main room which was covered with white sparkling lights—it was like passing into a star-covered universe. Music was playing—a romantic pop song from last year and flooded my mind with bittersweet memories. Flickering candlelight, lace-covered tables...Everything was so beautiful! It hurt my heart.

It took me a second or two to notice other people were already there and the first person I noticed was Ashleigh. Totally gorgeous! She was standing next to Jason and he looked--wow!

He was so handsome in his tux! OMG! If he wasn't such a jerk I'd be totally head over heels in love with him—too bad good looks don't equal a good person--which they don't. Caleb and Mitchell went immediately to the refreshment table and even they looked really nice--dressed up in their suits--clean and hair brushed. Did I mention "clean!" :) The parents, of course, looked nice as well--very posh in their new clothes and even the moms were wearing makeup.

Dad yelled, "Okay, let's get this party started! The two graduates must start the dancing—so you two get out there!" So with Caleb and Mitchell pushing Jason, and Tricia pulling me to the dance floor, Jason and I danced the first dance. Well Mom, Jason isn't much of a dancer, but he did try. I, on the other hand, can dance, but it's a little weird dancing with all the parents looking at us. But it was only a minute or two and then everyone was on the dance floor dancing like crazy. It's funny how parents love to dance. I guess it isn't only kids who like it. So we spent the night dancing and eating and laughing, and it was wonderful!! Most of the dances were fast dances as slow dances were a little awkward for us kids. The adults loved them though. I felt sorry for Dad as he didn't have you to dance with, but I danced with him and so did the moms. Everyone danced with everyone else and nobody sat on the sidelines. Mitchell was dancing like a crazy nut--all goofy looking and silly, and having a really good time! Even Ashleigh was having a good time. It was so nice to see her and everyone else smiling and happy and clean and dressed up. I wish we could live like this forever! Jason and Caleb danced slow dances with both me and Ashleigh (and their mom). Jason and I talked about being seniors and finishing school and how it was such a relief being done with school. It was nice talking to him--fellow senior and graduate. Like I said earlier, if Jason weren't such a jerk, he'd be pretty cool. He's so good looking! He was on his best behavior and when we danced, I wished I had a boyfriend holding me. I really wish I had a boyfriend. It felt sooo nice to have his strong arms around me, holding me, my head on his shoulder and when he talked to me his mouth was so close to mine. I wish I had a boyfriend who would hug and kiss me and care about me--to walk me home, to talk to in the evenings after the work was done, to meet in secret, to have secrets, oh...everything... But it was just Jason and Caleb. Caleb was a little awkward about slow dancing, but Tricia said she'd been teaching him. He's such a nice guy--polite but still a bit goofy, like he's still a kid, but not a kid.

So we danced the night away and by the time the evening was over and we went back to our homes, our hair was messed up and we were all a bit sweaty, our outfits were rumpled, and there were no refreshments left. It was <u>wonderful</u>!! The stars lit our way home and as I look out the window, I see them shining above us in the sky.

I'm so tired. I think I'll have to write about graduation tomorrow. Goodnight Mom. I love you.

Your favorite daughter
Meg

PS: I didn't say it earlier, but prom could've only been better if you'd been there. I know the stars shining above me tonight are shining on you as well. In spite of everything--all the bad and all the hardships, light and goodness still shine through.

May 31

Hey girl,

I am exhausted!!! Graduation was today. Mom and I went over early to take down Prom decorations. We left some of the lights and the archway, but moved the tables.

Janet gave a really nice speech and they got framed diplomas. We had music for them as they did a happy celebration dance on the way out of the room. I could tell Meg was really excited. Jason seemed happy too...I guess. It's hard to really judge his emotions. A mystery he is.... BUT Meg was all in tears and her whole family was too. I bet she wishes her mom was here. I know it's hard wondering where she is...or if she's even alive. I guess even though you're gone, I know you're safe and in a good place.

Jason read a stupid poem he wrote.

There was a young man from Laurel.
Who thought that school was just awful.
He struggled and fought.
By his mom he was taught.
Study hard and finish is the moral.

Yeah. That was his speech! But everyone laughed and I don't know what he could've said that would have been any better. It's so him!

But seriously, I need a nap! We were cooking all day yesterday to make sure we had enough goodies for prom and graduation and I'm worn out. I promised Adam I'd go fishing with him later so I better recharge. That boy requires my full attention when we're by the creek.

Blue skies and pooped,
Ashleigh

June 1

Dear Mom,

Well, I 'm a high school graduate! I smiled so much yesterday that my cheek muscles ache. I'm sooo happy I finished! It's <u>such</u> a good feeling that I'm done. And such a relief! I know I'll be studying for the rest of my life--especially as I'm going to study medicine, but high school and all the qualifications and requirements are DONE!!! I just keep taking these big sighs of relief and smiling. LOVE IT!!!

We had graduation in the already decorated clubhouse and it was great! I don't know how the moms did it, but there was more food! Jason and I wore our graduation gowns and silly flat hats and marched into the "auditorium" to Pomp and Circumstance. <u>I LOVE that song!!!</u> Mrs. Kinsey gave the first speech cuz she is (was!) our teacher. Her first sentence was "Oh, brave new world that has such people in't." That's from Shakespeare's *The Tempest*. She went on talking about how we're the generation who truly <u>will</u> change the world. She said the difference between this year's graduates and last year's is that our world truly does depend on how WE make a difference; how WE will literally be building this brave new world. Then she talked about how all of us need to continue our education--from the littlest to the oldest--and she quoted Plato. "The direction in which education starts a man will determine his future life." And what we learn and how we implement our knowledge will determine the future for all humanity for all our years to come. She ended with a quotation from Kettering's *Seed for Thought*. "We should all be concerned about the future because we will have to spend the rest of our lives there." and that spending the rest of our lives with this wonderful group of people will be very special indeed. It was a cool speech. It inspired me and made me want to cry all at the same time. The Kinsey family looked so proud of her! She's so much happier now than she used to be. I think teaching has helped her a lot. She gave Jason and me a copy of her speech so we'd have it to keep. (I saw Jason put his copy down and his mom picked it up. I have mine with this letter so you can read it when you come home.)

Then Jason and I gave short speeches as well. I talked about how being able to finish school was important to me, and that I'd depended on both Dad and you and Mrs. Kinsey to graduate and for everybody's support in more than just education. And I knew I'd be depending on my parents and the rest of the adults and the community for the rest of my life. (I also kept the full copy of my speech for you.)

In case you're wondering, we didn't have a salutatorian or valedictorian as there were just the two of us and we all know that Jason wouldn't have been ranked in the top of the class. I'd probably not have been one of the top two, but I was a lot closer than he would've been! And to be honest, if he was given class rank just below me, I'd have been ticked off. I worked really hard for my grades, and he barely made it through high school. So if he ranked up with me by grades and awards--I would have been really really angry. Mrs. Kinsey knew how I felt and she understood so I don't think she even considered having the valedictorian and salutatorian. Graduation means a lot to me. Jason just didn't care that much. He said he didn't really see the point, like it wasn't going to help him in any way and he wouldn't be going to play basketball anywhere so big deal. To me, graduation is a big deal. And if/when life gets back to normal, I'll have credentials to go to college! Yeah, like that's going to happen. :(

Then Dad and Mr. Kinsey gave us our diplomas (hand written and framed by Mrs. Kinsey) and shook our hands and gave us big hugs. Jason and I picked our recessional song, and decided to dance out of the room, so we'd practiced our dance number yesterday. It was <u>fun</u>!! And Jason's actually fun to dance with—believe it or not! Everyone cheered and Adam and Ava loved it cuz all the adults were yelling and laughing, so they yelled and laughed louder than anyone. Everyone threw confetti and streamers on us as we danced through the balloon arch. Then everyone else danced and the day ended up with food—of course! What's a celebration w/o food! The moms had taken canned ham and smashed it up with eggs and bread crumbs and stuff and made "ham"burgers for the men to grill. It was an almost normal meal for an almost normal situation for an almost normal wonderful graduation day. Makes me smile even now thinking about it. It was such a happy day!

I wish you'd been here.

Your favorite daughter
Meg

Like precious flowers
children spring resiliently
from darkest winter

janet kinsey

June 3

Dear Mandy,

I went out to the barn with Dad again today. I thought after I helped him feed everybody then I could saddle up Thunderbolt and go riding. On. My. Own. I haven't been riding alone FOREVER! But nooooooo....here comes Tricia. Yap, yap, yap, yap, yap. She was asking all these questions about the horses. Which one's older? How can we tell who's who? (seriously...they are totally different shades of brown and one is a boy!) When did I start riding? How did I learn? Good grief!!! Then she looked confused and unsure when she started to saddle Sadie, so what could I do? I had to help her out and then I got all into explaining all the tack and saddle and...well basically everything! b/c she had no clue.

She's been helping out at the farm a lot and is really into knowing more about the animals. She said that she'd been reading a lot about horses at the library and had been riding the horses around the property. I must've given her a crazy look b/c she started stuttering and said Dad helped her saddle Sadie and led her around while she rode a couple a times. She said she knew it was good exercise.

So......I told her I'd teach her how to ride properly. I know! I know! I can't believe it either! But she was looking at Sadie with that same longing I remember having when I was a little girl, wanting so much to get up on that horse and just go racing with my hat flying off over my shoulders! LOL. Yeah, I remember that look. Of course, my dreams of racing never came true but running around the farm and out in the fields is fantastic! And I'm sure I won't mind a little sidekick every once and while...as long as she doesn't do something stupid like try to jump a fallen tree and get herself killed! Maybe I can train Thunderbolt to back kick Jason the next time he's being a jerk. Thunderbolt's leg would probably get strained from all the kicking though! hahahahaha.

Gotta go...Mom wanted me home to watch the little ones.

Light drizzle, but feeling whatevs,
Ashleigh

Caleb

    I love dogs. They are always honest and want to please — unlike Jason. He is so selfish and never does his share. I'm glad Mitchell is here. He helps— even if he is a kid.

    Training dogs is so awesome. I could do it all day!!

June 6

Dear Mom,

   Well, the honeymoon is <u>over</u>. This high school graduate spent the day working in the garden, dirt under her nails, and sweating like a pig. But wait a minute...pigs don't seem to sweat, so why do we say "sweating like a pig". Not that I've seen too many pigs--I don't go out to the farm much. But you know who <u>does</u> sweat--boys and men! O...M...G... Dripping wet at the end of the day. You should see Dad and Mitchell when they come home in the evenings! Thank heavens for antiperspirant! So the saying should be "sweating like a man." But if it comes to a contest about who <u>stinks</u> more--men or pigs--pigs have it hands down!!! They stink soooo bad! Yuck!!!

   If K-Pox hadn't happened, I would've been at the beach this week with Jen and Rachel. We would've been out on the beach, tanning, looking at boys, jumping in the waves, eating wonderfully yummy food full of calories, going to clubs and dancing in the evenings...we talked about this weekend so much. And now I'm digging and scraping away in the garden. I know I shouldn't complain though. I have no idea where Jen and Rachel are--or even <u>if</u> they "are"--which I don't think they are. Well, I can't dwell on this. It's too hard.

   I've been able to put my "medical expertise" to use a little bit. I've been putting band aids and disinfectant on Mitchell and Caleb almost every day, and making sure everyone uses sunscreen and hats. Of course, the moms are doing this as well, but I think Caleb and Mitchell like to come to me--especially Caleb--as I'm not his mom and it seems less "baby-like." At least that's why I think they come to me. But I don't mind. It's fun to take care of people. As long as it stays small stuff!!

Tricia's totally into farm work and I don't see her til evening--if then. Some of the animals are having babies or had babies and she's all about the whole vet experience. She's so much less whiny than she used to be, and stopped wearing sandals to the barn! She wears boots, but they're very cute boots! :) She's also taken up riding, and is getting lessons from Ashleigh. She's found every book on horses that she can, and she's reading like crazy. They've asked me if I want to join them but I totally don't want to. I really don't like horses. They look pretty from far away but up close--they're so big! And they smell. I tried riding back in summer camp--remember that? And I was so scared of falling. "Don't worry," the instructors said. "Just be firm and they'll do what you want." Yeah...that didn't happen. The horse went where it wanted to. Anyway...I had enough then. The only reason I'd want to ride is so I'd be doing something with them. It'd be fun to spend time with Tricia and Ashleigh--just us girls. But I can't get over my fear of horses--and I don't like the idea of spending all that time on a sweaty stinky horse. I'd rather read about horses than ride them. :) But Tricia's practicing with her big ole saddle and trying to learn to lasso things.

Naturally Mitchell and Caleb have to get involved in riding and lassoing as well--to the irritation of <u>everyone</u>. I think we've all been lassoed at least 10 times a day. IRRITATING!! When I asked Mitchell why he doesn't rope the posts or trash cans or anything but me, he said he has to practice on real moving things, and Mr. Grace told the boys to leave the cows alone--that they've been roped too many times!

Speaking of Caleb and Mitchell—Caleb's been working with this pack of dogs and is training them to do a variety of things. Some stay at the farm as guard dogs—to protect the farm from other dogs and people. They're big mean looking dogs. They scare me and make me think twice about going out to the farm. Not that they'd bite me (I think), but they do bark and I'm just not crazy about big dogs. And some he's training to fetch things and I don't know what all. I think he's got about 10 dogs. Of course Mitchell's helping him and wants to have a dog at the house "for protection" he says. I don't want one. They're messy and bark and poop all over the place. Mitchell says that he'll take care of it, but he can't clean up after himself, so how will he clean up after a dog?! I think they should keep all the poopy things out at the farm. I hate stepping in poop!! So far Dad's agreeing with me but I think he's weakening. He better not! I told Dad that if he lets Mitchell get a dog, I'll move to the empty house next door. I'm almost 18 and it wouldn't be a bad thing for me to have my own place anyway!!! So...so far, no dogs. Mitchell's not happy and spends whole hours not speaking to me. No dogs <u>and</u> no Mitchell yacking. Win win! :)

When not at the farm Ashleigh spends her work time in the garden with me and we talk a little bit. But the garden's big and we're often working on opposite ends. We both miss our friends and when we do talk it's often about what we used to do. She talks a lot about her friend Mandy. She turns her head sometimes cuz she doesn't want me to see her cry, but geez, just cry in front of me already! It's not like I haven't cried about missing you in front of her. But she's kinda hard to get to know. I think she's really smart and just not sure what to do with this "brave new world". I remember being 16 and thinking I knew everything. I know I'm not totally mature now, but I'm not 16 anymore, thank goodness. I used to think she was just prickly to me, but I noticed she's the same to most of us--except Jason. I don't really know what to think about that situation. Jason acts like he likes her one day, and then the next, he's rude to her-- like he's rude to almost everyone most of the time. If she's confused about his behavior, she has every right to be. He's just jerking her around, but that's what he was like in school. Same ol Jason. It's all about him. Sometimes I think I see some maturing (like the way he behaved at the prom, dancing with all the girls and moms and being on his best behavior; helping the dads on the farm all day and working really hard), but then he does something stupid--like flirting with Ashleigh before dinner and turning his back on her by dessert. One of these days, I'm going to tell him off--and to leave her alone. Not that it'd do any good, but I'd make me feel better.

Well, I'm tired and have another long hot day in the garden tomorrow. Love you.

Your favorite daughter and sweating high school graduate
Meg

June 7

Dear Mandy,

Work work work. That seems to be life now. I feel like the Amish. Don't they just work all the time? Of course, it would've been nice to have an Amish person who survived to show us the ropes on all this gardening and no electricity stuff. Seriously, they're probably still around somewhere living just like they did before. Maybe we'll meet them someday!

Anyway...school's over for the summer so that's nice. We work in the morning...gardening, taking care of the farm animals, cooking...all that. Then we rest a little bit during the early afternoon when the sun is so hot. We read in one of those survival books that it's good to slow down during the hot parts of the day b/c then you don't lose as much water from your body. Dehydration is our enemy!

Jason goes around and delivers everyone's water in the mornings. He's like an old-timey milkman! Sometimes I try to answer the door when he comes. But that means that I have to look cute and some mornings I'm just too tired. And some days...well, it's just so weird. There are days when I'll be at the farm or wherever and Jason and I will chat and laugh and he'll act like he really likes me. He's definitely flirting. I'm not stupid...I mean I don't see him giving sassy looks and joking with Meg all the time, so it has to mean he likes me more than friends. But then, I'll see him the next day or even later the SAME day and he completely ignores me! It's like I don't even exist. He talks to everyone else BUT me. So fine, I just talk to everyone else BUT *him*.

It just twists me all up though. I don't know what to think. I know when he talks to me and flirts, my stomach gets all fluttery. I don't feel as nervous around him anymore and I even flirt back pretty boldly sometimes. Woman power! But it's just so confusing! I see Dad and Mom and they're always off doing their separate things and honestly, they've always been

142

like that. They don't have to be together every minute of every day. So maybe that's how it is with relationships? I guess I just hoped for <u>more</u>. Like in the movies you know? The boy falls head over heels in love with the girl and will do anything for her. And they want to spend all their time together. I know it's not real, but I thought the feelings would be real...like they want to be together or be around each other. Seriously, it'd be better to be with the Amish. All straightforward courting and all that. You like her, she likes you. Now get married and pop out some babies. Not that I want babies! Or to get married!!! I just like the idea of belonging to someone.

Well, I better go. It's time to start cooking. I can't believe how fresh carrots taste! And peas! Who'd have thought that peas are so fantastic! I blame it on the gross store-canned food. I actually like canning and preserving stuff with Mom. It's not complicated and it means we're planning for the future.

Windy and hungry,
Ashleigh

June 9

Dear Mom,

　　Life has been really busy lately and I've been too tired to write. Mostly spending time in the garden and putting rain barrels on as many houses in the neighborhood as we can. Having the barrels for irrigation and home water use will be so convenient! Won't have to haul water from the farm as often. Of course, that's only if it rains. But every little bit helps. I've also been working with Mrs. Grace and Mrs. Kinsey canning early vegetables like beans and peas. Talk about a lot of work! But we can't count on our store vegetables lasting forever. Ashleigh's arranging our cans by expiration date so we use them in order.

　　I like spending time in the garden. The moms and I spend a lot of time weeding, harvesting, canning, and preparing food. We have a lot of community meals at noon now cuz it's easier. We like to prepare lunch together--it's easier and more efficient and not as lonely. And those working on the farm or other places all drive back to lunch together, and then they all go back out to the farm together. So it's easier for them as well. We still meet for our own separate meals at supper. Which is nice cuz that way we can catch up with the latest news. How well is Tricia riding? How well can Mitchell rope? Are Caleb's dogs learning anything new? Is Ashleigh speaking or not speaking to Jason? Is Jason helping out w/o being told, or is he sulking about the task he was given? Tons of stuff to keep abreast of! Seems funny what we now find important news. I guess this is what the pioneer communities were like. Small communities and all in each other's business! :) We also talk about how the solar power options are coming along and when/if wind power will be something we can do. We're also thinking about digging another

144

well--just in case the ones we have now go dry or get contaminated. So Dad has been reading the manual on how to use this well-digging machine. That kind of stuff makes me bored just thinking about it—but Dad loves it. He really does. The dads hang out and talk about this boring (but necessary) stuff all the time--even in the evenings after work. It isn't unusual for all the guys to be hanging out talking about power and cars and other boring things. Those not interested in power options (like me) talk about anything else—science, philosophical questions, general stuff. Tricia and Ashleigh wander from one group to the other—trying to find the least boring group. Mitchell and Caleb usually hang with the dads if they're not out working on their fort, training dogs, or some other type of adventure, but Jason usually disappears after supper. No one cares enough to ask him where he goes or what he does. Or if someone did care (like his mom or Ashleigh) he wouldn't say anything anyway so why bother asking.

I don't know whether I find it odd or not that I seem to be finding myself wanting to do typical "women's" work. Is that cuz I'm innately better at these things due to strengths and aptitude? Or is it cultural and I've been caught up in an ages old propaganda campaign? I don't know. Part of me wants to not do "girl" stuff and wants to go hang with the guys and build generators and dig wells. Not because I want to build generators but because I don't want to be categorized into the type of work I'm doing just because I'm a girl. I want to do what I want to do because I want to do it--not because it's expected. So part of me wishes that I wanted to do "guy" things, but in reality, I like doing the traditional girl things. Of course I like being the doctor—so would that be considered uni-sex? Sort of one size fits all? It used to be only men could be doctors and now it's both men and women. So I guess I don't do everything by traditional sex roles. Lately I've been spending way more time gardening and next to no time doctoring (except for bandaids). I'm not that crazy about digging in the garden, but I'd rather do that than spend all day with Dad and his work. So...nature or nurture? I don't know. Just don't force me to spend my whole work day with Dad! :)

You know, Dad's really not the same man he used to be. I know I've said this before, but he's such a different man now. He's really nice. Not the "he's my dad so I love him so he's nice", but he really is a nice person--someone I like to talk to. He's actually funny sometimes and has a weird sense of humor-- which I never heard much before when he was on his computer all the time. But he spends time with me and Mitchell and of course, Mitchell just loves spending time with him. They do "guy things" with power stuff and Dad even tried riding horses one day. But he told me later that he agrees with me--horses are big and scary and he'd rather walk or drive. But if this is the man you met and fell in love with, I can see why. I think you'd fall in love with him again!

Gotta go. I'm tired and have to get up early to be in the garden before the heat gets too bad.

Your favorite daughter
Meg

June 13

Dear Mom,

I've decided to call the adults by their first names. I know it's been awhile, but I just couldn't do it at first. And when I started, it felt funny not to say Mr. and Mrs. Whoever. But I felt that after I graduated, it seemed more strange for me to be so formal, cuz I was technically now one of the grownups. So...it was hard changing from Mrs. Kinsey to Janet and Mr. Grace to Donald. But no one seemed to notice, (though they probably did and didn't say anything) so the change went pretty smoothly. Well, Ashleigh noticed right away and asked me why I changed over and I told her. She thought I was old-fashioned for not doing so in the beginning, but I felt more comfortable doing it my way. So, in case you're wondering why all of a sudden the adults and I are on first-name basis, that's why. But I must admit, it still feels weird.

Your favorite daughter
Meg

June 17

Dear Mandy,

So after Dad and I added some more worms to our compost bin (THRILLING, right?? The party never stops around here), I went with him out to the barn and took Thunderbolt and Gypsy out for some exercise around the farm. It's nice to feel connected to something bigger than myself AND be away from all the responsibilities. Free to just be me for a minute. Me and my horse...HI-HO!

I'm going to take a little nap. Then after my "siesta" Mom and I are going to sneak out and get Dad a Super-Grill. That's a funny word. I wonder if there's anyone still "siesta-ing" in Europe...maybe we're "siesta-ing" at the same time!

We're going to get Dad the grill for Father's Day...one with a smoker and a side cooker thingy and all the bells and whistles. Won't cost us a thing! Just load it up! Jason, Caleb, Meg, and Mitchell are going with us because we're picking one up for Sam and Donald too. Hopefully all three grills will fit in the truck! It was Mom and Janet's idea, but we need the boys' muscles! We're going to hide them in the Baxter's garage until Father's Day. We just had to go today b/c all the dads are working on the solar power panels out at the farm and they won't be back for a while.

Hopefully Jason's too hot to wear a shirt today...I mean the weather's too hot...he's always hot. I'm sleepy. On that note, I'm going to catch some zzzzzzz's and dream of sandy beaches far from here.

Hazy and dreamy,
Asheigh

June 18

Dear Mom,

 Guess what! We're building a swimming pool in the river!! We're taking turns learning to use the backhoe and digging a pool with a deep part for us older people and a shallow part for the little kids. We're going to bring all sorts of cool yard stuff from the local hardware stores so we'll have cement tables and benches and plant holders and paving stones and we'll be spending time in the evenings working on it, after our usual work. And we're all going to be working on it together! This is gonna be fun! We're usually split up during the day working on separate projects. This is one project where we can work on something together that's only for fun--not survival related. Yay! Even Jason is getting into it. He wasn't crazy about sharing the backhoe, but Ashleigh, Tricia, Mitchell, Caleb, and me all wanted to learn to backhoe, so the parents said we could. Which made Caleb happy—getting over on Jason. Jason sulked, of course. :) We're still working on the plans, and the parents are talking about damming off the swimming area and only allowing a certain amount of water in. They said it'd also be safer so none of us will float away downstream--not likely the way the water's running right now—getting close to a dribble. But after a storm, the river can get kinda high. So our decorative stuff will be set up higher on the bank--just in case of a flood.

 To celebrate the beginning of the pool, we had a bonfire after dark and us teens sat around and talked about all kinds of stuff like what will happen when all the houses around us collapse into shambles and we're the only houses left standing. Caleb and Mitchell stood up and made those muscle arms that boys do when they think they're strong and yelled, "Last people standing!!" It was funny—totally goofy, but funny. And then we started talking about how many people were dead in those houses and we'd be finding their bones years later. And Jason said we wouldn't find bones because animals would've gotten into the broken down houses and dragged the bones away. Yuck! Gross! And of course that conversation led to ghost stories and how the dead people here turned into zombies and looked all gross and bloody and wandered around town looking for living people to eat. So in the middle of the ghost stories we hear this noise in the woods behind us. We turn around to see what it is, but after staring into the bonfire it's hard to see in the dark. Then coming out of the woods we see this tall, pale, monster creature stumble-walking towards us. Ashleigh and Tricia screamed. I inhaled so hard I about died of a heart attack. Caleb and Mitchell jumped up and cursed. Then we all realized it was Jason and we yelled at him and Mitchell and Caleb chased him around the fire, pulled him down, and pretended to beat him up. By then we were all laughing so hard we could hardly stand up!

That got us talking about who we'd let in our new community—not wanting zombies to move in. I mean we talk big about what we'd do if someone came in and that we'd have to approve them and everything, but we couldn't really do that—they'd already be here. So then what? Since we were in a silly mood we came up with silly requirements for any new people: good looking doctor or dentist, bringing supplies like potato chips and candy, super nice and willing to help with chores (especially mucking out stalls), ability to build off-the-grid energy units—and the list went on. Mitchell asked what we'd do if our new person didn't have any of those things and was a horrible person—how would we handle that? Now this is

150

a question we've all thought about and talked about, but we've not come to any conclusions. He suggested jail, but who'd take care of the inmate? Clean up the poop and pee and feed them? Can't exile them—who'd keep them from coming back? If community shame and personal pride weren't going to work— what would? Jason said he didn't understand why everyone should have to follow our rules anyway—as long as they minded their own business, they should be allowed to do as they wanted. The rest of us disagreed. If they want their own rules, they need to found their own community. The discussion started getting a bit heated so we decided we'd set our zombies on them and that'd take care of them. But the problem is <u>not</u> an easy one to solve, and unfortunately, may have to be solved someday as there are no zombies to eat the bad guys. The fire burned down to glowing embers and the conversation died down as well. It was a nice evening—friends around the campfire discussing heavy and silly issues.

Your favorite daughter
Meg

PS: I don't think Ashleigh liked the conversation about town people turning to zombies, because of Mandy. She still misses her a lot. If you had died here, I wouldn't like to think about people calling you a zombie either.

PPS: Working the backhoe was fun--more fun than I thought it would be. Being able to move all that dirt around with the push and pull of some levers is amazing. But it wasn't something that I wanted to keep doing all afternoon like the guys and Ashleigh did. They totally got into it.

June 25

Dear Mandy,

OMG. It is SOOOOO fantastic!!!! We had our first dip in the swimming hole today! It was AMAZING!!!! I was a little nervous at first because I had to go out in front of everybody in my bathing suit (Eeeek!) BUT I went to the store a couple days ago and tried on like 1000 suits to get just the right one and I found this fabulous purple and green two piece halter. It's super cute and it's kinda sporty too, so at least I knew I didn't look slutty or it wasn't going to (gasp!) fall off when I tried to jump in or anything. That would've been SOOOO embarrassing! It's just...you know, worrying about what other people will think...or look at. Or maybe they'll notice my butt's a weird shape or my boobs are too small or I have hair on my back (I don't!!!), but you know! All those things that you just hate about being a girl sometimes!!!

But I wasn't talking about that! I was talking about swimming! SO we dug the swimming hole out last week. We all took turns using the backhoe...Rosie the Riveter baby! And that was tons of fun. But then we had to wait while the parents made sure everything was cut out the way they thought it should be and the creek was re-routed properly around it so it was still flowing. And THEN...showtime!!!!!

It's big enough for five or six of us to be in it without all banging into each other. We even had rafts to lay on in the sun and paddle back and forth. I don't remember the last time I had so much fun. Oh! And JASON was SO much fun today! He was being super flirty. Like splashing me and chasing me around. He even grabbed me and fell sideways in. Thank goodness it's pretty deep! Of course, Mom gave me a look and said we'd splashed the little kids, but they looked fine to me! The dads made a shallower section so the little kids could splash around. And whatever, it felt good to feel Jason's hands around me on my bare skin and be close to him...feel his breath on my neck...Gives me the shivers just thinking about it! We got on the big raft together and just kicked around...letting the sun warm us up. I was really glad he was in a good mood today. He made me feel special. I could've laid there with him forever...

You know...the other fun part for me too was just imagining where everything was going to be. Like...where we're going to set up the tables and the umbrellas. I thought about making a little sandy beach area for the kids. There's tons of sand at the store and they could build sand castles. Maybe I'll throw some shells in there too. Who knows if they'll ever get to see the real ocean. Maybe one day. We can take a drive... But for now they have Laurel mini beach and can enjoy that right in their own backyard :-)

Well, off to organize inventory. Canned tuna is calling my name!

BRIGHT sunshine and serenity,
Ashleigh

July 4

Dear Mandy,

So I'm in BIG trouble apparently. Honestly, I think everyone just needs to loosen up. It was just a little firework or two...well, okay it was more! But I didn't think everyone would get so crazy about it!

We were having our 4th of July shindig and everything was fine. Mom and Janet arranged games, we grilled, the kids were having a really awesome time. We even got to go swimming, so it felt like a REAL 4th of July, you know? Like when we used to take the boat out to Lake Clairemont and go swimming and tubing and just eat whenever we wanted. Remember when you came with us? You really liked riding in the front of the boat. And it was fun hanging around a bunch of guys we didn't know and being flirty and laughing at the concession stand...we could be whoever we wanted and nobody knew any different. And remember when we said we were cousins...we thought about saying we were sisters, but with my dark hair and your strawberry blond hair we didn't think anyone would believe us...so cousins it was. And then we'd be out on the boat for the fireworks and we could see all the other boats with their strings of lights, just swaying in the water...

So okay, our 4th was totally not THAT good, but it felt nice doing some 'normal' things and being around the water. The water hole is looking pretty awesome since I've been helping with it. I mapped out a design with Dad one night. He was surprised I was interested...but I just kept getting this picture in my head of what it should look like and I wanted to see if we could make it happen. So we decided where all the tables should go and umbrellas and the little 'beach.' We talked about trees and shade and getting sun and plants and drainage and runoff, which was not as fun to plan, but it was fantastic seeing the plans and design all come to life! I was pretty proud when we were there today. I can see now why Dad liked his job of designing buildings and stuff!

When it got dark, we all went over to the clubhouse and lit a bonfire outside in our fire pit. I totally felt confident hanging out with the kidults (that's what I'm calling us now...we're still kids sometimes, but we have to be adults too...so kidults!) AND I especially felt confident hanging out with Jason. There were times it just felt like we were in our own little world...just laughing and playing...for HOURS. No work. All play. It was such a good day. Then we went and had dinner and we were all just sitting around and waiting for it to get dark so we could light the sparklers. Adam and Ava had never done them before so I was showing them how to write their names and...and I just started thinking that the kids were not going to get to see fireworks that year. Jason had found some at the fire station, but everyone said we shouldn't shoot them off for fear of 'outsiders' or fire or whatever! So that meant no big display...nothing to oooo and aaaah over...On the 4th of July! I mean isn't that how we Americans show our country's pride? We fought for independence against England...the beast of tyranny! And we WON! Men and women fought and died and their blood is still in this earth. Isn't that just like K-Pox? It's just a different beast of destruction? Haven't we, the ones that survived, fought and won? Haven't we won our independence from this disease that wiped out so many? And aren't WE re-building our own lives just the way the patriots did?

I was just about to say something to Dad to beg him to let us shoot off the big fireworks...but then Jason came over and said, "Hey, you want to see some BIG sparklers?" And I knew he was talking about shooting off the fireworks and I totally wanted us to...for the kids, for us, for all that we've been through. So we snuck away. I told him we should set them off by the swimming pool b/c there was an open area and I figured there'd be water nearby just in case. We were only going to shoot off one or two...just to see the sparkle and remember...

So we set them up and BOOM! Jason lit the first one and

155

it was SO loud! It had a long fuse and we lit it with a sparkler so we had time to run behind the tables, but it still made me jump. I think Jason was shocked too because we kinda looked at each other and didn't say anything for a minute, but then we both got these goofy grins on our faces and we started laughing and I said, "Do the other ones!!!!" So Jason ran out and lit up another one! It went WAY up high and was purple. PURPLE! See! It was a sign! We were supposed to do it! I could just imagine how the kids must've looked seeing them. My heart felt so big in my chest! We lit the last three at the same time...like a finale you know? But of course one of them didn't go as high. It was still beautiful though. I couldn't have asked for a more perfect end to the day.

Well...almost perfect. All of a sudden I hear Dad shouting and Jason yells, "Just tell them I did it! Go! Go!" and we both took off running. I almost made it back to the house but Dad is quick! Somehow he saw me running and called for me to stop. I almost kept going...but I got scared. He ran over to me and asked if I was okay and was I hurt, and then he must have known...he got this really mad look on his face and said, "We'll talk about this in the morning. You will NOT leave for chores and you will NOT leave the house until you talk with your mother and me. Do you UNDERSTAND?" I could totally tell he was P-Oed, so I just nodded my head and off we marched towards home.

I went right up to my room and then I heard Mom and the kids come in. She asked Dad if I was ok and I could hear Dad's mad voice and her shushing him and then she came up the stairs with the kids and put them to bed. When she went back downstairs I could hear them talking. I know it was about me, but I didn't care. I heard Adam's little voice calling, "Ashleigh?" So I stuck my head in his room to tell him I was back. He said, "Did you see the sparkles?" and I told him yes. He asked me where they came from, so I told him they were just a little magic for him and Ava. He said, "They sure were loud magic!" and I laughed. I went and gave him a hug and told him goodnight.

So see...it was totally worth it. Even if I'm going to be in BIG trouble tomorrow. What can they do now anyway? We'll see I guess.

Firework smoke and sleepy,
Ashleigh

July 5

Dear Mom,

  We just had our 4th of July party. It was pretty fun but really irritating at the end because of stupid Jason—but I'll get there. First, we started the day with a barbecue. (By the way...I'm so glad there's still potato chips around. I love chips!! And they totally make a picnic! I don't know what we'll do without chips. There'll be some serious problems when that happens.) Anyway after lunch we had a spoon and potato race (Mitchell won) and a 3-legged race. I was paired with Dad and we won. And the younger kids played hide and seek with the littlest guys. I helped Adam and Ava hide and find the others. We had races and a hula hoop contest and a jump rope contest. I can still sorta jump rope—but not as good as I used to! Tricia's way better than I am. Then we went to the swimming hole for hours and we all got a little sunburned. The day was soooo much fun! Jason was being nice to Ashleigh so we didn't have to put up with their silliness--well, except for the flirting silliness-- which is easier to deal with than the sulking/ignoring silliness. The longer we're here, the less we seem to notice our age differences. Tricia's acting older and is much easier to be around than she used to be. Caleb's more mature than Jason most of the time. Sometimes when Caleb's around Mitchell they both act like total kids, but most of the time they resemble human beings. So anyway, after the swimming we went back to the clubhouse and ate some more and waited for dark so we could use the sparklers. We wrote in the air, and twirled around, and watched the little guys get all excited. Everything was so much fun and relaxing and the day was just about perfect. But...this is where the stupid Jason part comes in.

He found some fireworks that shoot way up in the air and burst all beautiful colors. He'd asked if he could shoot them off for all of us but we had already voted NO in a community meeting as they could attract strangers. Apparently Jason decided that he didn't need to follow community rules. So he and Ashleigh disappeared. None of us really thought about it cuz we're used to them wandering off. All of a sudden we hear a loud POW and whistling sound coming from the swimming hole and see a big fireworks explode in the sky over the tops of the trees! Yes, you read that right! A firework exploding and seen over the tops of the trees! Man, I don't think I've ever seen Jason's dad look so angry. His mom and Caleb and Tricia looked so embarrassed. Then Jackson looked around and saw that Ashleigh wasn't there and muttered something to Caroline. Dad told Mitchell and me to go back home. Mitchell argued and said he wanted to see the rest of the fireworks but Dad gave him that look that meant "Don't argue with me!" and we walked (very slowly) back to the house—so Mitchell got to see the rest of the fireworks. There were five fireworks total and then total silence for the rest of the night. I guess we'll find out what happens to the <u>idiots</u> tomorrow.

But it made me think. What <u>do</u> we do when someone in our community breaks our rules? We're all becoming adults and we can't have a community where everyone just gets to do what they like. Especially when their behavior can hurt us! I mentioned this to Dad this morning at breakfast and he said he agreed— that we'll need to discuss this with the group, and that I should begin to think of solutions to share. This will involve all of us and we should all be a part of the solution. Yuck! I don't <u>want</u> to deal with problems and solutions. Why can't everyone just act properly and then we wouldn't have to have consequences for misbehaviors. So instead of dreaming about the nice day we had, I have to think of what we can do about people who flaunt rules. What a DRAG!!! Sometimes I just <u>hate</u> Jason!!!!! What does Ashleigh see in him???

Your favorite daughter
Meg

July 5

So I can't believe it! I'm stuck in my room! Really?? Like I'm in time-out! Ugggh! So ticked off right now I can hardly breathe!!!! Mom and Dad were just waiting to pounce on me the second I walked downstairs this morning. They didn't even let me talk! They just started in on what a bad choice it was to shoot off the fireworks and how dangerous it was and how someone could've gotten hurt. I tried to explain that I was going to ask Dad first, but then Jason just said to come and I went. Then they started ranting and raving about making my own choices and not following someone else and I started yelling back about how they want me to act like an ADULT, but then they don't let us take part in the decisions!!! AND they still treat us as kids so what choice do we have???!!! But it's like they weren't even listening! Or even cared WHY I did it? I was trying to explain about the patriots and the kids and all that we've been through, but they just kept going on and on and on about safety and not letting our emotions get so out of control. Aaarrrrgggg!!!!! Like they even KNOW what emotions are! Seems to me that they're cardboard people that don't experience anything! They just spew venom at me and don't even understand how much it all hurts and how that one thing...that ONE thing of seeing something familiar just made it hurt less for a minute. They don't even get it. Jason understood! But they don't care. They don't care about ME!!! They don't care about what I think! And now I'm sitting in my room until it's time to go to this stupid community meeting where everyone can tell me what a loser I am. Well, you know what I think about that??? Screw IT! SCREW THEM! SCREW THEM ALL!!!!!!!!!

Humid and ANGRY,
Ashleigh

July 5 – AGAIN

Hey Mandy,
    I'm sure you're tired of me blabbing today, but I had to tell you this.
    We had to go before the WHOLE TOWN today. The little kids were playing and not paying attention, but still...they were there. It felt kinda like we were on trial even though there was no judge or jury or anything...and honestly it seemed like all the 'grown-ups' (because apparently I'm only a grown-up when it suits their needs for manual labor) had already decided on what they were going to have Jason and me do as a consequence for setting off the fireworks. But I guess they wanted to give us a chance to speak. Of course after what Dad said....but wait let me tell you from the beginning.
    We all went to the clubhouse this afternoon. I was already completely ticked off from my fight with my parents this morning. But then having to sit with my parents like a little kid...it was completely embarrassing and humiliating! I felt like I was going to be put in the stocks next and they'd all throw rotten tomatoes at me! Donald was leading the meeting and Janet was taking notes (Yes! Taking notes! I even got stripped of my historian duties...when I saw that I just wanted to break down and cry. Isn't it enough I have to be in the meeting of shame??? Do they have to rub my face in the fact that I can't even take notes either??!!). Jason didn't have to sit by HIS parents!...maybe he was 'representing himself'. He's been saying he was going to move out of his family's house, but I have no idea if he did or not. Who knows.
    So Donald started the meeting and told everyone that the emergency meeting was called to discuss the unsafe actions of Jason and Ashleigh on July 4ᵗʰ. He said this meeting was not intended to humiliate anyone (too late!!!), but to discuss and determine consequences.
    Then he went on to say that, fireworks HAD been

discussed and the community had voted to wait until next year. (And YES, I know I voted no to begin with...but I changed my mind ya know?) However, Jason and I had ignored this decision and set them off anyway. I started to totally freak out at this point! I mean, I guess I figured they weren't going to leave me in the woods to die or kick me out or stone me to death, but I didn't know what was going to happen. I really didn't think it was all that serious, but obviously it was EXTREMELY serious. I just thought we were having fun! I tuned out for a minute because I was trying to hold it together. I HATE crying in front of people. But then Donald stopped talking and said Dad wanted to speak. Wait...Dad???

I was hopeful at first and I almost wanted to look up. But after he started talking I realized he WASN'T going to defend me. He started to go on and on about the community and the importance of being connected to one another and supporting trust. I was PISSED!!!! Of course he'd take the community's side! That's what he always does! It's always about the importance of his work or his customers or his workers or his STUPID reminder post-it notes or whatever, except ME! "Sorry Ashleigh, can't do that because I have work stuff. Sorry Ashleigh, you'll have to figure that out on your own because I'm meant to serve others and not pay attention to you!" I couldn't believe he was doing it to me AGAIN and in PUBLIC! I was so mad I completely understood that saying about spitting nails...I could almost taste the metallic anger in my mouth.

But THEN!! But THEN!!! He turned to Jason and me and started to apologize!! I think I gave myself whiplash looking up. He said he was sorry for all the losses we had. He was sorry I had lost Mandy and a little piece of my heart with her. He was sorry all of us had to endure such hardship and pain that no one should have to experience. He said K-Pox robbed us of our childhoods, and he was sorry that he and Mom were just groping in the dark trying to figure things out too, and sometimes that was painful for everyone. He said that none of the parents raised

163

their kids to be ready for this world at the age of thirteen or sixteen or even eighteen...before they had more time to grow up. He said he was sorry if we had all let each other down...but it was no one's fault and that's why it's so important for us to stick together and fight for what we have now.

Dad said that he knew in his heart that God has a purpose for all of us and all of this. God has a plan even in the midst of the unknown. Because while it's unknown to us, it's not unknown to Him. He said we've all been hurt and damaged...but this community will be the foundation we need to build a new house for all of us. And he said that because he believed that so strongly, he also believed that if our house is threatened we have to protect it. And that's why we are here...to figure out how to protect our community...our house...our home. He said childhood mistakes are not little anymore and we can't afford to lose anyone so precious. He looked right at me when he said that and I started crying. I felt so bad.

After that the rest of the meeting was kind of a blur. Donald asked if we wanted to say anything. I managed to say that I just wanted the kids to experience fireworks...after all we had lost, I just wanted something to stay the same...but I was sorry for making everyone worried and going against what we had decided together. I felt bad after what Dad said, but I didn't want them to think I just did it to be obnoxious. I had a reason that seemed right at the time... I wanted them to know I wasn't just being stupid. Jason of course got up and started yelling about how he was old enough to make his own decisions and who were they to treat him like a little kid...I stopped listening. I wanted him to shut up and sit down! Weren't we in enough trouble?

There was a little more discussion, but then consequences were decided. I just wanted it to be over! Jason has to dig pits for the rest of the outhouses and I have to finish the landscaping at the swimming hole—AFTER doing our usual chores. Jason yelled a few more things and stormed out. Just dig the stupid outhouse pits and keep your mouth shut!

Community service is nothing compared to what my imagination had been coming up with so I'll take it. And besides, I could use the time to myself. I just feel crazy sometimes with all my emotions and worrying about what others think of me or what I think of myself. And it was nice the other day thinking about how the swimming hole would look when it was done. Maybe Dad remembered....

Well, I'm exhausted. After this crazy emotional day I am going to bed.

Sunset and tired,
Ashleigh

PS—And Dad came and gave me a hug afterwards, which was nice. Then he had to get back out to the farm of course! But we almost had a moment....

July 6

Dear Mom,

Well, the community met and decided on a punishment for Ashleigh and Jason as a result of their fireworks stupidity. You could tell their parents must've met earlier to make the decision cuz it was definitely decided before we all met at the meeting. Which is fine with me as I had no idea what to do for a punishment. None at all. Actually the parents kept using the word "consequence". For the behavior, you have to have a consequence. Which to me is just another word for punishment.

And that's exactly how Jason felt. He and Ashleigh were there at the meeting, sitting by their families, allowed to defend themselves, but not allowed to have a say in their "consequence". Jason was totally ticked off! btw it was weird voting on a consequence and what to do with a fellow community person— especially a friend. I didn't like or want to vote, but it was the only thing to do. We have to have rules and order or then what?! So anyway, the decision was handed down by his father. Jason, as usual, overreacted and stomped off. Ashleigh sat there quietly with tears in her eyes and wouldn't look at anyone. You could tell she was really embarrassed and when the meeting was over, she ran back to her house.

The dads brought a bunch of mulch and landscaping rocks to the beach that day and she spent the rest of the day alone there. I wanted to go say something to her, but didn't really know what to say so left her alone—which was a part of the punishment/consequence anyway. But I felt really bad for her. She would never have done that on her own and it was Jason who got her into trouble.

But this whole episode is really making me think. It's like

our conversation at the bonfire when we were talking about what _do_ we do if someone does something truly bad? What Ashleigh and Jason did wasn't that bad really. And I don't see any of us doing anything really bad. But if we were a different type of community—what if someone stole our food or we had a man who beat his wife or a mother who abused her children? What could we do? Would it be like Jason said—that we couldn't _make_ him do anything? Because we can't really force anyone to do anything. What if Jason decides not to dig outhouse pits? I mean he probably will do the digging cuz he loves his family, but what if he doesn't? Would his mother say she won't cook any more for him? Or he can't live with them anymore? Could we banish people? Would we want to? But if we did, what would make them stay away? Nothing. We're just us. Could we put people in jail? What jail? And for how long? Using community service projects works best in our type of community, with our kind of people. But that wouldn't work for all people. There are some really bad people out there. Or at least there were. Hopefully they all died with KPox. But if they didn't...how would we deal with more severe crimes. Seriously, how _would_ we deal with it? We'd have to protect ourselves from being hurt, but _how_ we did it would be so hard to figure out. I guess we'll have to make those decisions when we get to that point. It'll probably be individually designed specifically for the person needing the consequence. But one thing Jackson said made sense (if you can ignore all the God stuff)—was that we have to protect our community, our houses, our homes. That really hit home with me. Like Dad protecting our house and us from those burglars that time. He was willing to shoot those guys to protect us. And he expected me and Mitchell to use the guns as well. So what

167

will it take to protect our community, our houses, our homes?

I'm going out to play with the little kids. I need some sweet innocence in my brain right now.

Your favorite daughter

Meg

July 13

Hey Girlie,

So it's my birthday today. I know you know :-), but it's weird not celebrating with you. No sleepover, no going to the quirky second hand store and taking pictures with the weird stuff...no laughing in the dark with my best friend. I miss you more today.

Mom and the kids are planning a cake and little gifts later. I'm thankful even though things have been weird. Tricia gave me a really pretty purple shirt with a matching purse, which was unexpected, but I love it. Caleb drew me a picture of the water hole...said it was so I could remember how it was now and compare it to how amazing it would look later. Awesome right? I have been feeling awkward about everything...but it was super thoughtful people remembered. Meg gave me the gift of free labor :-) She said she'd come help me with the landscaping and some company might be nice soon. It's been good to just work alone and not think..just BE...ya know? Even though there's not many of us, sometimes it seems like we're always together!

After my regular chores were done, I started at the swimming hole last week..just placing furniture and umbrellas and dumping out bagged sand to make a little beach for the kids. I'm going to have to figure out how to keep the sand from sliding into the water hole too much... I'm going to the library today to research plants. I had to ask the warden...eeerrrr...Dad...for permission to go, but he actually listened to me about wanting to plant the right things. So he said yes, just be back in a couple hours. Since the trial, or whatever...the 'consequence' meeting, he's given me some space...as long as I'm working, he lets me be. Of course this was after another talk with him and Mom about how I need to hang out with Jason less. They said, "at least until things settle down," but I can tell they really wish I'd hang out with him a lot less forever. It's frustrating when they can't just listen to how I feel, they always have to give me advice...and post it on sticky notes. Oh yeah, Dad has started to put a few up in the community...so embarassing!

But I get it, they're mad. They think I'm some dumb girl that got all caught up with some stupid boy and made stupid choices. They probably think I'm going to end up pregnant like all the other girls at my school who thought they were 'in love.' Well, I did get a little caught up and Jason just happened to be there and we did something stupid together, but I was protecting myself. We made sure we were away from the fireworks when they went off... and I'm the one who thought of doing it near water in case of fire...But whatever. I thought it was for a good reason at the time. I know, I know. Mandy, you would've stopped me before I even THOUGHT about going off with Jason and shooting fireworks by ourselves, but you're not here! And I just wanted to have some fun. How were you born so much wiser than me? I miss you so much!!!

Aaaarrrrgggg!!!! I'm so tired of thinking about all of it! Plants! That's what I'm going to think about. Plants. There'll still be the sandy beach on one side, but I'm going to build a border of water lilies around the edge and other plants that will naturally filter the water. Won't that be cool? A lot of the books talked about a pump, but the dads already lined the hole and added a pump when we first built everything. Maybe the pump can be solar powered? That would rock right? Then I think I'll transplant plants from different parts of the creek to put around the edge too. And I found these cool rocks at the stores. They will look really pretty. Oh! And cattails! Just a little patch...for the kids.

Then trees...I need something for a little shade. I'll research that next. Just call me Lucy Landscaper!

Partly sunny and motivated,
Ashleigh (Lucy! Lol)

July 14

Dear Mom,

Just a short note...Ashleigh's still working on her community service work and the beach is looking <u>good</u>! She really likes working on the landscaping so I have a feeling that the "consequence" for her was actually a fun thing. Which is fine by me—as she wouldn't have done anything wrong without Jason's lead anyway. She had her 17th birthday on the 13th. It was a little subdued and she didn't want a party—she felt ostracized and embarrassed so I just gave her my present—which was 17 hours of my labor at the pool area—one hour for each year of her life. She really liked that and we'll get to spend more time together, which will be nice!

And Jason dug the pits for the outhouses. He probably enjoyed his chore as well cuz he got to use the backhoe without Mitchell and Caleb clamoring to help him. And he had to be alone. So while his consequence was supposed to be a negative thing for him, it ended up not being one. At least I don't think so. Except for his pride, of course. He's still sulking—and being very obvious about it. What a jerk!

I'm glad the parents came up with those particular chores for them. It worked out well. Ashleigh and Jason didn't refuse to do their chores and it went well. Thank goodness. I was worried about what we'd do if Jason refused to do his sentence.

Your favorite daughter
Meg

July 17

Hey fancy lady!

I am amazing!! I am totally fantastic at landscaping! You should see the swimming hole! Well, duh you CAN see it right? Doesn't it look amazing??!!! I rock! There's the beach for the kids. Then I dug another offshoot with the backhoe so I could add some more water plants for filtration. Then next to the beach, Meg helped me put plants around the edge so the water would stay clear. Some of the books said that frogs would live in there eventually, which might be kinda gross if they jump on us when we're swimming, but also totally cool for us to see this whole environment grow! An ecosystem and I am the MASTER!!! Bwaaahahaha!

The pump helps the water from getting too stagnant, but now we're making it solar powered (b/c I am awesome and thought of it) instead of just running it off gasoline for an hour. Thank you very much, I'm a genius.

I dug up a couple weeping willows, and the trees look really pretty, even though they're little yet. Hopefully they'll grow fast and we can have more shade. It made me think about planting a few more things around your cross...make it a little flower garden...or FAIRY garden! How fantastic would that be??!!

There's only a couple more days I 'have' to work my community service. I'm going to keep working on it though because I love it! I know it was supposed to be sort of a punishment...but I liked the time alone it gave me to think and create. I'm going to paint a welcome sign with an ocean mural for the kids. They'll like it. Maybe I'll paint a girl mermaid and a boy pirate. This has actually been a pretty nice two weeks just working and focusing on one thing at a time. Maybe I can do some more landscaping around our 'town.'

At least I feel accomplished...like I'm actually doing something to contribute. Something more important than just counting the inventory.

I'm off to get paint!

Bright Sunshine with no tears in sight,
Ashleigh

July 31

Dear Mom,

Ashleigh and I had a conversation about religion. It started when I said OMG about Jason's behavior which made me think about what I was actually saying. So I asked Ashleigh when we say "Oh My God!" or "OMG" do you think that's taking the name of the Lord in vain—which is one of the 10 Commandments? I mean I don't think we're really thinking about God when we say it—just saying the words, but we don't mean anything disrespectful. Or does that make it worse cuz we <u>aren't</u> really thinking about God when we say it—just using His name for a silly saying? Is that what they mean "in vain"?

And Ashleigh had to think about it for a minute and said, "I don't know. I guess it is. I'm not allowed to say it at my house. But I can't even say Oh My Gosh at my house cuz it sounds too close to Oh My God." She said she thinks all that stuff is more about being respectful to God cuz He's the one that made us and cares for us. Kinda like...don't sass your parents. Not like he's going to strike us down with a bolt of lightning or anything. It's like swearing ...people swear all the time and maybe that's not "nice," but it's something that happens since we're human. And besides there's the whole forgiveness of sins for when you do mess up.

I don't know. Seems like if there are rules, one should follow them. But since it isn't my religion, it isn't up to me to care about how the rules are interpreted and followed—or not followed. I guess I should be careful about how I say things in front of Ashleigh's parents cuz I don't like to offend people but it's not like I say blasphemous things on a regular basis though. But it's fun having someone to have interesting conversations

with. Way more fun than talking to Mitchell!!
    Gotta run,

Your favorite daughter
Meg

August 5

Dear Mandy,

    I spent the day with Tricia and Meg. It was kinda spontaneous. I was going out to the barn with Tricia b/c she said Sadie was throwing her head a lot while she was riding, so I was going to watch her ride. When we were walking out to the farm we saw Meg, and Tricia asked her to come along too. After spending time working together, Meg and I have gotten closer and I was thinking then I wouldn't be stuck trying to figure out what to say to Tricia. I know she's not that much younger than me, but she still seems like it sometimes.

    So it was an awesome day. Warm, but the breeze was cool. I always feel like my moods are somehow connected to the weather ya know? Some cosmic force pulling me out of myself and into the clouds or the sun beams...I don't know. But anyways, it was great weather and everyone just seemed friendly and calm. On our way to the farm we got to talking about boys and how weird they are. It was actually pretty hysterical. I was telling this story of how Adam likes to run around the house naked and doesn't seem fazed by it at all! In fact, it's like he's so proud of himself and all his parts! Hahaha. Meg said Mitchell used to do that too and Tricia said she remembers Caleb jumping off the diving board at the public pool completely naked once! She said he'd stripped down before his parents noticed and yelled 'Cannonball!!!!' before he jumped so everyone looked over. I was laughing so hard by the time we got to the farm I couldn't breathe. Boys are so crazy!

    When we got there Meg and I stood by the horse pen while Tricia saddled Sadie. Meg asked how I knew about horses so I told her all about Mom and her growing up riding and how I've been riding since I was five. I liked it, I just didn't like all the practice and going to the competitions so I stopped riding competitively when I was 13. We never owned our own horse, just shared with a family who rode in competitions too.

We talked a little bit about Mom and Dad meeting and being from such different worlds, but they made it work. Meg said something about a true love match and I guess she's right. I never really thought about it before. I started to ask her about her parents, but then Tricia mounted Sadie and I had to tell her to make sure the saddle was tight enough b/c it was slipping a little bit to the side. She's gonna fall off and get hurt if she doesn't make sure it's secure.

We all decided to go on a ride after that...well, Tricia and I decided. Meg we had to convince. I don't know if she's ever been on a horse before! Which is totally crazy to me. But she was on Gypsy the old mare who's like twenty years old, so she's not going to bolt or anything. She just plods along with the other two horses we were taking, so Meg finally agreed. I was riding Thunderbolt of course and he likes to lead, so I was in front. It was pretty fun. I took them over to see the Kirkwood farm and down the ravine there. I've ridden that way so many times, but it was really nice to point it out to new people and tell them all about who used to live out there. I was like a tour guide! It really was a beautiful day.

Blue skies and happy,
Ashleigh

August 15

Dear Mom,

I had a totally interesting discussion with Jason today. I understand him a lot more, but I still think he's a bit of a baby and over dramatic. And he says that Tricia's moody! Geeze.

As usual for Sunday all us kids were hanging out in the clubhouse. For one reason or other everyone left except me and Jason and Ashleigh. We were just talking about nothing in particular and reading and relaxing. I kinda think Ashleigh wanted me to leave, but I was comfortable where I was so I stayed. Jason was talking mostly to me and hardly paying any attention to Ashleigh--which was rather rude. Finally she left and I could tell she was upset that he was ignoring her—again. I asked him, "Why're you so rude to her some days and so friendly other days? That's so mean."

He said "I'm not. I'm the same way all the time. Besides who cares how I am. How I talk to people is my business anyway."

I told him "Ashleigh cares how you are. And you <u>were</u> rude to her just now—<u>again</u>. And no, you aren't the same all the time. You're moody some days and happy on others. It's hard for any of us to know what you'll be doing or saying on any given day. I've heard you tell Tricia not to be so moody. You're way more moody than Tricia. Seriously Jason. What's wrong?" I said it nicely—not like an in your face kinda question.

He just looked at me. I think he was trying to decide if he was gonna get angry and storm out or actually answer. He decided to answer. "I don't know what's wrong with me. I know I'm a jerk sometimes. I don't mean to be. But I feel so trapped all the time living here." He stood up and started pacing around the room. "All my plans for my future are gone. All my friends are gone. I have no one to talk to and my parents are so focused on this whole stupid survival thing that they don't have a clue how I feel. I really counted on gettin' out of this town after I graduated and I'm stuck here for eternity. Eternity! I don't think I can stand it! Really. I don't think I can stand it much longer! I just feel like I need to get out of here!

I wanted to travel and meet new people and do all sorts of things. I thought I'd learn to sky dive and surf and go hiking. When I had money I wanted to buy a cool car and have cool places to drive to. Now I can have the car of my choice, just pick one up off the car lot, but there's nowhere to drive and if I did go somewhere, I'd have to have enough gas in the tank to get back. The people I know now are the only people I'll probably ever know and that drives me crazy! I can't stand the thought of just knowing this community forever—and no one else.

I really want to go find more people but Dad's totally against it—as are the other adults and you as well. But we can't just sit here and worry about what other people will do to us. Maybe they'll do stuff <u>with</u> us—not <u>to</u> us. How do we know? We don't! Because we can't go find anyone! We'll just sit here like these little meek cowards with no guts to do anything except take care of ourselves and pretend that the whole world is wonderful and fun and "brave and new." What a crock! We're not brave! We're cowards and hiding in our little world. I hate it!

I hate having only two girls my age. No offense, Meg. But you have to of thought about this too. If we're the only people in the world and the world continues on we'll need children. Well, you know... Ashleigh's a nice girl and I know she likes me and I like her, but I don't want to be stuck for the rest of my life with one girl. I'm too young. I should be dating lots of girls. I'm not ready to be a quiet, calm, happy family man. I have too much inside me that wants to explode and explore and just get the hell outta here! Seriously Meg, I really don't think I can take it much longer. But I don't know what I can do."

Then he stopped talking and pacing around the room. He clenched his fists and his teeth and said, "Sorry for bothering you and talking too much. I'm goin' out." And he left and walked off down the street.

I haven't ever heard him talk that much in my life. But I totally know what he's talking about. We all feel trapped in some ways...only I think that for some of us...we aren't thinking of it as being totally trapped—not any more. In some ways, this life is very freeing. I mean, we're stuck doing the same chores over and over and don't have much choice in what we'll be doing, but we do have a whole different, less hectic life than we used to. I think the parents are totally into this new world. I know Dad is. He was miserable in his old life—as much as he loved computers. But now he's a whole new person. Ashleigh's dad used to be so uptight and get upset about little things like how much toilet paper each family should have, and now he isn't counting things so much and he laughs more. We've learned to trust each other. All the parents are happier. Even Janet. She is smiling and just seems happier than she did at the beginning.

I don't feel trapped. Not really. Not anymore. I was very disappointed that I couldn't go to college. Still am. But now this life is getting more interesting. And even though we work really hard, it's less stressful. We don't have to multi-task so much. Go here, go there, text her, email that, go to class, study, go to work, go home, do chores, think about all the things I haven't done. But now I know what I'll be doing for the day and I work hard and I don't have to worry about other useless stuff. And I can make life as interesting as I want it to be--learn new things, start new projects—not being dependent on what the world is expecting of me minute by minute. I don't know if I'm explaining this right. But I'm getting used to being here. There are problems but we're working on fixing them, and it makes this life way more interesting than I ever thought it would be.

But I understand Jason more now. I guess I thought he was more resigned about this life—getting used to it, like I am. But it seems that he's going the other way—getting more and more stressed and upset. I don't know what he can do though. We made a community decision to not search for other survivors--at least this year. I'll bet if we lived back in the 1700s, Jason would become a mountain man--exploring the wilds of western America—hunting and trapping and living alone. Freezing cold mountains!! Yuck! I'd hate that.

I wonder if that's what you're doing right now. Are you a mountain woman working your way east til you get home? I hope you're not a mountain woman. That'd be really difficult. I like to think of you living with a nice family and making plans on how to get home. If I think about you trying to get back here and going through bad times—I worry so much that I get sick to my stomach. I have to think of you living somewhere safe and making plans. That I can stomach. And I can't think of you as not being anywhere. That isn't something I can deal with. So I don't.

So...I hope you're having a good summer with your nice family and helping them to rebuild their community. We'll keep building our community and it'll be ready when you get here.

I love you so much.

Your favorite daughter
Meg

August 15

Mandy
Boys ARE STUPID!!!! One minute he likes me—the next minute
he's an absolute JERK!!!! I HATE boys! I HATE HIM!!!! All guys
do is let you down! ALL OF THEM!! They only care about
themselves! About THEIR stuff and about what THEY want!
It's never about taking care of me or what I want. I HATE
feeling so lost! I hate feeling like my emotions are so CRAZY all
the time! I HATE IT! I HATE IT! I hate myself. I hate it all.

August 22

Mandy, you will never believe this...

There was a storm tonight after dinner...and it was beautiful! Lightning dancing high in the sky like magical tendrils...Huge sparkling spider webs of light that lit up the dusk sky and then the dark night. It was awesome! Dad said it was heat lightning...just a harmless storm in the distance. A bunch of us were standing in our garage just watching. It'd been a sticky, muggy, hot, damp day and we were feeling totally lazy. We'd all been hanging by the pool in the afternoon and found any shade we could b/c the sun was too hot to even be out in the pool. I wish those trees I planted around the waterhole were bigger! I totally got burned in this funky oval-ish shape where I didn't quite reach the middle of my back with the sunscreen. Uggh!

So I was glad when the sun went down and this beautiful show started. I mean, there were a few fat drops of rain when it was almost dark, but that only lasted a few minutes and honestly everything was so dry and so hot, the drops just made the air thicker instead of better. I think the earth said SLURP! Thanks for the drink! Can I have some more?!! But then we started to hear the deep rumble of the thunder even though we could still see the stars in the distance. It was so weird! Surreal. We started to count the time between the lightning and thunder like we did when we were kids, remember? Until they were almost at the same time! And then there was the sound I will never forget....this huge CRACK BOOM that sounded like a loud gunshot...like a million rifles all firing at the same time. You could almost hear the air crackle. We all stared at each other because we didn't know what to say.

But then Dad looked towards the farm, and started yelling, "I think it hit out at the farm. There might be a fire, we have to get out there!" I could tell he was worried b/c Dad NEVER yells. So he's running and honking and yelling and we're all jumping in the truck...I swear he was already stepping on the gas so Jason had to run and jump in. It was CRAZY!!!

My heart was pounding. I just knew something bad happened. I was sitting next to Meg and Tricia and somehow we all ended up holding hands. I honestly don't know if I grabbed their hands or they grabbed mine. No one was talking. I just couldn't stop thinking about all the horrible things we may find out there. So I just lowered my head to my knees. I kept thinking about when the stray animals ripped all of our food apart and how much we lost then. How much were we going to lose now?? I just couldn't stand it. What if the entire barn is on fire? What if we can't put it out? What if the horses are trapped and burn up? Are the crops already gone? What if the farm gas tank explodes and we all die too? What if what if what if. Where ARE the horses? It felt like it took hours to get there even though I know it's only a short drive. It was probably quicker too from how fast Dad was driving.

Then the truck jolted to a stop. The crunch of the tires almost stopped my heart, but I knew we had to get out and help. I was afraid to see. We all dropped hands and jumped to the ground. I remember thinking about the dust that flew up when our boots hit the ground. It was still so horribly dry, we hadn't had rain in ages. The dads were handing out buckets and yelling to be careful.

Then it felt like everything went from slow motion to hyper speed! It wasn't the barn!!! The lightning had struck the walnut tree next to the barn and the branches had caught fire. I was so thankful for a second because a tree is just a tree right?...then we realized that the wind was whipping sparks and bits of flaming branches everywhere!!! Especially towards the barn and the horse paddock! OMG! So I started to run towards the fire. I didn't know what I was doing. I hadn't even filled my bucket! I just knew I had to get there! Jason grabbed my arm and yelled, "Ashleigh!! Wait!! You have to fill your bucket!" I swear I looked down thinking magic water had appeared. He pulled me towards the water pump and we all started filling our buckets and running towards the tree. We were dumping water on everything we could! Just trying to soak things so they wouldn't burn! We were running in blurs from one spot to the next just trying to make those orange flames go out. I was desperately praying for a miracle. I just wanted those flames to stop!!!

Finally. Finally the dads yelled stop and we all stood there, panting and exhausted. The tree was still smoldering a bit, but we had done it! The fire was out! The barn was fine. The horse pen was damaged in places, but it can be fixed. And then! Wouldn't you know it? It started to POUR! Not drizzle...but raining cats and dogs!!! The tree sizzled as the water turned the last embers to smoke. Hallelujah!! God sent the rain!!! He was watching over us. Even in the midst of our struggle, He was there.

I don't know who started, but we all began laughing. First just these little chuckles of relief and then great belly laughs so hard we were bent over, watching the rain make rivers through the grass. We were just totally relieved you know? We'd been terrified. And now it was over. I was so ridiculously happy right then and I looked around at the faces covered with soot and dirt and now streaming with water and tears of laughter...I was thankful for us...all of us. It was an awful, horrible, terrible, gut-wrenching thing. But maybe it took that to remind me why we are so blessed.

There was a lot of teasing in the back of the truck on the way home. And it really felt like HOME for the first time...Home. This new life keeps teaching us and teaching us. And now I'm going to bed. Night.

Distant rumbles and EXHAUSTED,
Ashleigh

186

August 23

Dear Mom,

OMG!! We had a fire out at the farm!! It was so scary! Lightning hit a tree and Jackson thought it looked like it was out at the farm. So we...let me back up a bit. All us older kids were standing in the Grace's garage watching the lightning cuz it looked like fireworks. We were watching the storm get closer and the heat lightning looked so cool flashing around in the clouds—really amazing! And then the storm got really close, the wind picked up, and the lightning started crackling down and BANG! It hit something close. That's when Jackson said, I think it hit the farm! So we jumped into the back of his truck and he blasted his horn so the adults came out to see what was the matter. He said we were running up to the farm to see if lightning hit anything. Dad and Donald jumped in with us and we all flew up there. The big old tree in the yard was on fire and the strong wind was sending burning pieces of tree branches and sparks all over the place—including towards the barn! We were totally freaked out and the dads got the water pump running and we all started running around with pails and flinging water to put out the falling burning tree branches. One of the burning branches crashed into the hay in the horse paddock. The hay burned so fast it almost exploded! The paddock fence started burning, and we all ran back and forth from the pump to the paddock splashing, flinging, dumping water frantically, and finally the fire died—drowned under our attack. Our adrenaline levels must have been running on super high cuz we moved so much faster and carried so much more water than we ever thought we could—we were totally scared we'd lose the barn and the animals, and so much of our food comes from the farm.

And then after all that running and throwing water and being scared of losing everything to the fire, the skies decided to dump the rain on us in torrents—like the gods were dumping buckets of water on us! So we all stood there in the rain, holding our buckets, and watching the soot and sweat wash off our faces and arms, getting totally drenched. And then we all laughed and laughed until our stomachs hurt. I'm not sure why we laughed so hard, cuz it wasn't all that funny, but we did. And it felt good after all that tension.

So we all ended up back in the Grace's garage—soaking wet, but grateful that the fire was out and everything ended well. We stayed talking until the rain fairly quickly drizzled to an end and then walked back to our homes, shivering from the quick change in temperature and looking forward to putting on dry clothes.

If it isn't one thing...it's another! What a life! I love you Mom.

Your favorite daughter
Meg

September 2

Dear Mandy,

So school's back in session! I'm kinda looking forward to it. Sounds like it's going to be a whole different format. Janet's talking about workstations and helping the little ones and doing more with subjects we like instead of just going through each subject like we did in the spring. She said it'll be more like a combo of a one room schoolhouse and home schooling. AND the best part is we only go a <u>HALF</u> day! So then we can be done for the day to work or whatever. Great, right?!

You know I'm thinking that by going at my own pace, maybe I'll even learn more than I would've in regular high school. I won't have to worry about busy work...I'll actually do things that matter to me and see how everything really works in the real world, you know? I'm sure there'll still be history and spelling and whatever, but I think it's going to be good. It's time for a whole new chapter to begin! Books. New chapter. Get it? Har har!

We had a Labor Day picnic this weekend to prepare us for school and fall and whatever. The food was good and we played flag football. And can you believe it, even little Adam and I played! Adam was adorable! I was on Caleb's team with Donald and Sam. Jason, Dad, and Mitchell were on the other team. They said it was even b/c Dad got the young guys and that made up for us having more on our team. I got Dad's flag twice. And get this...Jason tackled me—well, sorta tackled. Not I wouldn't have minded a real tackle from him...but I'd caught the ball from Donald (amazing right? who knew I was athletic?? I mean I played softball and soccer when I was a kid, but hey, I should've gone out for the football team! Maybe we could've won some games!) and I was running for a touchdown when Jason all of a sudden flew past everyone else and threw his arms around me. He yelled "Gotcha!" and then we tripped and fell and were rolling on the ground. It might've been my imagination, but it almost seemed like he lingered just a little bit before pulling the flag. I swear my stomach flipped like 100 times. He seemed so happy today. Caleb on the other hand was a little moody after that. Kinda stomped around and seemed really serious about winning the game. I don't know, maybe it's a competitive brother thing. He lightened up later though—after we had dessert. I pretended we were out of pie and hid it behind my back so he had to grab for his piece. We almost knocked over the table and of course my parents had to be jerks and tell us to settle down and stop horsing around...RE-LAX people! I thought we were ADULTS now, so stop bossing us around like we're little kids. We're not hurting anybody. Caleb and I got a good laugh out of it though. It was nice not to have to work.

Windy and ready for new starts,
Ashleigh

September 4

Dear Mom,

Well, school started again! I'm sitting in the back of the school room reading my medical books pretending I'm in college. Jason and Mitchell think I'm crazy for being in school again since I already graduated. But I told them that I would've been in college anyway so it isn't much different from what I should've been doing. Caleb and Ashleigh kinda understand, but Mitchell totally doesn't. Janet's teaching again and she'll be working with little Adam for half a day for his little one-person kindergarten class. How cute! Ava's staying home with Caroline for another year. One thing different from the old school is that instruction is from 8:00 to noon. Then we're done for the day! And at 10:00 we have a 10 minute bathroom/snack/recess break. That's a nice change from traditional school. As you can imagine—Mitchell <u>loves</u> those changes!

Jason isn't coming back to school. He's out with the men full time and they continue to learn what they need for new projects when it's needed. Dad's never without a book on some project or other and I see Donald and Jackson with books as well. I must admit it's fun to learn new stuff when it's used immediately for something concrete.

It's a busy time in the gardens and farm. Lots of harvesting and canning. It's fun and satisfying seeing all the filled colorful jars get put into the cupboards. We're dividing up the canned goods as we make them—by the number of people in each household. So we have pickles and tomatoes and beans and a bunch of other stuff. And if we want to trade some items for others we can do that. To be honest, I'd trade several jars of pickles for <u>anything</u> as the first batch didn't turn out so good.

But since no one really likes them, I don't think anyone would trade. The following batches turned out better—thank goodness!

I'm glad summer's over and I'm in school again. It makes life seem so normal somehow—school after summer vacation. And kinda makes up for not going to college. I mean I'd really rather be in college and have the world back to normal, but since it isn't, this is nice. I like having the continuity of life, having some of the old things as a part of the new life.

The worst part of my pretend college is that I don't have my friends in college with me. I'm missing them more and more lately. I know this is only temporary, that I'll get into the swing of things in a week or so, but it's hard right now. I wonder where Jen and Rachel are and hope they're still alive—though I know it isn't likely. But I can't let myself think about that too much. Too difficult.

Well, I'm tired (again) and off to bed. School tomorrow morning and canning corn in the afternoon.

Your favorite daughter
Meg

PS: btw Jason moved into his own place—next door to his parents (and close to his mother's cooking). To be honest, I've thought about doing that as well, but don't think I will. I like having Dad and Mitchell for company in the evenings—and if I get irritated with them I just go to my room. Hopefully his own place will help Jason feel better about life in general.

STRAY CLOTHES
FLAG STRANGERS.
-JG

September 18

What's up girl?!

I'm REALLY enjoying school! I know I've always liked to learn, but I really like the way we're helping the community by learning math and science and reading and all of it! I know my teachers always told us we'd use this stuff later...but now I really see it!

It's just like I've been thinking about...actually seeing nature work and how we fit into this world. I still struggle with why we have to live this new life...but I think it's okay! It's starting to feel like a real life and not just some crazy dream. I hope you like the little pumpkins I put around your cross for the fall. Ava helped me paint funny faces on them.

I'm super busy now with work, canning, school and all my chores! AND I'm making Meg some stationary with her initials at the top for her birthday. The other day at school Janet asked us to write a letter to someone (dead or alive) that we would like to have dinner with...I know the point was to get to know someone from history, but OF COURSE I chose you! But it was really cool because Meg came up to me later and said that she writes letters to her mom, just like I write to you. Crazy huh? It was nice to actually talk about missing you and hearing about her mom. The sad part for me though is her mom may be alive, but I can't say enough prayers to change what happened to you. I won't get to hug you again until I meet you in heaven. Still...I guess that means I have a super awesome angel on my side that no one else has. Bam! :) I think Meg understood why it's so hard for me to be friends sometimes. It makes me happy and horribly sad all at once... But I really hope Meg gets to give her mom all those letters someday. Even with what has been taken from us, I still hope we all find happiness. (Which would be TOTALLY easier if Dad stopped posting sticky notes at the clubhouse! Embarrassing! Like the last one he wrote about stray clothes blowing away?! I don't care if Caleb and Jason take their

shirts off wherever they are working...Yeah, they forget to pick them up and sometimes they blow away and Jason doesn't pick his up...but shirtless boys bring ME happiness...just sayin...)
   Ok, Gotta go! Life keeps truckin' on!

Cooler breeze and light spirit!
Ashleigh

September 20

Dear Mom,

Well, I didn't get what I wanted for my birthday—which was you. But I didn't really think you'd be back for my birthday. Maybe Christmas! The birthday was nice though. Dad and Mitchell fixed me a really nice supper and did all my chores. And we went target shooting and I got to have more turns than anyone else as a part of my present. I also got my own rifle—a Winchester 30-30 with an awesome scope. I know! Me liking shooting! I didn't like the 30-30 much at first but now I really like smashing things with those bullets. It's <u>totally powerful</u>!! So no one better get in my way—I can take them to kingdom come! BLAM!

Okay...that sounds a little harsh for a birthday entry. Don't worry Mom. I'm still the quiet gentle boring Meg, but I really do like target shooting. And I'm really good at it!

Ashleigh gave me some really nice stationary. Told me it was for writing to you. That was so thoughtful—makes me want to cry. I'm glad she's my friend now. I truly am. I need a friend to talk to and be with. Makes life less lonely and pointless.

So I'm 18 now but really who cares. 18 doesn't really mean much here. But I guess it's kinda cool that I'm legally a grown up. But like I said, doesn't really mean much...rather a letdown in a way. Oh well...happy birthday to me. :)

Your favorite daughter
Meg

October 6

Dear Mom,

I really love learning about plants we can use for natural medicines and other stuff. I spend hours reading. Like for instance...I learned an interesting thing about aloe vera. I just thought it was good for putting on cuts but it can also be a cure for baldness! Seriously! You rub the juice on your head, leave it for a few hours, then wash it out! Dad doesn't need it yet, but I'll remember this...just in case. :) And marigolds can be used for cuts and stings, fabric dye, a gargle for throat infections and a rinse for red hair! Learning about plants is really fascinating! I love it! Not sure if we'll use any of this, but it is fascinating.

Mitchell still fusses occasionally about going to school, cuz he wants to quit and be with the men all day. So when he starts whining and begging, Dad tells him how his reading and math levels need to be at a certain educational level before he can be included in their activities. And he needs to learn about government and how things work in the sciences—he has to stay in school so he won't be totally ignorant and embarrassed when he's an adult and making adult decisions. I don't know if Mitchell buys it, but Janet's making sure her students are learning lessons we can use in our new situation. Last year she stuck to how the curriculum was for the old way of life. This year all her lesson plans relate to community life. The math word problems solve for specific community problems. And when Mitchell, Ashleigh, or Caleb solve the math problems, their answers are used. English class is mostly reading and writing, and she has the students read books of interest. And they write reports on projects they're interested in and then present to the committees for review. Science and government are taught the same way. Mitchell worked on a project about how many bags of dog food the dogs will need in the next 5 years and the cubic yards of storage that will be needed for all those bags. (Rodents are getting into the dog food bags and storage is needed quickly.) Caleb worked on how much fertilizer and seed grain will be needed in the gardens and farm for next spring. Ashleigh's working on the beach landscaping and one of her projects was to work out how much more mulch and landscaping gravel and timbers will be needed to finish one portion of her garden. (She's totally into the beach landscaping and it's looking really cool! Who knew that her fireworks consequence would work out so well!) And at every committee meeting one of the students presents to the group. It's getting them involved in the governance of the group. It's pretty cool actually.

To help me learn and to help Janet, I'm going to have presentations about plants and other medical subjects. The first medical presentation I'll do will be on CPR and I've been asked to follow up with other basic first aid subjects. We decided we should all know basic first aid. I'm also working on a presentation about medicinal plants and how they're used. I'm looking forward to it. I have this small field guide about plants and when I walk in the woods, I take my field guide along. I've been picking up some interesting specimens. I'm going to try to use them for things like headaches or brew healthy tea and stuff. The dandelion tea I made was a total failure. I hated the taste. And anyway we probably have literally tons of real packaged tea in our grocery store, so dandelion tea will be at the bottom of my list of things to make again! :-) But it's hard to find fresh plants now that everything's dying.

I'll have to begin again in the spring when plants are new

and fresh.

Your favorite daughter
Meg

October 9

Dear Mandy,
    She's dead! I just know it! It's impossible that she just
wandered off and is still alive. She is gone. G-O-N-E. No one's
saying it, but it's true. I felt numb when Janet and Donald told
everyone tonight that Tricia is missing. Everyone immediately
formed a search party. Dad and I went out to the barn to
search. Meg, Sam and Mitchell searched around the houses. Then
Donald, Janet, Jason and Caleb went down to the swimming hole
and the woods behind there. When Dad and I got to the barn,
Sadie was missing and we knew Tricia could have gone
ANYWHERE on horseback. Dad called Donald on the walkie talkie
and we all met back at the clubhouse. Donald said we would have
to wait until morning b/c it was too dark to find their trail. Janet
started to sob and Caleb walked her home. Jason still kept saying
he wasn't quitting but his dad said no, he wasn't going to lose
two kids in one night. I couldn't stop the tears. Everyone is
stricken!
    We know Tricia's not the camping out type. She has an
awful sense of direction, but she's been walking to the farm
almost every day with Dad to help with the animals, so she has
to know her way around, right? She should be able to find her
way back? Right?!! I mean...I'm just so freaking ANGRY!!!! Why
would this happen?? She was JUST here today at lunch saying
something about not wanting to eat meat anymore and then
poof! Gone.
    God really has a sick sense of humor. After all we've been
through! After all we've done to keep faith and keep ourselves
going! He rips someone away again! AGAIN! Why isn't He
protecting us? Are we abandoned in this world?? His voice is so
quiet. Did HE die in the disease? Why doesn't He help us?? Why
are we left here to suffer? Maybe it IS the great judgment.
Maybe we've been left behind b/c WE are the ones that didn't
make it to heaven. Maybe we're not the saved ones...maybe we're

the ones who are waiting around to be judged again. But why? What did we do? What did I do? What did Tricia do? She's only 13!

Maybe it's not God. Maybe it's the devil. That maggoty snake! Maybe he's the one causing all this. Maybe he's trying to make us suffer when we just have to keep strong. God is with us. He has to be. He has to be, right? God is only love, not darkness. Aaaahhh! I'm just....I'm just....I feel like my heart is broken into a million pieces. God please! If she's alive, please send her back to us. We need her here. We can't lose anyone else. I beg you. Please Lord, don't let her be taken away! Please God. Please.

October 10

Dear Mom,

Tricia's gone! She and her favorite horse, Sadie, disappeared yesterday and they aren't anywhere to be found! Jason had gone to his parent's house and was arguing with them yesterday afternoon and Trish usually disappears during a family fight. So it wasn't til later in the evening that they realized she was gone. And now everyone's freaked out and left on search parties first thing this morning, and I was told to go to the clinic and wait. Cuz Janet is out with the search parties. Thanks a lot. Wait for what? But I decided to think of all the things that might happen to her while she was riding: she might break a bone—hopefully not landing on her hard head, or get bitten by a bug or snake (<u>no</u> cutting of bite area and sucking out poison), or get cut badly, or have a concussion or a sprain. Things in my first aid portion of the book that I did <u>not</u> study were what to do with an electrical shock victim or a heart attack victim or someone with an asthmatic attack. But if I need to, I can read those over pretty quickly. So I've been sitting here in the clinic by myself reading about the little I could actually do with broken bones and bleeding etc. and the information on how to use the cast material. I basically can't do much but put one of those removable casts with the Velcro on a broken limb, and make her comfortable. Check the bandage for tightness or looseness every 15 minutes or so. I have materials for all emergencies that I sorta know how to cope with and I'm as ready as I can be. So now I wait. And while I wait, I write.

Trish has grown up so much since we first met. At first she really took this whole end-of-life-as-we-know-it pretty hard. I mean we all did, but she was just sooo much more whiny about it. Back at the beginning when we saw her coming, we wanted to hide. Even then, she liked the fact that she could wear anything from any of the stores and dress extremely in style, and she still hates that there's no one but us to dress up for! It's kind of funny watching her wear her new outfits out to the farm to mess with the horses and getting all dirty. She's better now at choosing appropriate shoes and clothes, but not always. She says that just cuz there's no one left in the world, that's no reason to look pathetically out of fashion. So now she's wandering about in the country wearing who knows what. I hope yesterday was a day that she dressed sensibly, but you never know. I keep imagining little Tricia wandering about in her cute boots and tripping over rocks and crying. It makes me want to cry too.

Mom, Ashleigh keeps talking about how God could do this to us, to Tricia. We were at the clubhouse and deciding what to do and where to go and she starts in about God again. To be honest, I wish she'd quit talking about God. I don't see how God, if there is one, would allow this crap to happen in the first place. What kind of deity would allow K-Pox or hurt children or any of the other stuff that goes on—or has gone on in the last thousands of years. I don't want to be argumentative or mean, but geeze, I wish she'd just keep her mouth shut. I don't get it. I don't want a god that allows terrible things to happen. If I had to pick a god it would be one of the animist gods—perhaps a god of the trees—just standing there and being. I'm not sure what it would do, or could do, but it wouldn't <u>hurt</u> and <u>kill</u> people. Us kids in the community have had long discussions about religion and some are true believers in God and others of us aren't and some aren't sure. When it looks like we're going to get really mad at each other, we just quit talking or say that we agree to disagree. But it's definitely a point of contention. And Mitchell listens to all sides and keeps asking me what I think. I'm honest and tell him that I truly don't know the ultimate TRUTH. Does anyone? But when something bad happens, it really makes me aware that my true belief is that we are on this planet without any deity watching over us or caring for us.

Well, enough of this. I'm going to go outside and see if there's anyone around. I'm bored and scared sitting here by myself and worried sick. If there is a god up there somewhere, I hope he or she lets Trish come home. But when (not if) she gets home, I bet it'll be cuz she took care of herself and made it home on her own strength—not some god-given miracle!!!

Your favorite daughter
Meg

October 10

Dear Mandy,

She's back. God, I'm so sorry I doubted you...and yelled at you. What a miracle though! Apparently Tricia wanted to take Sadie on a long ride b/c she was really mad at Jason and just wanted to get away. What was she thinking?? She went out there all alone and she didn't even tell anyone where she was going. She should've known better.

So she was out taking a ride and something spooked Sadie. She bolted, throwing Tricia to the ground where she landed smack on her arm and then ran off. Tricia said it really hurt and her arm started swelling almost instantly. She forced herself to get up and walk. I can't even imagine. After a while she was in too much pain to walk much further so she sat down under a big tree. Thank goodness she was wearing a few layers with a sweater and jeans. Still trying to be fashionable, but I guess it was good this time! So she used her t-shirt to wrap her arm and kinda make a sling. Then she tried to rest a little bit, but it got dark and so she just waited all night in the dark! Then the sun came up and she started walking back to town. I was right though, she said she knew where she was, she just followed the road. That's where they found her.

The search party was only gone for a couple of hours then all of a sudden we heard the truck motor as it was coming down the street. They stopped in front of the clubhouse and Donald was shouting. It was hard to hear what they were saying, but then Donald climbed carefully out of the truck holding something...and I saw Tricia's boots. Good grief, those crazy colorful boots she wears all the time. And I knew it was her. She was covered in dirt and I started to cry. I couldn't stand to see anyone else dead. But then I heard him saying, "She's ok she's ok, it's just her arm." What a miracle!! I think we were all imagining something waaaay more awful.

Donald and Janet took her in the clinic where Meg had set

out a bunch of stuff...you know like stuff for wounds and whatever. I think she was preparing for the worst too! They were all so calm! I know they were trying to stay calm for Trish, but I was FREAKING OUT! We were all crowded around the door and we saw Tricia had made a sling for her arm out of her shirt. They said her arm could be broken, but then we had to go because Mom told us we should back up and give them some privacy.

I sat down with Caleb and we just grabbed each other's hands and held on tight. He was trying to be strong but tears were running down his face. I was sobbing too. I was just so glad she was back and I wanted her to be okay, but you never know. I know that Tricia's their biological sister, but she belongs to all of us now. We all sat outside the clinic and waited together. Meg said Trish should be okay when she came out later. Thank God for everyone's help. I don't know what we would've done if we'd lost her!

After all that craziness we still had to do our chores and Dad went out to the farm to feed everybody, and guess what? There stood Sadie right next to Gypsy and Thunderbolt...like nothing ever happened. She just found her way home. I guess that's what we're all trying to do.

Dusk and emotionally drained,
Ashleigh

October 10

Dear Mom,

Tricia made it back okay. She had a broken arm (we think) and her parents and I decided to put it in a removable cast and I told them the medical book said not to take the cast off for a month to six weeks. Janet and Donald asked my advice (a little) because they know I've been reading about medical stuff. But they made all the decisions. Everybody's saying how wonderful I am and how calm I was, but I'm not wonderful and I was only calm on the outside. On the inside I was screaming and crying like a baby. To be honest, Mom, I still am. I don't know if it's a broken arm. We assume it is because of the pain Tricia's having, but have no way of knowing truly. And we're not going to poke and move her bones about as that would do worse damage. So from what I could read in the books and what she was telling me, we decided to put the cast on her. I remember Sally (do you remember her—short dark haired girl with an offbeat sense of humor—she's gone now) she had a broken foot once and she had to stay off her foot for about a month, so we figured if a real doctor said it was right for Sally, it could be right for Tricia too. So she's in a cast and following me about, thinking I'm wonderful. I'm _not_ wonderful. I'm just scared. I hope nothing happens to anyone else, but I expect it will—life being what it is—hard and miserable. Oh, and her parents asked for some pain medication for her so she could sleep—which I got out of the hiding place and gave to them.

I've been studying a lot in my medical book and learning more about what can go wrong with us—and there's a _lot_ that can go wrong. I've also been back to the doctor's office to make sure that we have all the things we might need in case of emergency—like bandages and needles and thread for stitches (shudder) and prescription pain meds. I've only told Dad where the prescription pain meds are so they aren't a temptation to anyone else. You never know what people might want to try. Anyhow, it's not easy being the one people count on for medical help. I thought it might be kinda cool, but it isn't really. It's more a heavy responsibility and scary. We have to be true adults now and make serious decisions. Cause we have to be ready when the parents aren't here anymore. They'll get old and die someday. Or get sick or hurt. Will I be the true doctor then? I guess so. That whole issue is just too sad to think of. Our parents gone? It's hard enough without you. I can't imagine a life without Dad too. Won't think about it right now.

    This whole business makes me want to go to bed and stay there!

Your favorite daughter
Meg

October 11 Emergency Meeting Minutes

Present:
  Donald, Janet, Jason, Caleb and Tricia Kinsey
  Jackson, Caroline, and Ashleigh Grace; Adam and
    Ava Parker
  Sam, Meg, and Mitchell Shultz

Meeting convened due to Tricia's accident

Medical: Everyone will be trained in basic first aid as soon as possible.

Survival techniques: Every community member will be required to learn survival techniques, such as how to identify food in the wilderness, how to build a fire, how to use a compass and track their way back to town. Everyone will carry a weapon and be trained in the use of knives, bow and arrows, and guns. Guns can be used to alert the community if you are lost and other weapons can be used to hunt for food, if needed.

Community responsibility: Additionally, everyone will be required to spend time in each job area to have a basic knowledge of how different parts of the community work and fit together. The community stated it was highly important that everyone knows how to keep the community going when someone gets ill, or hurt, or dies.

Everyone will be responsible for checking in with family members, letting them know where they are going, making sure they are where they should be, as well as following basic safety rules. No one can afford to be careless.

Notes taken by Ashleigh Grace.

October 21

Dear Mom,

    I love walking in the woods now! I never was an outdoor kind of girl, and I'm going to be especially careful to not get lost or hurt, but the woods are so wonderful! It's so quiet and alone and full of wonder. If I believed in magic I'd believe that all sorts of good magic would happen in the woods in the fall. The colors are so bright, and not only the leaves, but the sky is so bright and blue. Sometimes the beauty of nature is so awesome I can hardly breathe. And I mean the word awesome in its literal meaning—full of awe. That's how I feel when I'm standing in a glade and the wind shivers the gold leaves out of the trees and I'm standing in a glorious golden leaf-filled moment of wonder. Or I walk down to the creek and the shallows of the water are a dark combination of browns and reds and deep burnished golds and a little silver minnow slips gracefully through the magic of color. I know some people don't like fall because it symbolizes death. But it so totally doesn't symbolize the end of things to me. To me fall promises the beginning of a new fresh future, that this is a time of rest and stillness to prepare for the coming spring. I truly do love the fall—even the rainy days. Rainy days are cozy and warm and a time for soup and family.

    On a more practical note...rainy days are chilly and we're all gathering up heaters and tanks of fuel. We've discussed using wood in the fireplaces but the parents said that fireplaces are not heat-efficient and that too much of the heat goes up the chimney. And the smoke (both the smell and the sight of it) might draw attention to us. So they're working on having houses properly vented so the fuels we use don't poison us in our sleep! Dad's going to try and make one of those gas heaters that looks like a fireplace work for us. That'll be pretty neat. Too bad we don't have fall magic to keep us warm! If I were the Fairy of the Woods I would wave my golden branch wand and make the house full of the warm glow of sunshine falling into an open forest glade.

If you're out there in the woods coming home to us, please find a warm safe place for the winter. I love you Mom.

Your favorite daughter

Meg

Caleb

Sad seeing all the houses empty. It's like a
scary movie everywhere. Weeds and trash and
broken windows. Going out at night is freaky —
always if the dead people will come back as
ghosts.

Oct 30

Hey Mandy girl!

We're getting ready for Halloween. The kids are gonna look so cute! They are SUPER excited. We're making caramel apples. Yum!

Sorry I haven't written more, but I've been crazy busy helping with costumes, target practice (I shot 2 cans off the fence in a ROW...like Annie Oakley!...well not quite, but we're all getting pretty good), and kids and blah, blah, blah. It was Adam's 5th birthday on the 19th and he got to pick all his favorite foods for the day. We made him a cake and Mom even let him have a tiny piece with his breakfast...he was SOOOOO excited!!! He sang a little happy song while he was eating...hysterical! I got him some chapter books and tulip bulbs we'll plant together, Ava picked out a puzzle at the store for him, and my parents got him a tool set and a BB gun! Can't believe he's 5!

But the coolest thing that happened today was Adam and Ava becoming 'official' Graces. :) So I know that Adam remembers his real parents and has this hazy memory of Dad finding them in the barn (btw, can you imagine how scary that would have been to leave the car after his parents were killed. He has never really told us what happened, but when we were cooking I kinda asked Mom about it again and she said Adam told them a story when the kids first came...something about a big crash, then his dad not waking up and his mom being really sleepy, but telling him to take his sister and find somewhere warm that had food. Then she fell asleep too. She probably saved their lives!! Was watching over them from heaven so they made it somewhere that we could find them...so crazy sad though...that's probably why he had nightmares when they first came here.) But back to the adoption thing! I guess when Adam has been practicing writing his name at school, he sometimes writes Parker, but then sometimes he writes Grace.

He told Janet that he is part of the Grace family so he should write Grace. Janet and Mom talked about it and after Mom and Dad talked to him, they all decided he can write Grace if he wants. We are not changing his name for good...there's no legal anything anymore anyway!...but we are going to add Grace as part of his last name (Parker-Grace). It's still important for him to know where he came from...and who knows, maybe his mom and dad made it through the accident and are looking for them like Meg's mom, you know? But today on his cake we wrote "Happy Birthday Adam Grace!" And Ava yelled, "Me Grace too!" So even though we will never take the place of their real family, we are all the same now. It kinda made me tear up a little. It's kinda hokey...but we all found 'grace' together. haha

K, gotta run! You know I love you!!!

Cloudy days with Heavenly hugs!
Ashleigh

November 1

Dear Mom,

    We had trick or treat last night! It was so much fun! First little Adam and Ava went out for Trick or Treats. Mitchell and Caleb went with them so the big boys got candy as well—which was ok with them! The little kids were so cute. They felt so grown up being with the big boys and not having their parents with them. Anyway, they went to our three houses and got candy. Then they went to the clubhouse and we had a Halloween party with refreshments, games, and dancing for everyone—LOVE the dancing!! Ever since the prom and graduation the moms are totally into decorating for different occasions. They found a bunch of artificial pumpkins and leaves and fall fabrics to decorate the main room. (They prefer artificial to real as it's easier to clean up. I get it, but it isn't as cool.) The weather was perfect—just cold enough to feel like fall, but not so cold (or rainy) to make it impossible for the little guys to have fun.

    Oh, let me tell you! We all had costumes! I was the Fall Forest Fairy Queen and wore a deep gold, long-sleeved dress with the jagged hem at mid-thigh and worn over brown tights. My shoes were gold with a low heel. On my head I wore a gold leaf crown (made with real leaves and paint and glitter) and I carried a gold and glittery branch wand (more paint and glitter). Little Ava was the Spring Fairy wearing a cute little pink dress with artificial flowers all over her hair and a little sparkly wand from the toy store. Trish was the Summer Fairy and wore a really cute short evening dress in a shimmery deep blue fabric--which she was totally excited about cuz she'd really wanted to wear a sexy dress for prom and couldn't, but her mom let her do it for Halloween! Ashleigh chose Winter—the cold and chilly

215

time of year. She found a really pretty silvery dress and a silver tiara. For her wand she took a cattail and spray painted it silver and sprinkled it with silver glitter. We all got ready together which was so much fun. Ashleigh's really good at costume makeup and helped all of us. She helped me put on makeup that made me look like a true fairy queen—shades of brown and gold eye shadow with sparkles, a brownish-red lipstick, and more sparkle in the face makeup and hair. I loved the way I looked. I wouldn't have had the nerve to dress this way if it hadn't been for Ashleigh and Tricia. We all looked absolutely gorgeous—if I do say so myself!!!

The guys dressed up as well. Mitchell dressed up as a pirate. Adam was a fireman. Caleb was a cowboy—mostly cuz he didn't really want to get in a costume—but we let him get away with blue jeans and a cowboy hat and his lasso. Jason came as a basketball star wearing his old uniform and dribbling a basketball. (Those basketball shorts are so baggy—do guys know they look like they're wearing skirts? Just sayin'.) Dad dressed up as a nerd and wore too short pants, combed his hair back funny, and put tape on his glasses. He was actually rather embarrassing looking and I thought he should be something else, but he wouldn't change. If I wear a costume I want to look nicer—not sillier or uglier. Caroline and Jackson came as a 1950s couple—she wore a poodle skirt and he wore a t-shirt with a pack of cigarettes rolled up in one of the sleeves. She had a pony tail and he had his hair slicked back. Janet and Donald were mad scientists and wore white lab coats and must've used a ton of gel to get their hair to stick out so much. They looked hysterically funny.

We danced and ate and had a wonderful time! I love

dressing up! I love to look pretty and sexy. Not that there's anybody to dress up for...but I've whined about this before so no sense going over it again. Whether there's anyone to dress up for or not, I still like getting all glammed up. And it was so much fun to have us three older girls talking and laughing together. I think we might actually become good friends—not totally yet, but someday soon. I look forward to that. I miss having good friends to talk to and have secrets with.

I miss you too Mom.

Your favorite daughter
Meg

Nov 11

Hey lady,

I really wish I had your advice right now. Mom and I haven't been getting along the greatest lately. I know she's worried about me and Jason hanging out. But it's like all the advice she gave was 'Watch yourself.' Really??!! NOT helpful. I think he's hot, but I don't know what I'm supposed to do...I want him. I want to us to be 'dating' you know, but I'm scared! Sometimes I don't understand why he's so hot and cold...sometimes he's a real jerk, but then other times he's nice and just seems like he only wants to pay attention to ME...and I really like that you know? Mandy, I wish you were here...you'd have something more intelligent to say than "Watch yourself."

And I've been so tired and emotional from all this clean-up we're doing. We decided to clean up the houses within a 1 block radius. That way we can make sure animals and rodents are not getting into our supplies and houses, but since we're leaving the houses off the main highways alone, they'll still hide and protect us. Sam said something like "The decay will be our ally and our protection." Kinda dramatic...but poetic I guess. I'm looking forward to doing something else that doesn't completely wear me out. Ugh.

Shiny Sun, but grumbly heart,
Ashleigh

November 16

Dear Mom,

It's already mid-November. The skies are dull gray and it rains a lot and it's getting cold. It's just plain miserable most days. I must admit it isn't too magical anymore.

I hate being cold. Do you remember Great Aunt Sally used to say that she hated November. She called it Blue November—she felt so blue and sad when November came. The leaves are off the trees, the year's winding down to a close. I used to think she was nuts cuz I loved the months of November and December. They're the holiday months—Thanksgiving and Christmas and days off from school and presents and big family get-togethers with food and lots of desserts! But now I understand her a little more. The year's disappearing and another year of life is gone. People you love aren't around like they used to be. I'm glad she died years ago so she didn't have to live through all this. If we think of where we were last year, we've lost so much.

We're talking about having a Thanksgiving Day feast—keeping up the tradition and sometimes I wonder what there is to be thankful for. I guess I'm thankful that we're still alive, but am I really? It has to be easier to be dead and not worry about having to survive. Some days it's just so hard.

Jason feels the same way and we talk about how discouraging it all is. We've been talking more since our major conversation back in the summer. We meet occasionally at the club house in the evenings. He usually does most of the talking and sticks to the same theme--we're all a bunch of chumps for staying here and not to go looking for something, anything out there. One of these days, he's going to look for other people, he doesn't care what anyone thinks. I understand what he's saying, but I totally don't agree. We should stay here. But we both agree how hard this all is. And how we wish things were back to normal. But they won't be.

We all seem to be down lately and find different ways of coping. We were all doing so well at Halloween and now, in just a couple of weeks, we've gone from happy to miserable. I think a lot of this has to do with Tricia getting hurt. Seeing her wearing that cast makes us feel more vulnerable and we're reminded <u>again</u> how fragile life is—that we've lost so much and could lose more. We've had so much good luck since we found each other and had such a good summer and early fall that I think we forgot how tough life can really be. Not tough as in working hard in the hot summer garden or dragging buckets of water from one place to another or doing household chores without proper electricity. But truly tough as in people being sick or hurt or dying. So we young people are having a hard time coping. I think the parents are doing okay. They have all their years of life to fall back on and aren't as easily freaked out. At least I think so—not that they've said anything. And they probably wouldn't say anything to us anyway. So for all I know they're just as down as us kids are.

Jason copes by wandering off a lot and sometimes staying gone overnight and doing who knows what. Mitchell whines about not having tv and video games when he's down—says he's tired of exploring and he'll sit and play solitaire with a deck of cards for hours. Like me, Ashleigh writes in her journal, rides, and takes walks. Caleb trains his dogs. We're bored with each other as well as tired of this life. Maybe next year this will all seem normal, but right now it isn't. It's still just hard.

Trish's been following me around a lot lately—if she isn't

at the barn with the animals. She's really interested in medicine and said she wants to be a vet. She might be a good one. She's been reading some of my medical books and is starting a little clinic at the barn so she has supplies in case she needs them. It's kind of cute really. She will get her cast off next week and she's excited about that! I'll be there to help as the resident "doctor-in-training." Like it takes anything to remove a velcro cast. I find myself smiling when I think of her so maybe there's hope for me not being depressed for the rest of my life.

She still likes to spend time in the stores going "shopping" when she's down—says she can't stand the thought of dressing like a rag bag. You know, to be honest, seeing her dress up nice, makes me dress nicer than I would've done, and dressing better makes me feel better—most days. And I've been known to go shopping with her. Ashleigh went with us one day—which was fun. I'm glad we three girls are getting along better now. I'm not as lonely as I used to be.

You know Mom, just talking to you always makes me feel better and thinking of how we're all getting along and toughing things out is a good feeling. The group will be meeting in a few days to talk about Thanksgiving and I'm feeling more like participating now than I was. I suspect that Mitchell will want turkey and he and Caleb are talking about shooting a wild turkey. We'll see how that idea flies (ha ha). I guess we'll have to start thinking about Christmas presents. Especially for Mitchell.

Well, I've got to go. It's about supper time. You know what? I still really don't like making meals. But I'm glad that Dad, Mitchell, and I share the duty or I'd just hand them a jar of peanut butter and a box of crackers. :)

Love from your favorite daughter
Meg

Nov 17 Meeting Minutes

Present:
Donald, Janet, Jason, Caleb and Tricia Kinsey
Jackson, Caroline, and Ashleigh Grace; Adam and Ava Parker-Grace
Sam, Meg, and Mitchell Shultz

Committees gave reports and current recommendations:

Shelter and Warmth: There is enough propane and gas heaters for everyone to use in their homes. Everyone should conserve energy to last through the winter. Fireplaces will be used as a last resort.

Power: Sam reported all available car batteries should be stored in a central location to make sure the batteries are not corroding or going to waste. We can use adapters to power small appliances if necessary.

Food and Water: Caroline discussed provisions for the upcoming Thanksgiving celebration. Some discussion was held about having a Thanksgiving dinner or not. A vote was taken and it was agreed that Thanksgiving will continue to be a tradition. The meal will be potluck:
Vegetables: Potatoes and canned green beans from the garden
Meat: Chickens from the farm, possibly wild turkey
Dressing: Boxed stuffing from store
Dessert: Pumpkin pie and cookies
Janet also reported the school children will be presenting a Thanksgiving play.

Safety/Security/Health: We continue to clean-up and repair houses and buildings we use (1-block radius, farm, storage areas, etc).

Survival lesson at this meeting was how to build a campfire.

Those going out of the living area should carry a lighter or matches in case fire is needed.

Minutes recorded by Ashleigh Grace.

November 19

Dear Mandy,

OMG!!!! Can you believe it??!!! There are others out there! We are NOT alone! It's amazing! Praise God for His many surprises and miracles! I feel so happy! Don't get me wrong. They're kinda old and definitely snarky about a lot of things....well not Noni, but Kenneth is totally t-ed off about having to be a part of a group. BUT if there's two people that've survived this long on their own, there HAS to be more people out there! Maybe even more families! I know Meg's desperately missing her mom and maybe this gives her hope!

Let me tell you about Mrs. Rebecca Oswald and Mr. Kenneth Sudley!! Rebecca said we could call her Noni. She said that her mother used to call her that as a little girl. In one of the African languages it means 'gift of God.' I like that. Even Meg didn't roll her eyes like she usually does when the big G is mentioned.

So the Scouts were out hunting. They were following a deer and went way further than they'd ever been before. All of a sudden Mitchell said something about smelling smoke...then he started talking with Caleb about cookouts and hot dogs. But Jason said to shut it b/c he also smelled smoke. So they kept walking and saw a stream of smoke over the trees. And Bam! There's this house with smoke coming outta the chimney!! Caleb said they couldn't believe it! They just stood there, totally shocked. Mitchell asked if it was on fire somehow from lightning. And Jason made some snotty response about how the smoke was only coming out of the chimney, so it HAD to be people. Caleb said he wanted to investigate more so started to walk behind the house so he could peek in the windows and Mitchell followed. But when he turned around, Jason had run up to the front door and started knocking and yelling "Hello! Is anyone in there? We're from town. We're survivors too! Hello??" Then they heard a man shout, "Get away from my door you hoodlum! You leave us alone!

If you try to come in here I'll shoot! I have a shotgun aimed right at your head!" Caleb started running, dragging Mitchell behind him, and yelling for Jason to follow them. They didn't stop running until they got back to town. "The Oswalds!," Jason gasped, "That's their name, it's on the mailbox." A couple of us were at the clubhouse and we all heard them shouting that they'd found someone!

What was amazing to me was that I KNEW her...not just the name, but Noni was the town librarian and used to work with Mom on a bunch of fundraisers! And I knew where she lived outside of town! Mom and I had gone to her house once to pick up cookies for the church bake sale. I used to talk to her all the time when I was at the library. So I ran to Mom and told her what happened and asked her please, please, please go talk to the Oswalds. She KNOWS us, I said, they're probably just scared! I mean who wouldn't be?? You think everybody in the world's dead, then all of a sudden some loud mouthed punk comes banging on your door and yelling for you to come out. We're lucky Mr. Sudley DIDN'T shoot him!!! (He is actually Noni's COUSIN, not her husband...but I'll explain that later). So Mom ran off to find the other parents and explained the situation and pretty soon, Dad, Mom, and I are marching off towards the Oswald's house with provisions...food, some batteries, water...Mom always says you should never show up empty-handed.

We talked on the way about who should knock. Mom said it should be her since she knows Noni. Dad argued a bit... he was worried about her getting shot! But eventually he said okay. She's pretty good at convincing Dad about things sometimes...it's like a magical power. I mean, look at how she convinced him to let everyone move into our neighborhood. ANYWAY...so when we got there, Dad and I stayed at the gate of the white picket fence. Mom said we shouldn't swamp the porch with too many people, especially after Jason freaked them out. Jason, what an idiot! Who goes running up to strangers and bangs on the door! Doesn't he remember how scared we all were when we thought we were alone???

So Mom goes up and knocks gently on the door and says "Mrs. Oswald? It's Caroline Grace. I'm here to help." We hear a man yelling about getting off the porch, but then Noni calls out, "Caroline? Is that you? You're alive! Oh Kenneth, put that thing down! The Graces were a nice family!" And then Noni was opening up the door and hugging Mom and they were crying and talking about how amazing it was that they weren't alone. Mr. Sudley, Kenneth, ...was standing there a little awkwardly holding his shotgun. But then Dad walked up and shook his hand and told him how happy we were to see them. Dad said I had to stay back at the gate, but I couldn't wait. Noni saw me and walked down the steps to hug me too. I started crying and didn't even care. It's such a miracle!!

We stayed and talked for almost an hour. Noni invited us inside and we talked about the community we had. They were pretty shocked there were even more of us (and that we knew the loud-mouth who scared them to death...well not to death). We told them all about our community rules and how everyone's been assigned jobs and the farm and everything! They told us Mr. Oswald died from KPox and that Kenneth came to live with Noni as they were the only people in their family who survived— at least that they know about. Turns out Kenneth even knew Mr. Flint (the guy who owned the farm) and said he'd always said good things about Dad. That helped, I think. Even though they seemed happy that we were there, Kenneth still seemed pretty wary of being in the community with all the others. I'm sure he was wondering about a community that let hoodlums like Jason in. His expression was downright pained when Noni started talking about how they lived this long alone...their garden, canning vegetables...it's like she was giving away national secrets. What really got him was when she started talking about their storm shelter! Apparently they had a bunch of food and supplies stockpiled. Noni said Kenneth used to be military so he'd prepared for the worst. Kenneth cut her off when she started to get up and offered to show it to us. "That's enough Noni!" I thought the veins were going to pop out of his head! I think she didn't realize how upset he was until she looked over at him. Aaawkward!!!

Finally Dad cleared his throat and said we were just happy that they were alive and he knew we'd all been through so much, but we'd be open to having them join our community so we could work together. BUT we'd also respect their decision for independence if they chose. I know I looked at him like he was crazy when he said that. Who'd want to be alone??? Kenneth seemed to calm down though when Dad said that. Noni just looked worried. Dad asked if we could all pray together and Noni started to cry again and said that would be wonderful. Dad thanked God for letting us find Noni and Kenneth and thanked him for our many blessings, but he also asked God for knowledge and courage for us and for our new friends to decide what to do now that we've found each other. It was a nice prayer. I think Noni appreciated it...even Kenneth didn't look as grouchy after we said Amen.

We left then. Told them we'd be back tomorrow. I can't imagine them not wanting to be part of our community though. It's crazy if they want to stay out in the boonies on their own! I felt like I was dying of boredom and loneliness before we found the other families! I'm really glad we found Noni and Kenneth. I'm so glad Mom listened to me about talking to them. After all, I am an 'adult' now right?

Whew! I'm exhausted after all these new things. Who knew, right? Just thought it was going to be the same ol' same ol', but life still has surprises. See ya.

Cool breeze, but hopeful,
Ashleigh

November 20

Dear Mom,

A lot has happened since I last wrote! We have new people in the settlement and Jason left! I'll start at the beginning. First the new people.

Yesterday the Scouts were out hunting/goofing off and saw smoke coming from a house they hadn't noticed before. Jason went up to the door and banged on it and Mr. Sudley said get away or he'd shoot Jason's head off!. Why Jason had to go and get all loud and bang on their door, who knows. What a jerk! Long story short, Caroline knows Mrs. Oswald from the library and is all excited about us being here. Mr. Sudley doesn't seem too happy about it right now though. He's always grumbling when I see him, but it's only been a day so he may just be getting used to us. But Mrs. Oswald loves having other people around. At first she was upset about all the library books being gone, but when she heard we had them stored at our homes and where we work, she was pleased the books were being used. She said she could help me find more on first aid and emergency stuff. She's a nice lady. She said she'd help teach reading at school and work with little Adam and Ava. Mr. Sudley is still standoffish, but I understand not warming up immediately. I don't think I would.

Then Jason—still totally hyped about finding new people—decided he'd go off and find more people—against the wishes of the rest of us. Of course it was a total fiasco—him yelling at everyone and burning rubber as he tore out of town in his pickup. So who knows how long he'll be gone or how far he'll go. Then Donald had the horrible job of telling Janet that her stupid son just left and didn't bother saying goodbye to her.

Just as she is starting to feel better and not be depressed. What a mess. He makes a mess wherever he goes. Idiot!

And Ashleigh's angry, and I totally get it—even though she wants to hate him, you can't turn off your feelings overnight.

We're still going to have Thanksgiving Day. When we first talked about it a couple of weeks ago Jason thought it was stupid to give thanks for having our world come crashing down around us. Caleb agreed with him, but I think that was just because he wants Jason to respect him. But Janet said that the first Thanksgiving was started to give thanks for the good things they <u>did</u> have, for the fact that they'd <u>survived.</u> It wasn't held to give thanks for their cool stuff and wonderful lives. So after a vote we decided to have Thanksgiving Day whether some people wanted it or not. And Jason isn't here now, so who cares what he thinks.

You used to tell me to not worry so much, that most things don't turn out as bad as you think they will. I'm going to keep telling myself that. Over and over again.

Your favorite daughter
Meg

Nov 20

Dear Mandy,

     Sometimes I just don't understand Jason and why he acts SO crazy! I thought he'd be happy we found other people, but this morning he and his dad were having a HUGE argument in front of their houses. AWKWARD...we could hear everything they were saying! Jason was totally yelling at his dad about going to find others. It's like nothing is ever good enough! Donald said NO. Jason said YES and he didn't care what everyone else thought..."We should go look for MORE people RIGHT NOW! Come ON!!" He was getting crazy animated too. Donald and Dad were trying to calm him down saying 'No Jason, we have to think this through. We have to think of the safety of everyone. We have to wait.' But the more they talked, the louder he got. It was intense! We all just watched Jason. It was like he was possessed. His face got all red, he was clenching his fists, and he had this crazy angry look in his eyes...He was totally freaking out. He said, "I hate all of you in this backwater dump! I can't stand being here anymore. I'm gonna leave! We need to find other survivors and get out of this hellhole! NO ONE can make me stay here! I hate this stupid world and everyone in it!"

     I thought he was going to push Donald b/c he was all up in his face...I think Dad did too because he was telling everyone to back off and give them some privacy. But I could see Dad's face...that narrowed-eyed look he gets when something isn't right. And he was all tense and he kept shooting looks at Sam too...like they were going to have to break up a fist fight. It was scary. But then Jason turned, stalked to his truck, jumped in, slammed the door, and revved the engine, yelling "I don't care what you say! I'm outta here you LOSERS!" He peeled out and left us choking on the smoke. Caleb started to run after him, "Jason! Come on..." But Donald said, "Let him go Son! Let him go. He'll be back! He's just angry. He'll be back." We all stood there frozen.

I couldn't believe it! I just burst into tears and ran to your cross. I had to be with you. All the hateful nasty things he said! Mandy, he said he hated EVERYONE in this small stupid town. I guess that means me too??? I know he'll be back tomorrow and probably be sorry for what he did and said...but Mandy, I seriously felt my heart shrink up into a little tiny ball and it just...hurts so bad. I thought he didn't hate ME?! I thought I was special! But he said EVERYONE...and that means me too. I hope the stupid jerk runs out of gas and it rains on him and he gets HUGE blisters on his feet walking back. My heart is broken.

Cloudy, rainy, and cold—just like my heart,
Ashleigh

Nov 24 Meeting Minutes

Present:
Donald, Janet, Caleb and Tricia Kinsey
Jackson, Caroline, and Ashleigh Grace; Adam and
  Ava Parker-Grace.
Sam, Meg, and Mitchell Shultz
Kenneth Sudley and Rebecca Oswald

Absent:
Jason Kinsey

We welcomed two new members to our community. Mrs. Oswald and Mr. Sudley were discovered and invited to join us. Jason left the community and we will wait for his return.

A brief meeting was held for committee reports.

Shelter and Warmth: Clean-up of neighboring houses has been completed.

Power: All batteries (including cars) from houses explored by the Scouts have been stored. Also, gasoline and other fuels have been stored in several locations. Gasoline is still available from siphoning from cars around town.

Safety/Security/Health: Weapons training continues. Competitions will start soon. Discussion was held surrounding future new survivors and the best way to welcome them to the community, especially if Jason finds new people. We decided we would hold to our previous decision that if new people are found someone needs to meet with them and then they can be invited to our community with group approval. It was decided that if they didn't meet with group approval, we'd have to figure out what to do on a case-by-case basis. It was acknowledged this would be a difficult situation in all cases.

Food and Water: Supplies are in good order and being used conservatively. New food items will emerge with planting in the spring and from animals at the farm.

Other: Since Jason is no longer available to fulfill his job duties, his chores will be redistributed to others. Mr. Sudley said he'd take on some of Jason's chores. Mrs. Oswald said that she would take over care of the library, including pest control and taking care of the books so they are preserved for future generations. She will also help in the school.

Final plans were made for the Thanksgiving dinner.

Meeting was adjourned.

Minutes recorded by Ashleigh Grace

November 26

Dear Mom,

Well, we had Thanksgiving with our new neighbors and without Jason. We all thought he'd come back, but apparently we're not cool enough for him. Poor Donald and Janet. They're so upset, but tried to hide it from Caleb and Tricia and the rest of us. Not that it worked—we could see they're upset. But we tried to pretend that everything was fine. They've had a tough autumn—Tricia breaking her arm and still in her cast and now Jason leaving. How sad for them.

It was nice having new people in the group! It kept our minds off Jason—sort of. We had really good food too. Caleb and Mitchell killed a wild turkey, as they promised! But we also had a couple of chickens from the farm. (Tricia would absolutely not be there for the execution—her words, and said she wouldn't eat any chicken. And she didn't.) We had potatoes and gravy and packaged stuffing and canned beans and corn. We even had pumpkin and apple pie and bread that Janet baked. Soooo yummy!

Before the dinner Janet and her students put on a play—including little Adam. He is sooo cute. The play was all about a turkey (Mitchell) trying to escape the townspeople so he wouldn't be dinner and everyone ordered pizza at the end. Very cute!

And then we all sat around the clubhouse and ate and talked and ate some more. We were all so stuffed and we talked about the "good old days" and what we'd like to see in the future and about whatever was on our minds. The guys and Ashleigh played touch football in the afternoon. Ashleigh told me it wasn't the same without Jason though. Poor thing. She can't decide if she's totally ticked off at him or heartbroken. She's probably both.

I know I'd be.

In the evening we were all still at the clubhouse and someone suggested a Monopoly tournament so some people played Monopoly. I didn't. I'm not very good at it cuz I don't like to see people lose all their property. But we also played poker (with chips, not real money) and I played that cuz I don't mind winning when no one has anything to really lose. I don't know why losing chips in a poker game isn't the same as losing at Monopoly—maybe cuz in poker you have to make your mind up quickly, cover your emotions, and it's all over very quickly. Then you go on and play another game. In Monopoly you have to plan to bring people down over a long period of time and watch as they (or you) slowly lose all your possessions. Short and sweet is the way I'd rather go. And I'm pretty good at poker. Dad beat me, but I came in second.

The clubhouse was warm with the heat from our heaters and lit with glowing gas lamps. The room smelled like turkey and the spices from the stuffing and pies. It was such a good feeling for us to have a restful, peaceful, fun day. Children laughing and the two littlest ones running around looking for attention. We have heat and supplies to last through the winter (and for years to come). We have friends. And that night, at least, we felt secure—at least as things stand. Jason being gone takes some of the peace out of our hearts, but we assume he'll be back soon and things will go on as usual. None of us knows what the future will bring, but otherwise the night was so pleasant and peaceful and happy.

We've had such a rough year and having this evening was so needed. Even Mr. Sudley smiled and said he thought the food was very good. Caroline said she thought we should have another

Thanksgiving feast on the day we met for the first time. Anyway, we talked about it and decided we would. So on April 26 next year, we'll have a Founding Day and celebrate one year in our new settlement. Goodness, was our first meeting only seven months ago?! It seems longer than that. I guess cuz we've been living this weird new life since early spring it feels like we've been at this for ages. It's odd to think that Adam and Ava won't ever remember what life used to be like. Even Mitchell will have more memories of this new world than the old one. But that's a good thing. No use dwelling on what we don't have anymore.

Christmas is coming up and the adults are all smiling and telling us that Santa will be coming. Like any of us believes in Santa! Well, Adam and Ava. But not the rest of us. But I can't help but be excited along with Mitchell. I wonder what Dad has planned. I have to think of presents to get for Dad and Mitchell. The grownups decided we should all draw names for the young people gift exchange. (I'm a "young" person still. For Christmas purposes I don't mind!) So I got Jason's name. Geesh! What do you get for a egocentric, grouchy, depressed (and absent) person? It'll take me the whole month to figure that out! Assuming he shows back up! I might luck out and he won't show up until after Christmas and I won't have to get him anything. No...I don't really wish that. I know his mom would miss him terribly.

I'm learning to crochet and am making you a shawl. If you aren't here by Christmas, I'll hold it for you until you get here.

Love, love, love,

Your favorite daughter
Meg

PS: Trish got her cast off yesterday and she is definitely very thankful!! She wanted me to remove the cast without her parents being there, but that wasn't going to happen! She told me that she'd been taking the cast off a lot when no one was around so she didn't think it would be a big deal. But we did it the right way and her parents did the honors. Her arm looked all skinny and white. Guess it'll take awhile before it gets back to normal.

November 26

Dear Mandy,

So today was Thanksgiving. It felt a little off without Jason there...like someone had died or something...you know? Just like...there was an empty space...but whatever! It was his choice to abandon everyone! Caleb told me his mom and dad took a car and went out looking a few times for him, but they can't figure out which way he went or where he's holed up and they didn't want to just drive around and waste precious gas. So they are just crossing their fingers, praying he's not hurt, and praying he'll come to his senses! I still can't believe he'd ditch his family. I would NEVER leave mine. I know my parents get on my case and are really annoying sometimes...and don't always let me be who I am, but I'm not stupid. They love me and they're all I have left. WE are all we have left!! Jason's a moron if he can't see that. We're probably better off without him making so much trouble. I wonder if he's even thinking about his poor mother...Janet seemed fine at times, but then you could see her fighting back tears at other times...It made me mad. Mad for how he's hurt her, mad for treating his family this way...mad at myself for thinking I was in love with him. Mad that with all we've been through, he's still one of those people who's selfish and only looking out for himself. I mean...we've lost SO MANY people, you'd think people would learn to stick together. Even when we've survived huge obstacles, Jason's still not satisfied. What a jerk!!!

But enough about egomaniac Jason! Today was a day to be grateful. Mitchell and Caleb actually found and killed a turkey! They said they'd seen some wandering around in the woods, but I never thought they'd kill one! It was really good! Everyone brought yummy food! Even Noni brought apple crisp! De-lish!

Kenneth and Noni were living in Noni's house outside of town and Dad was picking them up in the morning because Kenneth started helping out at the farm and Noni comes in to help with the library, school, and childcare. But a couple days ago, Noni decided that it was too much trouble to keep walking in town or getting picked up, so she convinced Kenneth to move in town. They're staying at the clubhouse til they pick which house they want. Good thing we cleaned up the houses around us! And Noni likes to be around the little kids too. She said something about seeing the future reminds her that not all has been lost. It's a nice thought.

We played some games together and just got to chill. We even played some flag football. Of course I kept thinking about when we ALL played back in September and it made me sad...stupid brain.

Oh! I forgot to mention how cute the Thanksgiving play was! It was about a turkey that was trying to escape from being the main course. It was hysterical...Mitchell was the turkey and he was running away from Caleb. We were all the hungry townspeople. Mitchell even pretended to have an anxiety attack while the town doctor (Meg of course) gave him all these breathing tricks to calm down. Then Caleb came running in and he had to run off again. Tricia saves him at the end with adoption into a traveling circus that had a turkey acrobats. Adam got to play one of the clown acrobats with Ava. Tricia helped Adam with his lines and it was amazing to hear him talk in front of everyone. Since they've been with us, they have totally grown up. But today he was so proud! Puffed out his little chest and said "I am the lead acrobat (he really said at-robot...lol) and I must have this turkey for the show!" Then Tricia said to Caleb "I will pay you twice the fee" and that worked out because then all the townspeople could order pizza from the hot pizza girl—me :), which is what they really wanted anyway. It was awesome. We got a standing ovation! :-) All the parents were proud and everyone had a good time.

I kinda felt like a Pilgrim today. I totally understand why they were so thankful after they went through death and starvation...having to start over building a brand new community.

It must've really been a struggle to leave <u>everything</u> they knew behind. I can't even imagine how strong their faith must have been to face what they did. I wish my faith was like that. Some days I feel strong that God is with me and with us, but other days I'm just so confused. I don't know...But I do know that today was a good day to give thanks and be grateful for all the blessings we DO have.

No clouds in sight and truly thankful,
Ashleigh

Nov 28

Dear Mandy,

You'll never believe what happened today. I had this HUGE discussion with Meg and I've actually started thinking of her as a close friend...almost like somebody I could FOR REAL open up to. Mandy, I know you'd have liked her too. We were walking back from the farm. I was helping Dad and she'd gone out there to ask something about gathering seeds for something to plant in the spring or whatever. But Dad had to run back to get a part to fix a stall door so the truck was gone and we were done with our chores, so I said I'd walk with her.

We started talking about Tricia and riding the horses. We both said it's amazing how much she's grown up in the past year. Meg said she's gotta give it to Tricia. Even with everything that's happened she seems like she's comfortable with who she is and looks pretty good most of the time. I agreed and then we started talking...I mean *really* talking. I told her I envied that confidence a little...I mean even though there are no cliques anymore or anyone to tell you what you're supposed to wear or what you're supposed to do...I still feel so ugly and stupid sometimes. Shouldn't I just feel lucky to be alive no matter what I look like? Not like any of the celebrities made it through the disease...oh who am I kidding! They probably did...a whole group of them survived and now they live all together in one of their beautiful mansions in a utopia of perfect-ness. They probably still have maids and people who get food for them while they work out all day to keep their perfect figures and fabulous hair. All the while not knowing there's a whole other group of us people out here who have dirt under our nails most of the time and smell! Meg laughed when I said that. But you know what? She said she's just as confused about how she looks, who she is, and or wants to be as I am sometimes.

We decided that it doesn't seem like the guys ever feel unsure! How annoying! I mean look at Dad! He's been posting his 'sticky-note reminders' at the clubhouse...embarrassing! I would feel totally awkward, but he doesn't...and Jason and his moodiness...don't get me started. Then Meg said that her mom told her no matter what, we have to think for ourselves b/c boys don't always have the same feelings we do. Obviously! If Jason would've cared about any of us he'd be here right now and not off throwing a temper tantrum somewhere. And Meg's totally mad at Jason for leaving too. Anyway, by that point we were back in town and we had to go, so it was fine. I had a pretty good time today.

Crisp wind, but content,
Ashleigh

WATER AND RESOURCES
ARE LIKE DIAMONDS =
PRECIOUS AND RARE.

PROTECT THEM
          - DAD

November 30

Dear Mom,

It's been a little over a week since Jason left and he isn't back yet. I'm so nervous about him bringing someone back with him, but it doesn't seem anyone else is as worried as I am. I guess his family doesn't care who he brings back as long as he returns. And maybe the others are concerned but don't want to dwell on what we can't know or change. But that doesn't stop me from worrying. I talked to Dad about it and he said he's concerned too, but we couldn't really do anything until we know the situation. But we decided to re-hide our medicines and extra guns and ammo—just in case—and not tell anyone. No one was supposed to know about our hiding places, but we'd gotten kinda lax about it and everyone knew where everything was. It was a community decision ages ago that only a few people know where the real stashes are. No one saw us move anything. And I'm not writing down where anything is in case someone reads these letters. But if someone reads this they'd know we actually have meds hidden, so I'm gonna hide my letters to you too.

What a stinky way to live. All secretive and scared again now. I really <u>hate</u> Jason and what he's done to us! Life has been so difficult for so long and just as we're getting used to this whole new world, he decides that he can't live without more people?! And he had to do it <u>his</u> way—even though we'd all <u>voted</u> that searching for more people wasn't the right thing to do at this time. What a total jerk!!! <u>I hate him!!!</u> <u>I hate being scared!</u> I hate thinking someone might come and destroy our new life. I liked our new life. And it could all be gone. Forever. Maybe he'll come back and not have found anyone. I hope so. If I believed in God, I'd be praying big time for Jason to come back—lost, lonely, and ashamed of himself. But knowing him, he'll just keep looking until he finds someone. Maybe...well, I'll just stop with all the maybe's cuz we just don't know what will happen, and I think that's the worst part. The not knowing.

We're all chipping in and helping with Jason's chores. Donald and Janet are working extra hard to make up for his not being here. So is Caleb. It's like they're embarrassed that he left us with extra work. But it isn't their fault. Jason's always been the difficult one—even before K-pox. All the trouble he was in at school and being drunk and stuff. Enough of Jason. I'm tired of thinking and talking and writing about Jason.

But there isn't really anything to write about or think about. So I guess I'll write again when there's more news or we've moved on to other troubles or issues.

Your favorite daughter

Meg

PS: Mitchell's doing fine. He isn't that upset about Jason being gone and we're not mentioning our fears of strangers too much to him and Tricia—playing it down so they don't worry too much. He's generally happy and healthy and 13—OMG a teenager! You'd be proud of him. Well, his hair needs cutting, so he looks kinda shaggy. But other than that, you'd be happy with how he's growing up.   :)

Dec 5

Mandy!

OMG...OMG....OMG. I don't know what else to say! Jason found people!!!! AGAIN! Men people! Two grown men who no one knows anything about...AND he brought them back and just drove them right through our community like he never heard the procedure for new people!!!! Someone has to meet them first, then they need to be invited in by the community...just like a membership to a club, dude! But no, not Jason. Mr. I'm-too-good-for-rules-and-I-don't-give-a-damn-about-others-safety Kinsey. He just led them right into our neighborhood with Luke and Clarence following in their truck and yelled, "Welcome to Paradise!" as they got out of their trucks. What a schmuck! And he had this SERIOUS smug look on his face the whole time he was pointing out all the houses and introducing everyone. I wanted to smack him! I'm sure most of us did...we were all in shock. One good thing was that both trucks were full of food and supplies. Of course a lot of it was junk food, but there were dried beans and some more canned goods too. Meg was excited about the chips hahaha. They also brought back this newspaper article...but let me get to that in a minute...

We had an emergency meeting to discuss letting them in....but really what was the point of talking about that since Jason had already basically given them keys to the city and showed them where everything was! I didn't put any notes on what people said, but let me just tell you that Kenneth and Dad were NOT happy. I knew Dad would be upset because he's totally suspicious of people AND he doesn't like rule breakers! Jason's sooo NOT his favorite person... But Kenneth even said things like 'we can't just let any hoodlum come into our town...How do we know they're honest and won't just kill us in our beds??!!" It was so sweet!!! He really does like us!

It's just such a hard situation. We have to stick together because we're survivors you know...but it'd be crazy to believe that ALL survivors are nice people like us...let's face it, some things just don't make sense. Lots of good people got the sickness...bad ones too so we don't know.

Oh! I wanted to tell you about the newspaper article. Luke and Clarence found it in one of the towns they passed through. It was the Boston Times and all about K-Pox. How it started, how it spread, and all the gross stuff that happened when people died. Honestly, it was hard to read b/c it was like we were living through it all over again. The horrible memories of watching people we love die...Mandy, I still have nightmares about that night I last saw you... But the annihilation too! We had heard some reports on the radio before we lost the signal, but it said almost 90% of the WORLD's population had been wiped out. 90%!!! That's horrifying! But it also means 10% survived! It said most of them were in families sharing the same blood. I saw Meg looking at me and I knew exactly what she was thinking... it means her mom's alive!

The craziest thing about this whole deal though is that there ARE more people out there! There could be whole communities like us. Wow...

Frosty morning and Shocked,
Ashleigh

Dec 5

Dear Mom,

Jason is an _idiot_! _A total idiot_! He brought two guys who we don't know to our town. Brought them right in without asking permission. Didn't ask. Didn't check with us. Just brought them in.

So we now have Clarence and Luke living here. For all we know they are axe murderers. He told them all about our food storage and apparently even mentioned that we have guns and ammo put aside. One of them asked (I don't remember which one) about them getting to have some of our guns and ammo, and Dad told them that they seemed to have enough guns with them already and didn't need anymore. So it was dropped. But Dad is right. They both came in with pistols in holsters (like they're cowboys or something) and rifles slung over their shoulders and more stashed in their belongings and the truck. Like they needed more guns!

Jason looked so proud of himself, bringing those idiots back with him. He was talking about all the good things that would happen cuz we had more man power. We can do this and we can do that. And Luke is in construction and he can build stuff. Yeah right! For all we know he can't build anything.

I find it so weird that I was just telling you how much I like our new life and getting comfortable. Now I feel like I did back when we were hiding and being afraid to come out to even get food and water. We work our way up to this peaceful life without being scared all the time...and now we're all scared again. Well, _I'm_ scared again. I think the dads are just angry. They're barely being polite to Jason and Jason's being rude and defensive.

<u>*What an idiot!!!!!!*</u>

Your favorite and scared daughter
Meg

December 5 Emergency Meeting Minutes

Present:
   Donald, Janet, Caleb and Tricia Kinsey
   Jackson, Caroline, and Ashleigh Grace; Adam and
      Ava Parker-Grace
   Sam, Meg, and Mitchell Shultz
   Rebecca Oswald and Kenneth Sudley
   Jason Kinsey

Potential new members (not present at meeting):
   Luke Boden
   Clarence Dyer

Emergency meeting convened due to Jason's return with two outsiders.

Safety: Discussion centered solely on the two men who Jason brought back. Their names are Luke Boden and Clarence Dyer. Jason said they met in Harding, a town about 80 miles southwest of here. Luke and Clarence said they'd been moving from town to town in the previous months, searching for other survivors and living on the supplies they found. They'd done a search of most of the houses in Harding and had found no survivors. They'd come out of their house when they heard Jason's truck driving through town. Jason stayed with them for almost a week before returning.

   Luke reported before K-Pox, he was an independent contractor doing all kinds of odd jobs. Clarence worked at a factory. Clarence had parents and a sister in North Carolina and was thinking about going there to see if they're still alive. Luke said his parents had died and he didn't have any siblings.
   Many issues were raised about letting these outsiders join our community. Since the details of those discussions were personal opinions, they are not recorded. However, the ultimate decision was to let them stay. They will be given the house next to Jason's.

Rebecca and Kenneth will also be moving into town this week and have a house next to the Shultz's.

Minutes recorded by Ashleigh Grace.

Dec 6

Dear Mandy,

Okay...so day 2 of new people. Luke and Clarence went out to the farm with Dad today. We're teaching them the ropes. They agreed to do chores and take turns with the animals so Dad's going to show them what to do. He'll stay with them the first few times to make sure they know what they're doing.

They're both in their 20s...Luke is 22 and Clarence is older...like 25. Luke is kinda cute too! He's got a dimple and he smiles a lot. It's kinda nice. Clarence is NOT cute...he's scruffy looking...well, they both are, but Luke looks so much better now that he's shaved and everything. Clarence has long, gross, stringy hair. The guys here are pretty clean-cut, I mean Mom cuts almost everyone's hair. We may be some of the last people on earth, but we aren't cavemen (and women!) you know?? Tricia would go berserk!

It's still hard to figure the newbies out. Luke seems really nice...he asks a lot of questions. Where is the food supply, who takes care of hunting, how do families talk to each other...stuff like that. Mitchell eats it up because it's like an older guy's really paying attention to what he's saying, but I can see Caleb staring at Luke...like he's not sure if he can trust him. Then Luke and Clarence came into Sav-More the other day to drop off the supplies they brought. They asked a lot of questions about how things were stored and what kind of supplies do we have and do they have to 'check things out' like at the library or do they just take stuff if they need it...it seems weird that new people are getting in on our stuff. There's a part of me that doesn't want to share, but I know that isn't right. So I have to get over it. And besides...Luke is cute and all and it WAS a little exciting that he was paying so much attention to what I had to say. It's probably just the weirdness of having new people.

And you know, I was thinking about Jason and I realized

that I really didn't miss him much when he was gone...It was a relief to know that. And now he's back...I have no desire to have anything to do with him. Especially since he brought these other people back without even asking! He only cares about himself. He doesn't give back to the community, to me, to his family...he just takes and takes and takes. I see my parents taking care of each other and giving back and forth. That's how it's supposed to be. You know Mom and Dad might be a pain about rules, but they really work hard and try to make our family and the community better.

With Jason, I'm not really sure what I got back. I feel like I gave him a personal side of me and he never gave me anything from him...not feelings, not nice-ness, not even a second look when he decided to take off! He was just totally into how HE was feeling. I want to be wanted by someone...to belong to someone and have them belong to me. But he was totally careless...I don't think he ever really wanted me. He knew I wanted him and he took advantage. I was too stupid to care...but I'll know next time. I'll know what real love is.

Sunny and strong,
Ashleigh

Dec 10

Dear Mom,

The idiots, I mean Jason and the new guys, are trying to fit in, and they're beginning to make some headway, but Ashleigh and I are still suspicious. Speaking of Ashleigh, she's really really mad at Jason and barely speaks to him. Totally different than she was a month ago. I feel sorry for her. I know how it is to really like someone and have him not even know you exist. When I was 16 I really thought Nick was so awesome and cute and wonderful! And I thought he liked me too, and it turned out that he just wanted to meet up with Madison. Remember Madison? Gosh we were best friends for years, and she was sooo pretty, and Nick wanted to go with her cuz of her looks. And so that got between us and I got mad at <u>her</u> and I should've been mad at <u>Nick</u>. What's worse is that we were never friends after that. What a shame, cuz Madison was ten times better than Nick. Girls sure do make fools of themselves for boys. Anyway, totally off subject.

Luke and Clarence are trying to be helpful so they might be okay. But I'm waiting to see how things go. Apparently Luke is fairly good at construction and Dad and him are talking about how to make a water mill for electric generation. Luke's been over several evenings to talk about the mill and other projects. Dad's opening up to him, but Dad would be friendly to anyone who liked building things. We're being careful when Luke and Clarence ask some questions, cuz we're still getting to know them. I look forward to getting past this stage and learning to trust new people. Of course, I'm sure that Jason answered <u>all</u> their questions before they even got here. And Dad and I are glad we moved our meds and munitions while Jason was gone. I guess the moral of that story is—plan for the worst as it <u>will</u> happen!

I'm trying to be open and not too unfriendly, but I'm having a hard time warming up to them. I guess Luke is okay. He tries hard to be charming and I have to admit that he <u>is</u> good looking. And a stupid part of me is thinking that he may be the only man (besides Jason who's an idiot) who's even close to my age—in case I want to get married someday. But now since we know there's more people out there, I don't have to be stuck with Luke or Jason. But the whole situation's just awkward. Mitchell's happy with the new guys and he doesn't see anything wrong with them. He thinks I'm being mean to them. I think Caleb's still on the fence about them. I haven't said much about Clarence, cuz I don't like him. He's dirty and cusses too much, even around the kids. The dads don't cuss—well not too much. Even Jason tries not to—sometimes. I also don't like Clarence cuz he's snooping in all the unoccupied houses when he thinks we're not paying attention. We already checked the houses months ago and left most things as they were, in case people came back. And we told Luke and Clarence that. But I saw him come out of a house and his coat looked too big—like he was hiding things in his coat. Now seriously, what's he gonna do with a bunch of stolen stuff? There isn't anybody to sell it to...no eBay or Craig's List to sell it for a bunch of money. He can hide it, but then what? So anyway, I don't like him. I talked to Dad about it and he said we'll keep an eye on him, but since I wasn't sure, he didn't want to confront him yet. But to say a good thing about Luke, he seems to understand the rules and when Clarence does swear, he tells him to knock it off—"Hey! Kids and ladies present!" Clarence just makes a face and mumbles sorry.

Jason still thinks he's the best thing ever in finding new

people for our community.

What an idiot!

Your favorite daughter
Meg

Dec 15

Dear Mandy,

I'm sorry I haven't been over to visit you in a while, the weather's been dreary. At least I have a little sparkle in my day...I have been decorating for Ava's 4th birthday and now we are waiting for Mom to bring her back home from Noni's house. Mom took her to Noni's for a 'princess tea' (sooo sweet) and I stayed behind to decorate her room like a fairy castle. All she wants is to be a fairy...like Halloween! So Dad and I have been glitter painting giant flowers and Adam is helping him hang up twinkle lights. We found one of those canopies to hang over her bed and new bedspread, pillows, the WORKS! She's going to freak! We'll have cupcakes later too. Four sparkly candles for 4 cute years. It's really fun to have little siblings to love.

The wind has been vicious lately! I was sooooo cold this morning. I just felt...chilled in my bones, you know? Meg says to stock up on Vitamin C, Echinesha...however you spell that...and these other things that she's raided the stores for to keep us healthy. Are germs gone now that no one is carrying them? I mean...if none of us have colds...we can't spread it right? Or do germs just live 'out there' somewhere and float around waiting to strike...like a secret band of ninja germs! Look out! Here comes snot!!! Hahaha. We talked about fruit and health-boosting foods in school one day too...made me think of sailors who used to get scurvy because they didn't have any oranges. Scurrrrrvy. I still think that's a funny word. Maybe that's why pirates had wooden legs and eye patches...

I'm so random! Maybe I have scurvy!! Haha. I do feel like I'm still learning in school so that's good. Janet makes us write, which I love, so I'm not complaining. I actually wrote a short story the other day about a girl who falls in love with a dragon, but they can't be together b/c every time they profess their love for each other he gets all worked up and breaths fire! But then! An evil magician takes over their world and freezes

258

everything, including the girl. So the dragon saves her by breathing fire over and over to keep her and the world warm...the magician is defeated b/c he melts from all the heat, but tragically the dragon is dying. So the girl takes the magician's wand and turns herself into a dragon too so she can breathe 'the spark' back into her love's heart. And they live happily ever after! Pretty awesome right??? I thought so. Janet said it was very creative...need to jump around less...but hey, everyone liked it. Caleb even drew me a picture of the girl and dragon.

Speaking of breathing fire at people...Jason and I have started talking again. He tried to speak to me a few times right after he came back, but I ignored him. Does he think I'm just going to fall all over him again?? But then I was taking some boxes over to the clubhouse and he was hanging around and asked me if I needed help. I tried to walk by him, but he said "Come on Ashleigh, you can't stay mad at me forever!" Then I told HIM that the people I want to hang out with don't just leave their family and community behind! And they sure don't call them stupid losers! I don't hang out with people who hate me. Of course he apologized and said he was just mad and frustrated and he was sorry for that junk he said. He just needed to get away to figure things out, but then he found the guys and...of course he wanted to come back to be with his family...and other people. So that's why he came back. He just wanted to be home.

I kinda felt like that girl in my story...the ice melted a little. Not all the way! Because I still think he's a self-centered jack-ass...but it was nice he apologized...and he helped me carry the boxes. He also asked if I wanted to take a walk later, but...I may not feel like it! He'll have to work a little harder if he wants to be my friend again. Who's stronger now buddy? We'll. Just. See.

Blustery and Stubborn,
Ashleigh

259

Dec 18

Dear Mandy,

So I know I said I wasn't going to get all stupid over Jason again...and I'm NOT! But we've been hanging out again...a lot actually in the past few days. Taking walks or just going to hang out by the stream, like we did that first time we really talked. He did apologize and I'm pretty sure he meant it. And maybe time away changed him. He certainly seems more...something. And it doesn't seem bad...we're taking it slow, just talking! Not about anything big...just about old friends or other people we knew.

Jason brought up a couple of pranks he and his friends had pulled and started making fun of some kid. I told him I didn't really think that was funny. I mean, the kid's dead you know? and then he said something like "Oh stop being such a baby, it's just a joke." Then we sat there for a while and I was trying to figure out if I should leave. But then he said he was really sorry and did I forgive him. It was really cute. Trying to make me smile and saying "Come on, Ashleigh, you're not mad right? You know you can't stay mad at me." And flashing me his totally sexy grin. So I said it was okay and I wasn't mad.

I don't know if I really did think it was okay though...I just didn't want him to be mad at me or think I was a baby. You know he put his arm around me after that...and held my hand. My heart was beating so fast!!

And you know what else I've been thinking? I don't have to let him make all the moves here, right? Who cares what my parents say! They've been saying these things like... "Watch what you're doing Ashleigh, not everything can be taken back once you've given it" or... "Not all people are meant to be trusted with everything"... Or Dad the other day... "No one buys the cow if you can get the milk for free." We WERE at the barn, but he was looking right at me...good grief! Totally embarrassing!! I'm not going to have sex with Jason or anyone right now! Remember you and I vowed to remain virgins until we were married. We even made up our own words b/c the other purity pledges we found online were so lame! It was after we had that guest speaker in health class, which was totally embarrassing b/c of all those HUGE diagrams she had with her! AND Jennie Lorens was uber-pregnant at the time. I remember the speaker saying something about protection's not always 100%. AWKWARD! But seriously, what would I do with a baby??? Don't get me wrong, Adam and Ava are fine, but I do NOT want one of my own. HOWEVER...Fantasizing never got anyone pregnant....right?

Snow flurries and daydreaming,
Ashleigh

December 20 Meeting Minutes

Present:
Donald, Janet, Caleb and Tricia Kinsey
Jackson, Caroline, and Ashleigh Grace; Adam and
Ava Parker-Grace
Sam, Meg, and Mitchell Shultz
Jason Kinsey
Kenneth Sudley and Rebecca Oswald
Luke Boden and Clarence Dyer

Discussion was held to determine Christmas provisions and activities. Brief committee reports were given.

Shelter and Warmth: Plans have been reviewed for putting out fires (in the woods, fire pit where we burn trash, kitchen fires that could spread, etc). Extinguishers will need to be checked and each family will have a detailed evacuation plan and meeting spot at the creek.

Power: Extended hours for generators will be from 4 – 9 each evening. One night a week will be designated for a community event, which will reduce fuel usage in individual homes. Scouts will continue to make trips to outlying homes and farms to siphon gas from abandoned cars and trucks and look for more solar panels, wind power stuff, and other alternative power items.

Safety/Security/Health: Weapons training will increase during winter months, with all community members being required to pass certain skill and safety tests.

Food and Water: Winter months will be used for spring food planning: how food will be grown, stored, and maintained. The goal is to no longer rely on supplies left in the abandoned stores and to become a self-sustaining community.

Christmas: It was agreed that power will be available at the clubhouse from noon to 10 pm on Christmas day.

On Christmas Eve there will be cookies to decorate and a Christmas Pageant at the clubhouse. On Christmas Day, everyone will celebrate at their own homes and then meet for dinner and festivities at 4:00—if they want to.

Family traditions will be upheld and Santa Claus will still bring presents Christmas Eve. All community members will contribute to stocking gifts and presents for Adam and Ava. The community gift exchange will take place on Christmas Day. All adult members will participate. The exchange list is being kept by Janet and will be kept secret until Christmas day.

Other: Luke said that he and Clarence appreciated us letting them into our community and making them feel welcome. He said that they would do anything that was needed to help the community thrive. Luke was assigned to the Power committee and Clarence will be working at the farm and both will work in areas where needed.

Meeting was adjourned.

Minutes recorded by Ashleigh Grace

December 20

Dear Mom

We had a big meeting and decided we're going to have a community Christmas at the clubhouse. We'll have C'mas morning at home with family—then the clubhouse will be open from noon to 10pm with electricity all that time. Such luxury! We'll have wood for the fireplace and we've decorated. It looks really nice! And us "young adults" as the parents call us, will exchange gifts. Gee Mom. I don't want to get Jason anything—he can be such a grouch. But, to be honest, he's not as bad as he used to be since he came back. But he can still be such a serious DRAG! Oh—that's what I can get him—a Grumpy doll from Snow White! That'd be so funny—to me anyhow. I'll get him that, but something else as well. Only I've no idea what. At least money isn't an object. Ha! Ha! :-) Thing is—we've all had access to all stores so we have what we want anyway. So getting someone something they don't already have or want is hard. And time is running out!

I'm crocheting Dad an afghan for C'mas and am almost finished. I've been working on it when he's not around so it'll be a surprise. I finished your shawl. I'm telling you now, but if you come before C'mas, I'll just keep this letter back so you won't know. I'm still trying to decide what to get Mitchell, but I better think fast! I did think about getting him video games since we have electricity in the evenings now, and we can use the clubhouse on Saturday nights, but they must've all been looted from the stores cuz I couldn't find any new ones. I really don't want to search old houses. They're so lonely. And I'm afraid that I'll bump into old bones and maybe rotten flesh. Yuck! That's so disgusting. Or I might bump into Clarence. Double yuck!

Luke told me and Dad that he and Clarence wouldn't participate in the C'mas gift exchange or C'mas celebrations— that they weren't family. But, if it was okay, perhaps they could come by later in the evening to see how the day went? Dad said of course they could! Luke looked at me for my permission, and I shrugged and said "Why not." I guess he's okay. I'm glad they didn't try to get in on our C'mas and he realized that they <u>aren't</u> family. Not yet. That will take a while. If ever!

Well, I have to run. I'll write more later.

Love from your favorite daughter
Meg

December 25

Dear Mandy,

     Guess what I did most of the day!...played video games! How crazy, right? The parents decided to surprise us and snagged our favorite video games from the stores before we could. Then we opened them up this morning and they had these huge screens set up at the clubhouse with game systems so we could play. Awesome, right?! It was pretty cool. We had a tournament going for a little while. I actually beat Jason on Downshift 5000! Then Caleb and Tricia totally kicked my butt for the championship, but I still got to tease Jason about losing to a girl. :) Mom said they'd been hiding the video games for months, planning for Christmas. So we had movies and video games all day!

     Let me tell you about yesterday. We all got together after lunch. Janet wrote a Christmas program which we did with the little kids. It was really cute. It was about an elf that kept falling asleep while he was making toys. Adam got to play the elf...he was ADORABLE!!! He was making these "kaaa-chooo" sounds to pretend like he was sleeping. Then Ava kept running in with hot chocolate to wake him up. It was so funny because Meg played another elf who was filling the mug and Ava kept looking in the cup like "Hey! Where's the real stuff?" Then she'd run over to Adam and say 'Here go!' Oh my goodness I thought I was going to die laughing. We were all co-worker elves who kept catching Adam sleeping and we had these funny lines like, "More work and no play, it's an elf-erific day!"...or Mitchell's was "Toys done are stupendous fun!" Lol. BUT the absolute best part was when Jason came in at the end. When we'd practiced he was just supposed to be the head elf who comes in with the 'Spirit of Christmas' to sprinkle over Adam and make him the fastest elf ever. Well...Jason came in as Santa Claus instead! He found an old costume somewhere! OMG! You should have seen Adam and Ava's faces!!! They were stunned! Jason was all "Ho-ho-ho...This will

266

make you the fastest elf in my workshop! Ho-ho-ho!" Ava totally froze and Adam just had the biggest grin ever on his face. He came up to Mom afterwards and said "Santa gave me real spirit sprinkles!" Ooohhh. Sooooo cute!!! It was really sweet of Jason. See, he's not always Mr. Grumples!

So we did that and then we decorated cookies. The parents brought eggnog and Mom and Janet started singing Christmas carols. We had CDs to play while we just relaxed. It was nice not having to go to work...like a real Christmas break! Donald had this hysterical Christmas music CD, but the words were all different from the original lyrics...funny. I don't know who sang it, but we were cracking up. But then it was getting dark and people went home for their own traditions.

At home we sang happy birthday to Jesus around our nativity like we do every year and Dad read the story for us from our family Bible. And even though Adam and Ava were asleep, we set out cookies and milk. You know, I know that Santa isn't really the one that puts presents under the tree, but I still like to think of him as the keeper of Christmas spirit. You know, like Adam said...he brings us Spirit sprinkles. It was a really good night.

So then, this morning!! We got up and the kids were so excited about the presents and the missing cookies! I have to admit I was just as happy watching them rip apart the wrapping. Mom and Dad must've stayed up late to put everything under the tree. I couldn't believe it when I opened up my presents...Downshift 5000! I looked for it when I went 'shopping,' but just figured it got taken way back when people were raiding stores. Almost all the video games were gone anyway, so I didn't really think about it. But there it was! Sweet! They got me some clothes too, a pocket knife, a new journal, and a couple books. I made Mom and Dad a scrapbook with the photos that we had stored in boxes. Good thing Mom used to print out pictures, because the electronic one are harder to get now. I wanted us to remember happier times. It was all the vacations we'd taken. We used to go every year. Who knows, maybe we'll go again someday. There won't be any lines at Disney! Then Mom and Dad made chocolate chip pancakes, which was awesome because we haven't had chocolate in forever! We let the kids play so we could cook for the potluck with everybody else at four.

Oh and the gift exchange! So the parents exchanged gifts too, but I don't really remember what they got. We "young adults" had our own party going on. I can't believe what Meg got Jason! So funny! She got him this Grumpy doll and even he laughed about it. She also got him his team's basketball State championship trophy from the school and a school t-shirt too. She must've broken into the school! I was impressed.

Caleb got me this totally awesome fountain pen and some parchment paper from the art store. I'll be just like Jane Austen! He got me ink and everything...too bad there's no way to send people letters. Maybe we'll start up the pony express again! Won't that be nuts?? All the ways we think we've 'evolved,' but then we'll have to go back to living just like they did back then. As long as we don't have to wear dresses all the time or those horrid corset things. I mean, really? Women died from those things!

So Meg got Jason, Caleb got me. Tricia got Caleb a book on medieval weapons and more arrows. Pretty sweet. I know he was pumped about it. He's actually really good at scouting and using his crossbow...and his rifle too for that matter. So he really liked that.

Mitchell got Tricia...Oh it was hysterical!!! He comes in carrying this huge box, wrapped all crazy with like four different kinds of paper and drops it with a big thud at Tricia's feet. Open it! Open it! He was sooooo excited about it. So Tricia opens it and it's blinding...literally! I mean Mitchell must've grabbed everything that had any kind of sparkle on it from the stores. Make-up, purses, shirts (not even all the same size...and definitely not Tricia's size...), bracelets, headbands, even a sparkly doll! It was AMAZING the amount of glitter that was packed into that box. But he was so cute! I thought his face was going to split apart with how much smiling he was doing. Oh...and then he asked her if she liked it with this little puppy dog look on his face. So sweet. Thank goodness she said she loved it! She gave Mitchell this big hug and told him she couldn't wait to try everything on. OMG, I think she made his year! I think he likes her!!

Oh! But then! Jason had Mitchell and got him a go-cart! Are you kidding?!! A freaking go-cart! I heard him say something to Meg that it used to belong to one of his friend's who's gone now. But that thing is LOUD! Mitchell was in absolute heaven. Dad and Kenneth weren't too happy...it's a waste of gas and too loud and blah, blah, blah...but Donald and Sam said they don't really get to be kids anymore, so leave them alone. I agree. Let the kid drive a go-cart on Christmas! Luke showed up when he heard the noise. Clarence didn't. But Luke was smiling and laughing along with everyone else so that was nice. He even had a piece of pie with us after that.

So who am I forgetting...Oh Meg! I had Meg. I know she's not much for cooking even though she does it because she has to. So I made her a coupon book for 10 free meals. Pretty awesome right? When she doesn't feel like cooking she just gives me a coupon and I'll make it for them! I really don't mind cooking and Mom said she'd help me. Meg really liked it. She looked a little relieved actually. Maybe it lessens her load a bit. That's what Dad always says about helping others.

And saving the best for last...Jason and I hugged. It wasn't a big deal and I'm not saying we're hanging out again! But I get the flutters when he touches me!

Well, I'm exhausted! I'm all snuggled by the fireplace at home, drinking hot chocolate (Oh yeah! That was in my stocking. Yum!) and writing with my new pen so I won't forget about our first Christmas in our new world. I think Jesus would be proud of how we celebrated His birthday today. Even with everything we've lost, we still brought some light into the darkness. Literally! lol. Merry Christmas to all and to all a good night.

Starry night, Holy Night,
Ashleigh

December 26

Dear Mom,

Christmas was so much fun! I didn't think it would be but it was. Mitchell was so excited about his presents. I gave him a first aid kit for his own and told him I'd give him lessons in splinting bones and stuff. He's totally psyched about learning medical stuff. Dad gave him a bunch of video games. Apparently the parents had taken all the cool video games from the store shelves ages ago so we kids wouldn't get into them and we got them for presents. That was very cool! Of course we played video games all Christmas afternoon. I gave Dad his afghan and he really liked it. So do I. I think I did a good job on it. It has some mistakes but you can't really notice them unless you know where to look. We had a quiet morning opening gifts and we put your gifts under the tree. I hope you come soon to open them. Mitchell asked if you were coming back and I said yes. Dad didn't say anything. Just kind of shook his head and looked at me. But I don't care. I'm keeping the hope alive. I need to, especially for Christmas.

Anyway, I finally did think of what to get for Jason. I did get him the Grumpy doll, like I told you. Everyone laughed when he opened it—even Jason did a little. The rest of us thought it was hysterical! And Mitchell and Caleb called him Grumpy all day—which really irritated him. But the real present was the school basketball State championship trophy that I took from the school lobby display case. I also put the signed team t-shirt in a frame and gave that to him. No one looks at that stuff at the school and he was on the championship team so he might as well have it. He totally loved it! He got this big old smile on his face and came over and gave me a hug. He said he wants to keep it in the clubhouse so we'll remember the kids on the team and the school as it was. I thought that was nice. Kinda made me want to cry to be honest. And I liked the hug. Perhaps I shouldn't be telling you this as you're my mom, but it felt so nice to be held by a man other than my father. He smelled so good, like shaving lotion and soap and shampoo. I hugged him back (he felt all solid and muscle-y!) and he looked down at me and smiled right into my eyes. I never realized how pretty his eyes are--blue with flecks of gray. Nice!

Anyway, Ashleigh came over right away and said that if hugs were being given out, she wanted one too. So I hugged her and she laughed, but she obviously wanted a hug from Jason. Jason laughed too, and gave her a hug. And then everybody started giving everybody else hugs--moms and dads, kids, friends, little kids, everybody. It was kinda cool really. Christmas should be a holiday of peace and love—no matter what religion you are--or aren't.

We shared a big community dinner about 4 pm—chicken, potatoes, gravy, veggies, pies, and stuff. And we played video games, the parents talked and drank wine, and we all pretended life was back to what it had been in the old days.

The evening ended with go-cart rides. That was fun! Luke came out for the go-carts and he seems to be okay. Since he's over at the house talking to Dad a lot, I'm getting to know him better. So when he came out to watch the go-carts, he stood by me. That was kinda nice. Maybe I could have someone—like Ashleigh has Jason. I don't know. We'll see.

Love from your favorite daughter
Meg

January 1

Dear Mandy,

    I had my first kiss tonight!!! With Jason of course! Not my first kiss ever, but my first real kiss. I don't think Bobby in 2th grade counts...I mean it was a dare and he missed half my mouth. And then there was Ricardo at summer camp last year. He came at me with his mouth open and it totally freaked me out so I turned my head and he ended up licking my ear! Yuk! So this is the official one! On the mouth, no licking, eyes closed...It was heaven. I was kinda freaked out b/c it all happened so fast, but whatever... Here's the scoop. Everyone was at the clubhouse for New Year's Eve. The parents were playing cards and having drinks, the littles were already crashed out in the corner b/c it was like 11:30, and the kidults were watching a movie. Oh yeah, we watched a zombie movie for fun...Really??!! I just went along with everyone b/c I didn't want to be a big baby, but I hate scary movies! And a movie about dead people coming back and trying to eat everybody??!! Totally freaked me out! Do you know how many dead people are probably around here??!!! It would be a freakin apocalypse!

    So after the movie we decided to go out and drive Mitchell's go cart before the midnight countdown. I really didn't want to go outside in the dark...seriously, that movie was crazy! I was kinda hoping Jason would want to talk or hang. So we're getting our coats on and then he was right beside me and whispered right in my ear "You want to do something else?" uuuuuhhhh, yeah!! Totally got butterflies. So I started to ask him what, but he grinned and said "Don't be a drag Ashleigh, just come on." Which was kinda rude, but I couldn't resist those sexy eyes!

    So we went outside and Caleb started driving the go-cart. It was pretty funny. There was some ice on the road so he did donuts and we're all laughing. Meg was standing next to Luke (who showed up again), but she got cold and they went back inside. Tricia stayed out and rode with Caleb. BUT there I was, shivering, totally disappointed that this was all Jason wanted to do, but then he leaned in and said "Come on." Now I totally know this is how I got in trouble before, but we weren't going to set off any fireworks...and I was so excited we were going to be alone, but kinda shaky too, ya know? So I'm following him in the complete dark, thinking zombies were going to jump out at any moment, and all of a sudden we stop behind the old Larsen's house. They had a porch swing out back and Jason sat down and patted the seat next to him. He asked me if I was cold. I said yes so he put his arm around me and we rocked in the creaky swing just enjoying being close. I was dying inside, it was so amazing...and he was being totally sweet. Then Jason hands me a beer! "Here, we should have fun too." I kinda laughed...I mean, being alone together is what I've been dreaming about, but I was nervous about drinking!! I didn't want to ruin it, but I don't really drink. I've tried a few times, but it tastes gross and, Mandy, you and I always thought those parties were stupid and dangerous, remember?

Remember that boy who always had the big holiday drink-fests? What was his name? Aidan? Jaden? Hayden. Something like that. He was a senior a few years ago, but he always had those blow out parties where everybody was drinking in the woods and running from cops. Of course no one ever got busted. I think the cops showed up one time and the entire football team was there. But they all played the game on Friday night. Remember his famous Christmas parties? Even after he graduated he had parties, well...til Kaitlyn tried to kill herself in the bathroom one year. She was one of the cheerleaders and I guess she was dating Hayden...Brayden?...whatever, but she caught him making out with some other girl and went nuts. It was crazy. You know all those things that seemed so big...all the drama with other girls. Who knew we'd be HERE just a year later?? I wonder if she'd have tried to kill herself if she knew she was going to be dead a couple years later...

So anyway! There we are, sitting on the swing drinking, and I'm feeling a little hazy, and Jason is smiling and he looks down at me and his eyes look all romantic and I knew he was going to kiss me! He leaned in slowly until our noses almost touched and then his lips softly touched my lips and I thought I'd melt right there! We. Were. KISSING!!!! His arms were around me and mine were up against his chest. We didn't kiss for very long b/c he said we should get back before we got in trouble again. We laughed...like partners in crime. It was amazing. I hope I did it right! Eeeek! Happy New Year to me!

Nighttime skies and Smiles,
Ashleigh

January 2

Dear Mom,

Well, Christmas is over and we have started a new year. You know I'm mostly happy these days. Not sure why. Just am.

I was thinking...it's weird that I used to like noise all the time. I wanted the tv on even when I went to sleep. I liked the sound of people talking when I drifted off. And I listened to music when I wasn't watching tv. And of course I talked and texted with my friends every minute of the day. And since we lost power, it's been sooo quiet. I had a hard time falling asleep when we first lost electricity. I heard every noise, every creak of the house, every bird tweet, every noise I couldn't identify, and it scared me. I could almost not work or do anything without the tv keeping me company. And now, I sleep so well when it's quiet. My mind knows all the normal night noises and I don't wake up for a bird or wind or whatever. Now that we have the video games and music again, I'm not that into it anymore. Not Tricia though! She's totally psyched about having her music and listens to it every time she can. And btw it's NOT my kind of music. Yuck!

Tricia loves to dance and when she plays her music she dances around. She's funny. She gets me to dance too, which I like, but sometimes I feel kinda silly dancing in the kitchen or wherever. It's different at a party—I totally get into it there! But she's all over the place and doesn't care what she looks like. She definitely dances like no one's watching. She's actually pretty good! She's made up dances to imitate all the people here. For me she mimics the way I move my hips and arms. I didn't know I did the same moves so much! She imitates Mitchell by wiggling all over the place—which is pretty much how he does look. Her

276

Jason dance is trying to act tough and sexy but embarrassed. Her Caleb dance is goofy and uncoordinated and totally out of time with the music. She's a good mimic and makes me laugh.

I like having her around. I like the company and she asks tons of medical questions and I like to answer them. Sometimes I have to look stuff up and that's good too. We're both into medicine. I like the pharmacy/medicine part more and she's totally into the blood and bandages part—which I can do, but not crazy about. When the animals have their babies, we're called to help out. She's going to be better at that than I am before too long. But just watching animals give birth makes me think about making sure that Ashleigh is on some type of birth control, cuz I don't want to deliver her baby—not yet anyway! She told me she and Jason are 'back together' and there's been some making out. Fingers crossed that things aren't too far along yet! I hope he's not leading her on and that he actually likes her. I really really hope so! She'll be so hurt if he's not sincere.

Anyway, back to medicine...I like mixing medicines and reading up about all the types of meds we've found in the pharmacies and homes. I've been going through my stock of meds and putting things in categories and alphabetizing and throwing out really old stuff. Most of the heavy narcotics were stolen when the riots were going on, but not all of them. Dad and I are still the only people who know where the serious drugs are hidden— Donald has some of the OTC stuff. We haven't had any reason to use anything too strong yet thank goodness. I hope it stays that way. But we do use meds sometimes, like Ava had a mild fever the other day and Janet has migraines sometimes. Most of the time we let our bodies fight things on their own.

Well, this is kinda embarrassing to tell you since you're

my mom, but I think Luke likes me. He's flirty and tells me I'm smart and I look nice and he finds me when I'm at the school studying by myself or working at home. It's nice that someone finds me attractive—finally! But part of me just wonders if it's because I'm the oldest girl and therefore his last choice. But he could've liked Ashleigh—she's cuter and more lively and fun. I'm the serious, boring one. But whatever! It's so nice to have someone interested in <u>me</u> for a change. It's been a looooong time. Don't worry Mom, I'm not getting serious, but a little flirting won't hurt anyone! :)

Luke and I are spending more time together. He'll come over—supposedly to talk to Dad, but then it ends up that we're talking. It's really nice to have a guy to talk to—someone who actually listens to what I say and is interested enough to ask questions. We've talked about the usual stuff—what were your plans before KPox and what do you miss most and stuff like that, and now we're talking about what we see this new world turning into. He's kinda like Jason in that he wants to search for more people and see who/what is out there. He thinks my wanting to stay hidden in a little community isn't realistic—that we'll have to face up to the real world and make tough decisions someday. Like what do we do if someone comes in and tries to control us or something and how would I handle that? I don't agree. I think we should be like small pioneer communities in our early history, people could stay somewhat sheltered for a while. I don't want to deal with tough issues. Luke says that isn't realistic and that we will have to make tough decisions. I wish he'd not talk about it. I like things the way they are!!

It's my turn to cook this evening and I'm using a meal coupon that Ashleigh gave me! I wonder what she'll bring?!

Your favorite daughter
Meg

Caleb

I don't trust this guy. Too friendly + too helpful. Sneaking around houses w/ Clarence. What are they up to? And he always carries a gun, why would he do that? We're not dangerous people!

Jan 8

Dear Mandy,

     I can NOT believe my parents are such JERKS!!!! I mean, really???? Grounded? And now a curfew??? You have GOT to be kidding me!!! I thought we were considered 'adults' now and had our own say in the community. I guess we're old enough to work like servants, but not old enough to make our own decisions, right?

     Fine. Then I'm not going to work today! Screw it. Somebody else can count how many stupid cans of soup and tuna we have. If you want to treat me like a kid then I'll act like one. They are such JERKS!!!!!

Cloud cover and Furious!,
Ashleigh

Jan 12

Dear Mom,

We had snow last night! About 6 inches and deep enough to shovel! Janet sent a message through Caleb that we don't have school today so we could play instead! Snow day!! It was fun to go outside and play in the snow. We all built snowmen/things. Dad, Mitchell, and I built a snow snake that had his head sticking out at one part of the yard, a bump of his body in the middle of the yard, and his tail at the other end of the yard. Mitchell's totally psyched about it! Ashleigh's family made a bunch of little snow men and women about 1 foot tall with sticks for little arms. Some look like they're talking to each other or walking or reading little books and other stuff. Very cool. Jason and Caleb made the biggest snowman of the bunch. They pushed this huge snowball around the yard for the bottom part, and then had to get the other guys to help them put the second large snowball up on the bottom one, and a ramp to get the head on! Snow days are fun!

After that we all shoveled our sidewalks. Luke and Clarence eventually came out of their house and helped with the shoveling. When we finished shoveling Luke and I were just hanging around in the front yard freezing to death so I asked him if he wanted to come in for some hot cocoa. He did. And it was nice—talking and laughing and we watched a movie with Mitchell and Dad. We sat really close to each other on the couch and he touched my hand occasionally. If Mitchell hadn't been sitting right next to us, who knows...So he also stayed for supper and went home right after that.

Mom, I have to admit that I'm conflicted. I want to like him—no, I do like him. I'm just not sure if I should like him. My

282

head is telling me go slow, I don't know this guy. Sure he seems nice, and he's really good looking, and the community likes him. (Well, except for Clarence. Clarence doesn't seem to like him much. They don't spend time together and Clarence rolls his eyes a lot when Luke talks, or just walks away.) So my head is saying whoa. But my body is saying "Hello cute tall guy with the pretty brown eyes!" I don't know. I just don't know. And Caleb doesn't like him either. But that might be just because Jason is so tight with them and he could be jealous.

Speaking of relationships... Well, it was bound to happen. Ashleigh's totally angry at her parents and is sulking. I guess she's been lying to her parents and she n Jason were sneaking out and meeting at night--and she's told me she's drinking too! I can't believe she'd do that! But she says it's no big deal. But it is a big deal. And Ashleigh said that she wasn't going to fall for Jason again. I don't know. I just don't know.

Anyway, her parents caught her coming in early one morning and were not pleased and put her on restriction—and boy is she MAD. "I'm an adult!! I should not be treated like a kid!! If I'm a kid I'm going to act like a kid. I'm not going to work. I'm going to be miserable!" But things would be better for her if she wasn't so obviously sulking! It's like Tricia's old personality morphed into Ashleigh. And Tricia's making fun of Ashleigh's behavior! Which makes Ashleigh even more mad so she didn't talk to Tricia yesterday.

It was Tricia's birthday today. Cake and party and a sleepover at my house tomorrow—Ashleigh and Tricia are coming. That should be fun! Well...if Tricia doesn't make fun of Asheigh and they start feuding. Fingers crossed they behave! (Mitchell's staying at Caleb's house so he won't spy on us. Yes, he would so do that! Irritating!) I gave Tricia a set of vet books from a nearby vet's office and some medical equipment that looks interesting. We're going to check all that stuff out later. Kinda cool!

Your favorite daughter
Meg

Jan 15

Hey Mandy,

So things are still going pretty well with Jason. Granted we haven't gotten to see each other as much after my parents caught me sneaking out last week. Don't even get me started on how ridiculous they overreacted. Good grief! You'd think they'd caught us smoking pot naked or something! Jason said to meet him late so we could look at the stars and just have a few drinks! Granted, he drinks WAY more than me...but no biggie! I just went out for a little bit...fully clothed, mind you!...and came back...again, clothed! I mean, yes, there definitely was some intense making out...the kissing has gotten a LOT better, :-) but that's all! I'm not interested in going all the way, even though Jason does seem a little frustrated when I tell him to slow down. He says I don't have to worry and he wouldn't let anything happen to me...that he'd protect me. He even showed me a condom he had in his pocket! He's got to be crazy! I am not ready for that...but then he says I'm the most special girl in his life...and my heart gets confused. Honestly, when I'm with him my body says Yes! Yes! Yes! But for some reason it just doesn't feel right yet. Mandy, I know we talked about having wild, mind-melting sex...on the beach, in a hammock, lol, but when we were older. AND we promised our first time would be with our husbands. I want to stick to that. But Mandy, I'm struggling.

Mom and Dad are no help at all. They gave me this 'big talk' after they caught me sneaking back in the house. Talk about awkward!!! Mom talks about everything in detail...aahh! We had that horrible conversation about periods when I was in elementary school and this was no better! They just talked about all the physical stuff and not going too far (Gross to talk about with your parents!) And then they went on and on and on about relationships and mutual respect and modesty, blah, blah, blah, blah, blah. But it's like I'm supposed to feel only one way or another and that's not true!! They've been married for what...like 100 years? They obviously don't remember what it's like to be a teenager and they don't think Jason is the 'right man for me' and they say I should wait, but they didn't even ask me what I thought or how I felt. And wait?? FOR WHO??? Mitchell??? I don't think so!!! Double gross!!!

I tried to talk to Meg about it when we had the sleep over, but it was kinda weird with Tricia there. It's her brother...and she's only 13, so we switched subjects pretty fast. I'm just so confused...especially in the moment. Like when Jason and I are making out, I WANT to. I want to just keep on kissing him and I don't really care where I'm supposed to be or what I'm supposed to be doing. But then at the same time, sometimes his hands get a little...roamy...and I start to feel nervous and don't want to do THAT stuff. I don't know. It's really frustrating. Shouldn't I feel comfortable the whole time? Then with Mom and Dad breathing down my neck and saying all this stuff about how God wants us to respect ourselves and respect others, and making sure the decisions you make now won't haunt you in the future...it's too much pressure! My parents keep saying 'do what's right,' but what the hell does that mean? Is it what FEELS right? Or is what I THINK is right? And can't that be the same thing? How do I KNOW when love is real and when sex is ok????

Then there's Caleb too. My heart is a traitor! I'm into Jason, right? But...when I'm with Caleb sometimes...I really want HIM to just grab me and kiss me too! There are moments when it looks like he might, but then he always has something else to do. I bet he'd be a good kisser. Ugggh!! Life shouldn't be so complicated!!!!!

Cloudy skies and confused!
Ashleigh

Jan 19

Dear Mom,

I don't know what to do about Jason. He's drinking again. He keeps away from the parents when he's had too much, but of course they know. Tricia said their dad told him to stop drinking and Jason told him to mind his own business. So they aren't speaking much either. Getting drunk won't help him with problems. He also asked me for some meds to help him cope — something to make him feel happy again. I told him to talk to his parents and if they say it's fine they can get him something. He got all irritated and said he shouldn't have to talk his parents cuz he's an adult. I said I don't care and he's mad at me. No big deal. He said Clarence was interested in meds too and that I shouldn't be the only one with access to what should be community property! I told him no way. Getting high won't help anything. And I'm not going to be a drug dealer!! Besides I always tell Dad what meds I give out. Jason got more angry with me and I told him if he asked again, I'd check with his parents to see if they agreed. He said he was over 18 and he made his own decisions. I told him that I was also over 18 and I made my own decisions and my decision was that I'd tell his parents. He stormed off. I just wish Ashleigh would fall out of love with him! He's too immature and messed up. He seems to be a decent person underneath his stupidity, but he makes decisions like he's the only one who matters. Like bringing Luke and Clarence back. That was all about him, not the community. No one has the life we planned, and we all have to deal with it.

Ashleigh and I had a chance to talk the other night — just us two. She wanted to talk to someone who wasn't a parent and for some sympathy. I can do that — provide sympathy and be a fellow teen, not a parent. I really do feel for her. It must be so hard to be in love, and know the whole world's watching and not being able to do anything without being under a microscope. And then she picked Jason to love (not that she admits it), and he's a train wreck, but that's not how she sees him. I've never been in love that much. I've had crushes on guys, but not been <u>so</u> in love. I kinda envy her a little in having such intense feelings. When she's happy—you can tell she's on top of the world. But then I watch her crash and I don't want to be in love. She's soooo confused. Poor thing. I couldn't do much except listen and say I support her. I wanted to say be careful of giving her heart to Jason—but she's hearing that from her parents—and it's too late anyway. Her heart is already his. And he's not aware of how he's hurting her or probably doesn't even care. How sad...

Your favorite daughter
Meg

PS: I wanted to talk to her about Luke, but it wasn't the time. She needed to talk about her problems and I'll have a turn eventually. But I'm conflicted as well.

Jan 21

Dear Mom,

     I went on a date last night! At least I think it was a date—if a planned, ahead of time walk can be considered a date. So... Luke found me in the kitchen the other night after supper and he helped me wash dishes—which was nice. And we were talking and he asked if I wanted to go for a walk after we finished. And I said yes, so we went for a walk through the old neighborhoods. We held hands and his eyes looked at me all flirty and charming when we talked—he has pretty brown eyes. And we talked about so much—serious stuff and the mundane! How quickly trees grow up in yards that don't get mown. How streets get weeds in them. What foods we miss the most—he misses restaurant steak and potatoes and I miss ice cream—the types with candy bars in them. He talked about his parents and how he felt when they died, and that he missed them. I told him I missed you too, but that I expected you to come home one day. So we walked and talked for a long time. It was so nice! He dropped me off at the front door and leaned down and gave me a soft quick kiss on the lips. Oh my!! Talk about my heart racing! So if a walk can be a date...I went on a date! :)

Your favorite daughter
Meg

January 24

Dear Mom,

    We're digging out of all the snow. OMG!! It snowed about 4 feet! and the drifts are really amazing! Mitchell's having a blast! He and Caleb found a sled and they're sledding and throwing snow balls and building a huge snow fort. I don't think we've had a snowfall this big since he was little. I'm sure the snow will be gone in two weeks but in the mean time we'll LOVE it! We popped popcorn in the fireplace and talked about the good old days and what we missed and what we liked better about the new life. Of course, we talked about you and how much we miss you. Dad said that what he likes best about the new life is actually having a life. He said he didn't realize how much he was missing—especially with us kids, but just life in general. What he misses most (after you) is the technology. He said he'd love to be able to search online for the information he needs for his energy projects, but laughed cuz his wish didn't make sense--if he had the electricity to search on line, he wouldn't need to be searching for energy information. :-) Mitchell said that he misses friends his age to play with, but totally likes hangin out with Caleb. What he likes best is no old-style school--it's better now cuz school's shorter and he learns important stuff for our life. What I miss most are friends and the conveniences that electricity brought us—like hot showers and turning on lights when you go from room to room, instead of dragging around a lantern or flashlight. What I like best is the relaxed pace of life--like we're back in the early days just after hunter/gatherer societies and getting into early agricultural communities. I really like the sense of community we have. I mean we have our disagreements but we're all much closer to each other now than we were to our neighbors before. We count on each other for safety, food, social life, everything. I like that.

Anyway, when we were all out shoveling snow this afternoon, we heard this loud roaring noise! Coming in our direction! It was scary—growly machine noise and loud and getting closer. The men moved towards the noise and told the rest of us to get back. Ashleigh, me, and the moms stood with the kids behind us and waited—holding our breath. And then around the corner comes Luke! He got the tractor and snow plow from the farm and was plowing a great path to our homes. He plowed everyone's driveways and our whole street. That was fantastic! Mitchell asked if he could drive the tractor so we all took turns driving and had a blast. Totally fun! Then the dads and Ashleigh's mom got into it too and between all of us driving the tractor and learning to use the snowplow, a lot of streets got cleaned up. When the streets were clear, we went inside and drank hot chocolate. I'm glad we don't have hard winters like people do further north. Snow is fun occasionally, but not all winter!

I think I've forgotten to mention that I'm getting pretty good at target shooting! We've been practicing a lot this winter. I'm really accurate shooting the bow and arrow and I'm also pretty good with my rifle and pistol. As you know, we have to target practice and I practice at least 2x a week. I learned how to hunt, but don't really like it. I just like to practice on targets, not cute fuzzy things with big brown eyes! I'm the second best shot (after Caleb). Ashleigh is pretty good too, but she isn't into it like I am. I beat Jason last time we had a competition and he had some excuse why, but I still beat him! Very cool. You know, some days he's a really nice guy. And then other days, he's a

291

total jerk. Dad said that when his hormones level out, he'll be an okay guy—if he quits drinking. Dad says weird embarrassing stuff like that. I'm just glad he didn't say it around Jason!

Mitchell's calling us for supper. It's always interesting to see what he comes up with. Last week he fried the squirrels that he and Caleb shot. Not bad--but I like deer better!

Your favorite daughter

Meg

PS: I've been thinking that I want to stay away from Luke a little bit. I feel like I'm rushing too fast. Or is it him that's pushing too fast? I don't know. I'm just not ready/not feeling it/not...something. Whatever—time alone without him crowding me would be nice.

January 28

Dear Mandy,

So here we are again. Day...I don't know...400 of the snow-in? At least I got to hang out with Meg the other day and talk and paint our nails. But come on! Are other people just happy sitting around doing nothing? I mean Jason can sit in his house and drink with Clarence, but he can't hang out with me? Guys are so stupid. At least Adam enjoys my company. We built another snowman this morning...well, it was really a snow dog. He was adorable, stomping around in his little snow boots. So when do boys turn from adorable into jerks? Is it like a rite of passage or something? They have to treat others like dirt and then they can grow up? I just don't know why Jason's so complicated! Maybe I'll just hang out with Caleb on movie night...see what Jason thinks about THAT!

How do married people deal with all the annoying crap in relationships? Do they just ignore it? Is that what relationships are supposed to be? You just ignore the bad? But what amount of bad is okay and when does it mean that it's not the right person? I mean Jason is great and I really like him, but I wish he'd pay attention to me or act like he gave a crap about me, not just when we're making out. I mean what about all those movies where the guy is hopelessly in love and running all over everywhere to get the girl...when does that happen? Am I not worth that? Am I not pretty enough? Am I annoying? I just feel so lost some days. And I hate feeling like this! I hate feeling so...needy. Aaarrrrrgggggh!

Well, gotta go...when I ran into Noni today she said she'd teach Meg and me to play gin rummy. :)

Snowy and pathetic,
Ashleigh

293

PS – Playing cards with Noni and Meg today was really fun. Noni reminds me of my grandma. We even got to talking about boys! Noni told us she met her husband at a community dance. She'd had a few boyfriends before that, but her husband made her feel the most like herself...the 'best Rebecca' she could be. Meg and I talked about that on our walk home. That's an interesting thought right? Instead of feeling so insecure all the time and worrying about what the other person's thinking. You just find the person that makes you the best YOU.

February 4

Dear Mandy,

We're going to have a talent show!! And everybody's in it! Mom and Dad are going to sing a duet. I heard them playing some old people music from the 60s the other night and laughing. All us kidults are going to do a newscast! Isn't that hysterical??!! With commercials and everything...like for cars that run on smelly socks...and trained squirrels that fill your bathtub with hot water. LOL. Meg and Jason will be the newscasters. Jason didn't want to do it at first, but Janet and I talked him into it...it wasn't hard really, he loves being the center of attention! I'll be the on-site reporter with Caleb, Tricia will be the weather reporter, and Mitchell's going to do something with Caleb and the dogs.

Noni's working with Adam and Ava on a song. I'm not supposed to know, but Adam practices at home with Mom and it's a little hard not to hear him! Jason, Donald, Sam, and Luke are helping with set design. Oh! and we are doing a fashion show. The guys don't want to participate! So Tricia is creating wild outfits for me and her and Meg, but classic ones for the moms...sparkly ones! And I think Dad has lost it! He was taking spoons out of the drawer today and was all weird about it! I asked what he was doing and he made up this really strange excuse about Kenneth needing something with a different sound...what?? And Caleb is drawing the programs so they should be awesome.

Speaking of Caleb...we walked out to his 'dog training' course after we did some target practice tonight. We were doing this funny thing to see if we could still hit the targets if we had to spin around or stand on one foot. Gotta have some fun! But the dog course...now that is fun and super amazing! Now that the snow is disappearing, he and Mitchell put all these obstacles out at the farm and we take the dogs through the course when the days are nice. We were talking about the dog pack and I've really learned a lot about dogs since Caleb has been helping me train Alice (Named from Alice in Wonderland. I figured we all kinda feel like we fell down the rabbit's hole). He said I could even take her by myself sometimes when I go walking.

He told me one of the smaller dogs tried to challenge the pack leader by growling and biting him, but he got put in his place! It's kinda scary to see them when they bare their teeth and snap and bite at each other, but Caleb says it's all normal. They have to make sure the pack is protected at all times and they do that by working as a whole team. If there were too many dogs trying to take over, the whole pack could be hurt, so it's better to have one clear leader, then everyone knows who to look to when they need guidance. Kinda like people I guess... I'm glad the dogs are part of our community. It'd be scary if all these dogs were just running around wild doing their own thing and threatening everyone! Maybe our pack will chase off the wild beasts so no one steals our food again! It was neat to see how much Caleb has accomplished and how we can all work together to protect our home. It's good to have friends.

Well, back to writing our newscast!

Clear and Sunny and feeling good,
Ashleigh

Feb 5

Dear Mom,

Our talent show is going to be so much fun! Some of us will put on a news show and Tricia's putting on a fashion show for us girls and the parents have stuff planned, but they aren't saying what. I like surprises when they're fun surprises!

I think we'll have to limit the amount of people on stage or we won't have anyone left in the audience! But that'd be funny to have the whole group of us on stage in one skit. Except Luke and Clarence won't be on stage. They aren't acting—though Luke is helping with set design. He's really good with building things. We're taking up most of the clubhouse for stages, dressing rooms, and storage. Fun!!

I'm working on some of the news stories. Ashleigh's totally getting into the talent show and I'm glad cuz it gives her something different to think about--other than Jason. I guess we all need something different to think about. It gets boring doing the same ol thing over and over again. Same ol people over and over again.

So...this is what I have so far.

"Good evening. This is the LPS (Last People Standing) evening news brought to you by Suzie Sow Kitchen Waste Dispos-All and Green Hose Water Heater Company. The lead story this evening is the talent show being held in Laurel tonight at 7 pm. There will be a number of entries in the show, including musical numbers, poetry readings, and surprises. This reporter has tried to get to the bottom of the surprise entries, but sources are not speaking at this time. We will report anything as soon as we hear."

"In other news, Ava is beginning to talk up a storm and

297

is saying the cutest things. She is also learning to run so the community should be on the alert for a running, talking, very charming little girl. She is not considered dangerous, but could steal your heart. In a related story, if anyone is interested in babysitting occasionally, Caroline would be interested in talking with you."

"And now a word from our sponsor—Hate to waste your kitchen scraps? Does your garden have enough carrot scrapings and potato skins? Do you think that your kitchen waste is wasted in your garden? Let Suzie Sow Kitchen Waste Dispos-All take care of this nasty chore. Just put your kitchen waste in a small pail, set the pail outside your door, and the Suzie Sow Waste Patrol will pick up your waste. No fuss, no muss, no bother. You will be left a clean pail to fill up again the very next day! Pick-up and delivery are free of charge! You can count on Suzie Sow being totally organic and will not hurt the environment. Call Mitchell for more details. Suzie Sow Kitchen Waste Dispos-All."

"Water is still a matter of concern for the LPS. The water engineers are continuing to improve the rain barrel water retrieval system. Extreme cold has the engineers considering various methods of keeping water from freezing in the barrels. Water heater insulators are being experimented with and the engineers will let us know how this works out. They continue to make sure the well is producing clear water and test the purity on a weekly basis. It is still recommended that water be boiled the recommended one to five minutes and then properly filtered. The engineers want to remind everyone that water is a precious commodity and not to waste it. So if you are trying to make a skating rink, please use water from the creek and not the drinking supply—Caleb and Mitchell!"

"Speaking of water, the Green Hose Water Heating System may be just what you need for your water heating needs. This system works whenever the sun is out and will heat water for a very comfortable warm bath or shower. While this system is not recommended in freezing weather, during above freezing temperatures, you can't ask for a better eco-friendly water heater. To find out more, please notify the Water Engineers and have a Green Hose Water System brought to your home!"

This is about all the "news" I have right now, but I'm thinking up more all the time and the others will be adding theirs as well. It's going to be so much fun. We can't take too long though as we all have a least one thing we're going to be in. Even little Adam and Ava are doing something with Janet. I'm really looking forward to the fashion show—and having Trish dress us up like models will be awesome! I wonder what she'll have me wear?

Must run! Have to work on the show!

Your favorite daughter
Meg

PS: Mitchell and Caleb are doing something with the dogs but it's very secret and they hide at the farm to work on their act. I'll let you know what they did after the show. :-)

Feb 12

Dear Mandy,

 I feel like I'm flying! I mean the talent show was AAAAWWWWEEEESOME! We had so much fun! Adam and Ava sang the cutest song! It was a farm song, so they had to stop and make animal noises too, which was adorable. They were almost yelling at the top of their lungs they were so excited. Their act was first, so we definitely started off on a good note.

 Then the 'community band' played...hysterical!!! I guess Kenneth used to be in a 'band' or group when he was younger, so he and Noni taught Dad and Donald ...but get this...they weren't playing instruments. Kenneth was playing spoons and SINGING!! Lol. That was what Dad was up to the other day! Noni was playing a jug, Donald had a washboard, and Dad was playing an old bucket like a drum!!! Honestly, it was really good!!! Actually amazing! And so good to see Dad and Kenneth BOTH smiling at the same time.

 Then it was our newscast and we were fantastic! :-) We had stories about community stuff, commercials for waste disposal (b/c I would TOTALLY pay for someone to deal with our trash), and then Caleb and I ran around for the 'breaking news'.... like Kenneth sneezed and Jason said "This just in...Kenneth sneezing!!!" Caleb then had a quick interview with Kenneth about how he felt and got reactions of others around him on the sneezing. Ava was sitting in front and said, "Germs! Germs!" and hid under Caroline's chair. I had another interview later when Janet coughed. I think everyone was afraid to make noise after that. Hahahaha. It was soooo funny!

 After that Mom and Dad sang...some old song. They dressed up like hippies and everything. Ha ha! Then Janet read a poem she wrote and made us all cry, so thank goodness the fashion show was after that! We had a little intermission, so we could get ready. Tricia had all of our outfits laid out and instructions on how to do our hair, makeup, and accessories. I was really impressed with her organization. It's nice to have girlfriends to laugh with again. AND get this!!!...Jason wants to see me later!!...BUT wait, I'm getting to that!

We looked totally fabulous during the show! Especially me!! Jason was definitely checking me out. And why not? I'm the hottest one up there, right? Lol. But seriously, Tricia picked great outfits for everyone... with sparkles on everything. Mom looked really pretty. Dad had a BIG smile when he looked at her...gross...hahahaha. Everyone looked amazing!

So today was great, and it's Valentine's Day in a couple of days...waaa-hoo! And Oh! that's what I was going to tell you...Jason wants to meet at "our" porch swing tomorrow! I'll have to sneak out (so lame!!! My parents are still saying I have a curfew, really????), but I'm going to meet him anyway! He didn't say why, but maybe he wants to give me a Valentine present early...not that I really expect him to really give me anything... but I'm sure he will! I have to finish mine for him too...but not tonight. I'm exhausted.

Oh I forgot to write about the finale. Caleb and Mitchell did this whole dog-trick show. It was incredible! He had them all sit, roll over, and hold up a paw. Alice did a wonderful job balancing a ball on her nose! Then there was one funny time when Caleb called out, "Bang! Bang!" and then Buster and Max and Lola all laid down and rolled over with their tongues hanging out and their feet up in the air. They jumped up when Caleb yelled, "Up!" Those dogs are super trained! We've been working on protection techniques, but we didn't want to scare anyone so he left those commands out.

It was such a great night. I am so happy. With more to come I'm sure!!!!!

Cloudless starry night and Elated!!
Ashleigh

301

February 13

Mandy,

    I am shattered with anguish. I need you here now!! Come back to me or take me with you!!! I can't believe I'm so stupid. What an idiot! What an idiot he must think I am! I'm just so MAAAAADDDDD!!!! And hurt and furious and so stupid, stupid, STUPID!!!!

    Of course Jason didn't want to give me a Valentine's present! Of course not! What a selfish self-centered, pond scum sucking jerk!!! And I'm the stupid idiot that fell for it. Mandy, you always told me. You always told me I'd fall for some stupid jerk that would break my heart because I believed too much in love that wasn't real. 'Movie love' you said, right? Well, that's exactly what this is! I am SUCH A MORON!!! He is SO not who I thought he was. I have been so blind!!! And a FRIGGIN ignorant naive dim-witted IDIOT!!! I'm sure he's laughing behind my back right now or not even thinking about me at all because he only thinks about himself! I HATE him! I HATE him! I hate myself! I hate it all!

Feb 15

Hey girl,

Sorry I lost my mind the other day. I just...couldn't hold it together. Today I thought I was better. Meg and I were going to play cards with Noni and I was trying to act normal even though I still feel broken on the inside...But on my walk over to the clubhouse I started thinking about how stupid I've been with Jason and how I was so blind to the kind of person he really is. Then my thoughts started spinning about everything that has happened with him and losing you and K-Pox and... I collapsed on the clubhouse steps and started weeping all over again! I just couldn't keep the pain inside.

So there I was...a pathetic ball of sorrow...and I hear these footsteps. The ground was slushy...muddy and wet and makes that sucking sound (like the hole in my soul!!!) every time somebody walks. That's how I heard Jason coming the other night when we met...big sucky footsteps for a big sucky suck-head. But anyway...there I was...weeping. And I hear the footsteps. For a second...just a second, I thought it might be Jason to apologize...yeah right. So I'm wiping all my tears away and...I don't know, trying to look brave, when I look up and there's Meg. I was totally expecting her to ask me what's wrong but she just said, "Let's go inside and talk, Ok?" So we sat on the leather couch in the game room and she gave me a big hug. I was trying to be so strong, but then it all came spilling out. The tears started all over again and I told her everything. EVERYTHING...

The other night when I went to meet Jason I thought it was going to be great! We were both on such a high from the talent show. Happy and laughing and just having a great time...so when he asked me to meet him I thought it was special. Aren't guys supposed to proclaim their love with some grand gesture??? Yeah right! So I get there after I lie to my parents...again! I told them I'd forgot to lock up the inventory log and since it wasn't that late I'd run over and make sure everything was put away.

I got to our porch before Jason and here come his big stupid feet...suck, suck, suck through the backyard. The mud was telling me right there! "He sucks! He sucks! He sucks!" Why didn't I listen???? And he's in a FOUL mood and I can smell the alcohol on his breath. I mean, I'm all happy and he's super pissy and carrying a beer! AND I'm stupid and think he's sexy in a brooding way...duh!!!

So I just blurt out, "Hey I have something for you!" and I hand him the story I wrote. You know the one about the dragon I wrote for school? Well, I redid it a little and put it in a frame for Valentine's Day. At the top it said "You Melt My Heart"...hokey I know, but I thought he'd think it was funny!. But He barely reads it...and then...he says, "I can't read some silly kid's story now," and thrusts it back at me, but it drops in the MUD!!! THE FREAKIN SUCKY MUD!!! And he didn't even care! He goes off about how his parents are treating him like a child and nagging him about drinking too much and hanging out with Clarence so much and even Meg is treating him like a kid! And he went on and on about how HE was the one who found the new people and HE brought back new supplies and now everybody's being totally rude to Clarence and they still expect him (Jason) to work when OBVIOUSLY he should be looking for more people!!! On and on and on... SERIOUSLY??!!!

I swear I must've been looking at him like he was crazy! I couldn't even understand what he was talking about. Why did he even want to meet with me? He just kept on and on and I realized....I don't even know this guy!

I mean, what's his favorite color?? Who knows?! What's his favorite candy? Who knows?!!! He doesn't like school, which I happen to love. He doesn't have any respect for community rules, which I kinda thought was cool, but now I realize HE is just unsafe and stupid. He wants to leave again....and that's the last thing I want to do. This is where I grew up! My parents and

304

the kids and our friends are here. There's no way I want to leave and die out there alone. What idiot wants that? Well, I can name one...

I screamed, "You are such a selfish jerk!!! All you care about is yourself and getting trashed! Why DON'T you leave again?! We'll take care of your mother whose heart you broke! So go off by yourself! Nobody wants you here anyway!" And I stomped off.

But now...I'm glad stood my ground and said no when he wanted to have sex because HE'S A JERK! And I feel so stupid that I even wanted to! Like one of those girls I never understood...how they got pregnant or ended up dating idiots. I understand them now! Maybe they were just too scared to speak up. I went along with whatever Jason wanted because I wanted him to like me. Because...I'm lonely...and I'm scared...and I AM a silly little girl and I've been acting like one ever since this...THING...with Jason started. I haven't been acting like ME and I'm sick of it! Completely, grossed out, SICK. OF. IT!

So I tell Meg all this! and she just listened. Didn't ask any questions. I don't even know how she heard what I was saying b/c I was blubbering like a dork. She handed me a box of tissues and said, "People do stupid things and we make mistakes...at least you can learn from them and move on. You know, I can see why you liked Jason, but HE'S not learning from HIS mistakes and that's the stupid part... he should know better. You don't want to be involved with him til he grows up." I nodded.

I'm glad Noni was late today and walked in after I had gotten control of myself! And I'm really glad Meg was the one who showed up today even though I felt like a complete fool. It made me feel better to talk to her. She'll never take your place Mandy, but she's one of my best friends here. I miss you so much...will these cracks in my heart ever heal??

Sunny, but heartbroken,
Ashleigh

Caleb

I don't like
Clarence. He
is kind of scary.
I don't think I've
ever seen him smile.

February 15

Dear Mom,

Ashleigh and Jason had a fight. Ashleigh told me all about it and she said she's been a moron and will never like Jason again and that he's a total sucky jerk (her words—not mine!). She gave him a story for Valentine's Day and he didn't even read it and dropped it in the mud! Then he went on and on about himself and how he feels—typical Jason style! Seriously!! He's such a jerk!! Does he think of no one but himself?! Ashleigh and I had a really good talk. Not like I'm all that wise in matters of love or anything, but it's nice to have someone to talk to! She eventually smiled and said she really appreciated having friends again. I know how that feels! I love having Ashleigh and Tricia as friends. It fills a hole in my heart that I've had since all my friends left.

I really like this life. It's so much more calm and peaceful than our life was before (well except for Jason and Clarence.) The only thing missing is you. If you were here, life would be perfect. I don't want anyone to ruin it. It's like we have a little piece of paradise on earth. We need to make sure that we protect this way of life and each other. We're all protective of each other and we need to stay that way. One big family that we protect and keep safe.

We're planning for Caleb's birthday party—the usual cake and presents. It's getting harder and harder to find presents for people—we pretty much have anything we want. I'm going to bake him some cookies just for him that he won't have to share!

Speaking of family, I gotta get going. It's my turn to make supper. Oh, I used most of Ashleigh's dinner coupons. I'm saving my last coupon for my birthday! btw Mitchell is trying to be more adventurous with cooking! You should've seen him with the rabbit he trapped! He got out a cookbook and tried to make a stew. Dad and I ended up helping him and it tasted good! Cooking together is fun—more fun than being in the kitchen by myself!

Your favorite daughter

Meg

February 16

Dear Mom,

Luke's been coming to the house after supper for the last couple of nights. People are starting to notice—and Ashleigh kinda smiles and raises her eyebrows when she sees me. I don't like the attention from the group...but I do like the attention from Luke. He's so nice _and_ he's sexy _and_ he likes me! We walk every evening and just talk and talk. I love it! I love having someone pay attention to me. I love feeling like life has this one normal thing left in it for me. I love feeling that I may have a husband someday and children and a future—Mom, don't worry, the husband probably won't be Luke, cuz I know we've just met and I don't feel like he's the "one", but at least I have hope again. I don't think I totally realized how much I was worried about not having a family, but knowing that I might have children and my own family someday makes me feel so _good_. And I absolutely love having him hold me close. And having someone to get dressed up for and to wash my hair for. It's wonderful!

But Mom, like I said, I'm not sure he's the one. I mean I do like him and his attention, but... I'm just not ready to be serious. And just cuz he's the only person here in Laurel at the moment, I don't want to settle for the first guy who comes along. I think watching Ashleigh and Jason these last months makes me really nervous about getting into a relationship. I see how miserable Ashleigh is...and wonder whether all those highs and lows are worthwhile. I don't think I'm ready for that. And after all—I might actually have choices in husband material! Is that not the _coolest thing ever_! Knowing people are out there somewhere is such a great feeling—scary sometimes—but great in other ways.

Your favorite daughter

Meg

PS: Dad isn't sure what to do or say about me seeing Luke—which is kinda funny. I know he wants to tell me to be careful and other fatherly advice but doesn't really know how to and he hints at things. I guess I need to put him out of his misery and tell him I'll be careful and do all the things he'd like me to. I'll tell him tonight—then he'll be able to sleep better! :)

PSS: I'm also not sure that I like that Luke carries his pistol with him all the time. We all have guns and know how to shoot, but we don't open carry. I asked him why he does, and he said, "Because I can. And you never know." I don't like that answer. It's just not right somehow.

February 21

Hey Mandy,

You'd be so proud of me! It's been a week and I'm still on a moron-free diet. I've seen Jason, but I'm staying away from that drama. He can ruin his life all he wants, but he won't ruin mine. I'm done! We're adults now right? And adults make choices for their own lives. Life is too precious to spend time with people who don't care about you. Sooo, so long stupid! Hope you have fun drinking beer with Clarence! Who isn't nearly as cute as me!

Today at school Adam was reading this cute book about a mouse that went on a field trip with dinosaurs. Marty the Meek! It was all about how they had to learn to be polite and how the mouse actually became the leader for everyone when they got lost, but he was humble and kind in getting everyone to work together. It was so cute! Adam got so excited at the end that he yelled "Marty the Meek saved everyone!" lol When we were walking home he was still talking about it, but I started to get confused because doesn't meek mean shy? So I dropped him off with Mom and went back to ask Janet about it. So she keeps this GIANT dictionary in the classroom so we looked it up. Ugh, I miss the internet! BUT it said that meek was 'enduring hardship without resentment.' Then we got to talking about that scripture in the Bible about the meek inheriting the earth and I told her I didn't get how unresentful and 'nice' people get anything. It always seems like the loud and nasty people or mean and nasty VIRUSES just come in and take whatever they want and the other people that are trying to good things just suffer!

I don't think she really knew what to say, but then all of a sudden she got up and grabbed this Greek dictionary she had behind her desk. She said she remembered her priest talking about something once. And get this! The Greek word for meek said it was related to war horse training! What?! Horses! And horse training?! I seriously felt like God was trying to tell me something. The hair on the back of my neck was all prickly! But

311

the word was all about how the military picked the strongest and toughest horses....the ones that were the most determined and passionate, but through kindness and love, they accepted guidance from their riders. They channeled their wild and rebellious nature into the service of one focused purpose so they could stand strong in the thunder of battle. !!!!!!!! Can you believe that?! I started to cry...How crazy beautiful and awesome is that?! WE...this town...WE are the meek...the ones that stand strong in the battle of this new world and we do our best to endure without bitterness because we just can't be buried. Too many people already are! We are the ones that lived and are trying to channel our strength into this new destiny....We are the meek that shall inherit.

Slate gray skies, but holding strong!
Ashleigh

March 5 Meeting Minutes

Present:
   Donald, Janet, Caleb and Tricia Kinsey
   Jackson, Caroline, and Ashleigh Grace; Adam and
      Ava Parker-Grace
   Sam, Meg, and Mitchell Shultz
   Rebecca Oswald and Kenneth Sudley
   Luke Boden

Absent:
   Clarence Dyer
   Jason Kinsey

Discussion about upcoming planting season and community care for summer. Committee reports given with projected spring projects.

<u>Shelter and Warmth</u>: Will make general repairs on houses and community buildings.

<u>Power</u>: Sam discussed the installation of more solar panels with the idea of trying to use more of that power for appliances and lighting.

<u>Food and Water</u>: Discussion re: planting and planning for food and supplies. The clubhouse garden will be dedicated to fruits and vegetables for canning and storing. There will also be an herb garden with medicinal herbs and a pumpkin patch. Crops for animal feed will be planted at the farm. (Feed for horses, cows, pigs, and chickens)

<u>Safety/Security/Health</u>:   Community   members   were reminded of summer precautions for hydration and good hygiene, especially for wounds in order to prevent infection.

Donald reported participating members passed their weapons tests. Caleb got the highest score in marksmanship with Meg coming in a close second and Ashleigh in third. Caleb and Mitchell tied for top scores in archery with Meg coming in third.

Meeting was adjourned with a community dinner.

Minutes recorded by Ashleigh Grace.

March 14

Hey spring flower!

SOOOOO glad spring is almost here! It's nice to have warmer weather, but not be hot summer yet when we just sit and puddle all day. Winter was FOREVER! It was too cold for walks and I really needed to get out occasionally! Today I cleared away the leaves and icky stuff around your cross. I'm getting ready to plant new flowers. I can't believe the pickles made it through the winter!!! :) I buried the jar halfway so it didn't fall over and break or freeze or anything. But I laughed when I saw it under all those leaves. All these people died...but the pickles are still fresh!! How weird is that?!

We'll start planting soon. We're planting tomatoes (yum!), peppers, corn, carrots...and other things...and pumpkins!!!! Lots of pumpkins for the fall! Won't that be fun! I'm excited about having the garden again. I don't mind working outside and it's nice to have fresh food. I don't feel so worried about starving to death like I did last year. I don't even spend as much time at Sav-More taking inventory because most of the food we are growing on our own and the other supplies (trash bags, bug spray) I just need to update every couple of weeks. Luke was asking me about gardening tools the other day, so I'll have to go back and see if we have extra shovels, garden hoses, batteries, and antifreeze like he wanted. It was a strange list, but whatever! I'm just glad even though we have grocery stores, we don't need them! Yay!!!

With all this talk of planning, I started thinking about the future. We'll keep planting, harvesting, and working. Sometimes I wish weeds and bugs wouldn't keep growing, but I guess they have a purpose too. I used to wish something would magically make everything go back to the way it was before K-Pox, but it's never going to change...kinda like those pickles. And I think that's ok.

It's the spring...it makes you think about new life and

314

moving forward. It's amazing how different 'forward' is now. It's kinda like we've moved backward, but are more forward than we were before, you know? We're all working together, looking out for each other, taking better care of the earth, recycling, not playing so many video games (boooo) or being on the computer. I wonder if it will somehow reverse all the damage we did to the earth before...Reverse global warming and heal that hole in the ozone.

And I'm moving forward too. It's been a month since Jason and I broke up and the hole in my heart is healing more every day.

Slightly cloudy and thoughtful,
Ashleigh

March 17

Dear Mom,

Totally confused!! I really like spending time with Luke. At least I think I do. But part of me says to slow down and not rush to get involved. The smart part of my brain is saying, "Who is this guy? You don't know him at all! And just because he pays attention to you, doesn't mean he's the guy you want forever." And the other part of my brain says, "Yeah, but he's cute and it's nice to be held and kissed and ... well, who knows what's next... and who else is there anyway and what could it hurt to have a boyfriend."

Ashleigh and I were talking the other day, about how difficult it is to have a boyfriend here. We were sitting on my back porch with our feet propped up on the end table, drinking warm Diet Cokes and eating chips. The guys were gone so we could talk without nosey boys listening. Totally the right mood for girl talk. I asked her how she was doing since she and Jason broke up which started us talking about relationships. She said she'd really liked Jason and might've wanted to marry him, but he didn't ever feel the same way. She liked the holding hands and kissing parts a LOT! So do I!! But we decided that going much further would be a big mistake because even with birth control available (and I could sneak it to me and Ashleigh if we wanted to be secret), it just wouldn't make sense to have sex. 1. There's still a chance that we could get pregnant—not good!. 2. When the relationship doesn't work out, you can't get away from them—they're here all the time. 3. What if there's someone out there who's better! When we came up with reason 3, that led us to describing our perfect man. My perfect man is about 5'10" to 6 feet tall and has light brown hair and brown eyes. He'd like to read and talk and spend a lot of time with me. He'd also like to spend time with my family cuz that's really important.

Ashleigh didn't even have to think before she said, "I don't care what color hair my perfect guy has, as long as he has dreamy eyes and ripped abs! He has to be kind and generous and like outdoor stuff like hiking and horseback riding, and be in love with this area like I am. He has to really just like me for who I am...no games. No drama!! And it's really important to me that he's Christian so we'll end up in heaven together someday."

Now to just find these perfect men!

Your favorite daughter
Meg

March 19

Hey Mandy girl,

So weird today...Caleb said something about seeing Clarence snooping around people's houses and taking things??? Caleb also said one of his rifles is missing and his dad got mad at him about not taking care of his stuff, but he KNOWS he put it back on the rack after he went hunting. He acted like he thought maybe Clarence had taken it. Why would anyone steal like that? So weird!

There's something weird about Luke too. I'm not sure and Meg spends more time with him than I do, BUT it's just a weird feeling I get when he's around...He's always looking a little smug and is very attentive to where everything is located. He asks a lot of questions...I don't know. Maybe I'm just being paranoid after everything that has happened, but hmmmmm...

Blue skies but suspicious,
Ashleigh

April 4

Dear Mom,

Mitchell has been talking a lot about religion lately. He's interested in what it all means—God, heaven, hell, Bible stories and everything, and said he wants to attend services with Caleb. He asked me and Dad if he could go. We said of course he could. As you know, Dad and I think alike on religion, but if Mitchell wants to check it out, he's free to do so.

He was asking me about heaven, but mostly about hell. It is a scary concept. Kinda like that old song you used to listen to: "I know there ain't no heaven and I pray there ain't no hell. Never know by livin', only by dying will tell." Or words close to that. I told him that I believe there isn't a heaven or a hell so not to worry. That we just die and turn to dust. So he asked, "But what if there is?" I told him that I have no definite answers to the world's major theological mysteries, that people have been questioning this very thing for eons. Then I sent him to Dad! Let him take that on! :)

So he's going to Easter services at the Grace's tomorrow. I doubt he'll get all his questions answered, but he needs to search for them on his own. To make up his own mind.

Your favorite daughter
Meg

April 5

Dear Mandy,

Another holiday come and gone. It's amazing how much time has flown by! Today was Easter. We ate, we played, we all got together and laughed and talked. Noni and Kenneth came to our house to have 'church' with us this morning. Dad gave the sermon, Mom sang a solo, then we sang together. It was comforting to hear the familiar Easter story. Kenneth read the scriptures with more feeling than I've ever heard from him! It made me a little teary actually. We invited everyone even though Meg, Sam, Jason, and the new guys didn't come. I was kinda surprised Mitchell came, but I think he was just tagging along with Caleb. It was definitely more low-key than our other holidays, but it was still wonderful!

I had a good talk with Meg later. We were watching the kids and she was telling me about doing an egg roll with her mom. I'd never done an egg roll before! That got us talking about Easter traditions and family dinners. Sometimes Meg seems so sad and I know it's because her mom hasn't shown up yet and there's no way to find out why.

You know it's different talking to Meg sometimes. Not in a bad way. I mean, talking about boys or hating our thighs is the same...but it's when we get into deeper conversations, like the one about her mom, it's...different. Even when things are bad or I feel hurt deep down to my bones, I still believe God is there. But with Meg, I KNOW she doesn't believe in God...so when she's hurting or questioning LIFE, it has to be hard for her not to have something bigger than herself to turn to. She doesn't have someone to turn to with prayers for answers or for healing...or prayers to take the hurt off her shoulders.

She says she doesn't believe in a god that does bad things to good people and needs proof of God's existence, not just some old stories. Faith doesn't cut it. She wants to work towards something, not just pray and hope it'll happen like a genie granting a wish. She said that prayers seem selfish...cuz it's like asking Santa Claus for toys...more about helping yourself than helping other people. And instead of just praying for life to be better, people should be DOING things to make it better. And why would God give the world all the evil things we deal with including K-Pox? She said she gets comfort knowing that when we're done with this life, we are done. That we are only a small part of the universe and that is all.

I totally get where she's coming from and I have the same questions. Why doesn't prayer always "work?" Why DO bad things happen to good people and good things happen to bad people? The way Meg talks, her mom was a really wonderful lady. Kind and loving and wanted the best for her kids, so where is she now? What if she survived K-Pox, only to get tortured and murdered for the Tylenol in her purse? And what if her mom DID die? Since they don't believe in heaven...where do they go now? Heaven? Hell? Purgatory? Some random space vortex?? Mandy, I know you're waiting on a cloud for me with bowls full of cheese puffs, but I wonder how that is for Meg...her believing that this life is it and there is no everlasting. The hard part for me is there's nothing I can say to make the pain of missing her mom go away...the constant hurt of not knowing.

I told her I struggle with what to believe. She looked surprised when I said that, but I do! My parents always tell me it's okay to question things. God gave us brains. So I don't think she's crazy or stupid for asking all these questions. And she grew up differently than me. I like talking to her about things b/c it helps ME understand or question more. I can't force her to believe what I believe, but I'll love her and pray for her anyway. She's my friend! And I kinda like to think that everyone ends up in heaven...won't she be surprised when we meet there!!! And her mom will be there too! With chips! Absolute heaven. I guess I'm not really sure about a lot of things...but for me, my questions are about HOW God works in our lives. It's NOT a question about whether or not He exists...Faith is believing, even when you have questions, even when you don't have proof.

God exists whether we believe in Him or not.

Breezy, but feeling warm,
Ashleigh

April 16

Dear Mom,

It's Mitchell's 13th birthday today! He's officially a teenager and so excited! Dad didn't seem as excited as Mitchell! :) This was a much better birthday than last year!! Remember last year he wanted a gun and Dad said later? Well, he got his gun this year. It's a 22 rifle with a scope and silencer and a ton of bullets. He was so excited! He's been shooting already, of course, but he always had to use Dad's guns. And now he has one of his own. Very cool! But I'm still a better shot and that bugs him! Ha Ha! And we had a community party with cake and stuff. So much nicer than last year!

Luke came by with a present too—more ammo. Not sure where he got it, but it wasn't from our lot. Mitchell took off immediately to show Caleb and go shooting. He's at a good age—still a kid but old enough to do grown up stuff.

Luke and I are still hanging out, but I'm not feeling the same. So it's easier to hold him off, but he's not a patient man. Which makes it weird to keep saying no. But something is just not right. And if I were to be tempted, I just talk to Ashleigh and she puts me on the straight and narrow! Sorry Mom, if this is a little too personal!

Your favorite daughter
Meg

April 20

Dear Mandy,

Whew! I forgot what hard work it is to be outside planting and organizing and building and who knows what else! Honestly, today I just wanted a hammock to lie in and relax. Enjoy the sun on my face you know?

We're also going to celebrate our first Founding Day--the day that we all came together and 'founded' this new life. I think it's a lovely idea. A new Independence Day! We've come a long way from eating only canned food and worrying about our next meal or how to have clean water. (or where to have toilets!! Ha!) I'm so grateful we have each other. Lately when I look at Adam and Ava I see all of our hopes shining in their eyes. And Meg! Thank God for Meg!!! She's been such a comfort with you gone and all the struggles with Jason and my parents and learning how to be a big sister to Adam and Ava. I don't know what I'd do without her...without anyone here! I swear I'd do anything to protect us. This is our home. Together we work, we bleed, we sweat, we cry, we laugh...We LIVE! Truly live! And no one can mess that up! No one!

Spring blossoms and grateful,
Ashleigh

BE RESPECTFUL
OF MEMORIES
LEFT BEHIND
-JG

April 23

Dear Mom,

Jason had his 19th birthday party today! We met at the clubhouse and had cake and gave him presents and stuff. I'm still not happy with him so don't really care about his birthday.

Luke has asked several times where I have hidden the meds and stuff. I've told him I don't know what he's talking about so he laughs and drops it. I'm not sure how to take it. Is he joking or serious? He's being really helpful with everyone here lately. And he's always talking about how well we have things working and how it's exciting being a part of a new society and he's really glad that Jason found them. That he hated the thought of being one of the only people left on earth. And he's been really helpful now we're getting ready to plant again. Luke's also good with Adam and Ava—kinda watches out for them just like we all do. Clarence doesn't notice the little kids unless they're in his way. But Luke will say stuff like, "Hey, where'd the little guy go?" And he'll play with both Adam and Ava. Most guys don't usually play with little kids. So that's cool. But I'm just not sure about him.

Your favorite daughter
Meg

April 26

Dear Mandy,

What a traumatic day!!!! Today we were at the Founding Day picnic. I brought the kids and they were playing like usual...everyone keeps an eye out for them. Most of the time there's no way they could be missed with all the yelling and running around they do...but all of a sudden Mom gets this concerned look on her face and looks around. Then she stands up and starts walking and looking and she's totally freaking me out. So I ask her what's up and she asks if I've seen Ava. Well, I start looking and we tell the others and we CAN'T FIND HER! Then Adam burst into tears. I swear I thought my heart was going to explode, it was beating so fast. So we're looking and looking...for like 30 minutes! When all of a sudden Luke walks out of the woods carrying little Ava!

Can you say OMG Thank Goodness!!!! And she was fine!!! I guess she just wandered off looking for flowers and went too far by herself. I was really surprised she wasn't in full-on-tears-melt-down mode, but there she was...big grin on her face with a huge bunch of dandelions in her hand!! Aahhhgggg!!!...It was so scary though. Worse than any horror movie. We all hugged her and hugged her.

After that, I totally don't know if I ever want to have kids. I mean, to be responsible for a-WHOLE-nother life??!! It seems so....HUGE...and what if you mess up? Ava's the closest thing I have to a little sister and I almost died when I thought she was lost. What if she was actually my kid?? It would feel even worse. Even though my parents and I fight, I know they're trying to protect me still...even though I can protect myself. I am learning from my mistakes! And honestly, I have great friends who are looking out for me too...Meg, and Tricia, and Caleb... Speaking of Caleb...we talked at the picnic today. He hasn't really seen Jason much lately—he's totally ticked off about Jason's drinking so much and still being caught up in his own stuff. He said Jason's been to family dinners a couple of times and goes to see his mom but that's it. Caleb's sad about how things have changed. He used to look up to Jason, but not anymore. He hopes Jason will stop acting so stupid! I wish he would too. Even though I'm not totally crazy about Jason anymore, I don't want him to screw things up with his family. Family are the only people REQUIRED to love you.

I'm just glad the day ended well. Thank goodness Luke went looking in the woods. Our group wasn't even near the woods during the picnic, so I have no idea how she got so far away and into the trees before we noticed. So crazy! Just glad she's back!

Storms in the distance and exhausted,
Ashleigh

April 26

Dear Mom,

We had such a scare today! Little Ava wandered off and no one could find her. It was horrible! We were all yelling her name and we spread out in all directions and do you know how hard it is to search for a little 4 year old girl in a very big area? We didn't know if she was close by or sleeping in one of our houses or had wandered off into the neighborhood. She was with us at the party and we were all supposed to be watching her. But everyone thought that someone else was watching so no one was. So you don't worry I'll tell you right now—we did find her and she's okay. Actually, Luke found her. I like him better now. We were all looking and spread out all over and he came back to the main search area with her on his shoulders. She was laughing and saying "I went for a piggyback ride with Luke and he gave me candy!" Luke said he told her he'd give her some if she'd stop crying and go with him, so we got some out of the candy stash and we all got some. It's a small price to pay for having our little girl back safe and sound. It scared us so bad!!! We're now going to delegate a child watcher and not count on group watching anymore. Scary Scary Scary!!!

I hate the idea of something happening to our little kids—or any of us. We're one big family and I don't want anything to happen to us. We all feel this way—very protective of each other. Even idiot Jason's part of the group. He might be an idiot, but he's a part of the family and our idiot, and I don't want him hurt.

Meg

PS: I forgot to mention...Clarence took off to North Carolina. Luke came by yesterday evening after supper and told us Clarence took off the night before—took a car and supplies and just drove off. I can't believe he didn't say goodbye or ask if he could have supplies or tell us what he took or anything! I told you he didn't have any manners! Well, I hope he finds his family. He didn't fit in that well here and I'm sure his mom will be glad to see him.

April 30

Dear Mandy,

    Today was a fun day. Even though it started off a little weird...Ava kept telling Mom that Luke promised her more candy if she was a good girl in the woods??? What?? We were totally confused! And do you know how hard it is to get a 4 year old to tell an accurate story? She kept talking about candy and Mom was getting a little annoyed because she had a million things to do, so the kids and I made homemade dog treats while Mom went to work. Then I took them to see Caleb after we were done. He was working with his pack. Puppies were jumping all over the place....SOOOO cute!!!

    Caleb and I started talking about Clarence leaving. I actually don't feel bad about it. One less person to worry about feeding...and he was creepy anyway. But how weird to be out there all by yourself! If we do start to travel at some point I hope we do it together. This community is my home and I'm not interested in leaving any of it behind. We've fought too hard to make it work. Caleb mentioned again he was pretty sure Clarence had been stealing. I thought about when us girls went to the Fisher's house for inventory and I saw their mantel clock was missing. It wasn't big, but I noticed it was gone was because when Dad and I went there for supplies before, it chimed SO loud. CREEPY! Like some ghost clock...reminded me of the bells during all the funerals. But it wasn't there the other day. Kinda like the empty gun cabinet at the Parishes and Dad's pocket knife he couldn't find at the farm.

    Why would anybody steal from us? It's not like money or possessions have any value anymore. So I'm double glad Clarence is gone if he was the one taking stuff! If he has that creepy clock, I hope it chimes all the way to North Carolina!

Partially sunny and sorta relieved,
Ashleigh

May 8

Dear Mom,

Luke is spending a lot of time with me and I'm really not sure I want all this time together. I still like being on my own some—to read and spend time with Dad and Mitchell, but he keeps coming over every evening. How do you tell someone to <u>not</u> show up? Well, I guess I need to figure it out. It's not that I don't like him. It's just I feel he's pushing me too much. I used to like the attention but I don't anymore and ...I'm <u>not</u> ready to be in a relationship. Maybe if he was someone else, but I'm just not sure about him. Maybe in time...or maybe not ever.

Life's going on as usual—gardening and school and studying. Jason's still having a problem with drinking but shows up for work when he's supposed to. To be honest, I think Luke had a talk with him and told him to straighten up. He's the only person Jason listens to. And Ashleigh's involved in the community garden and landscaping down at the swimming hole again. She really does like her landscaping--she's awfully good at it! She and her dad work together on stuff and it's nice seeing her not being all moody cuz of Jason. We're spending more time together and talking <u>a lot.</u> We're really good friends and when I want to giggle or worry about my relationship (or is it a NONrelationship?) with Luke, I know I can with her. It's nice. So now I have one of the things that I wanted— a girlfriend to talk to! Now I just need you home!

Your favorite daughter
Meg

PS: Luke keeps asking me for pain killers. I keep giving him the usual over the counter, but he wants more powerful stuff. I tell him I don't have any. That he should ask Dad. But he never does.

May 9

Dear Mandy

It's so nice not to be the one having guy drama! Meg and Luke had been dating and he was coming over A LOT! Apparently that's not a good thing though because Meg said that he's getting on her nerves. She told me the other day she just wished she could have some time alone instead of always having to chat or hang out with Luke. I hear her! Sometimes it's nice to drift away into your own little world.

I keep trying to tell her not to let him push her into doing anything she doesn't want to do. Not to feel like she has to hang out just because HE wants to. We may be primitive in the way we live, but the feminist movement still happened! I still think there's something off about him though. He is becoming more scattered in his chores. I overheard Dad talking to Mom about him showing up late or doing chores in places he wasn't supposed to be. And he eyes Meg like the dogs do when they are waiting for dinner. Definitely intense, but tense too...like he is looking for some way to attack? I don't know.. I feel sad for her though...she said she wishes she had her mom to talk to. They must've been really close. I feel weird talking to my parents about stuff, but back in the old days they were never around anyway, so I just never did...I always had you instead! And now we have the little kids to take care of and we talk a lot about planning...but not REAL stuff.

I want to be there for Meg though. I may not know the answers about boys and life and everything we have to learn as adults, but at least we can figure it out together. I won't let anything bad happen to her. Even if we don't believe we'll end up in the same place when we die...we can walk this journey on earth together. And I can pray for answers for both of us.

Green grass and friendship,
Ashleigh

May 13

Dear Mom,

    I wish you were here. I don't know what to do and Dad is <u>not</u> the person I want to talk to—it'd be too embarrassing. I'll talk to Ashleigh later, but I'm probably over-reacting. So...here's the problem...Luke keeps finding me when I'm alone, and he's been very friendly and I don't feel the same way anymore. We used to kiss n stuff. And that was nice...before. I liked his attention at first, but I told you he's been too friendly too fast. I dunno, maybe guys are just like this. So I'd been interested in him, but now that he's trying to get closer, it makes me uneasy and I'm backing off. But he keeps pushing. And there's just something about him that I'm not comfortable with.

    I'm probably making more of this than I should...I just don't know. So anyway, he knows I spend time in the school room studying my medical books after the kids leave class cuz it's quiet and I concentrate better when they're gone. Well, yesterday he stood in the door of the class and I felt trapped—me just sitting there and him in the doorway. I shouldn't have felt trapped, I should've liked him there, but I didn't. I said I had to leave and Janet was expecting me. It wasn't true, but he didn't know that. I walked past him and he didn't move very much so I had to brush past him when I walked by. If he was the "one", I should've been all excited when our bodies touched—should've wanted to stop and press against him—like I did before. But I didn't. It was beyond awkward. He thought I liked being that close to him and held on to me for a hug...put his head down for a kiss, but I just laughed, gave a little shove, and kept going. Last week I would've stayed. What's wrong with me! I don't want to be one of those girls who the guys say is a tease. I'd hate that!!

And today he came by school again. I didn't even see him at first. I was studying and he started talking and I about jumped outta my skin. He looked at me with flirty eyes and said I looked cute when I was studying—so serious with my books. I think I said thank you, but I'm not sure what I said cuz he made me so irritated creeping up like that. He asked me what book I was studying so hard and I showed him. It's about medications and he's really interested in that. He hovered over me to look and asked me if I had any of those meds and did I like to get high. High? Seriously? We've talked about this before and he knows I'm not that type. I looked up at him like he was crazy and he laughed and said he was joking—not to take him so seriously. And then he dropped the subject and started flirting again—telling me how cute I was and how if I wanted to go for a drive, he'd find a car and we could go driving around. I smiled and said no...that Dad was waiting for me, and got out of the door before he could get in my way.

I don't know what's wrong with me! Why can't I flirt back like I used to? He didn't say anything out of the ordinary—just normal talk, but something's just not right with us anymore. And I don't like being pushed!

So what do I do? Am I just being over sensitive? I don't think so, but I truly don't know if I'm being an idiot or not. Ashleigh can flirt without any problems, and I'm a total dork! But I think it's him, and not me. I don't like <u>his</u> flirting. I think I'd be fine if I liked him better. I used to like to flirt with him, and it was exciting, but I'm just not feeling it anymore. But I'll obviously have to handle this on my own. And I'll make sure not to study in the school room alone anymore.

But it's probably just me being a dork! I'll see what Ashleigh says.

Your favorite daughter
Meg

May 15

Hey you,

    I took the little kids riding today. Tricia helped me. It was awesome! Adam's been asking and asking to ride the 'horsey' and Ava is big enough now. They rode in the saddle with us, of course, and we only trotted around a bit, but I swear you should've seen the big smile on Adam's face! He said he was an actual cowboy now! Lol! I love those kids. I'm really glad they ended up with us. I can't even imagine what would've happened if they'd wandered off in a different direction and Dad hadn't found them. Some things are truly meant to be.

    Everybody's been so busy with spring planting and working. We haven't had a community activity in like a month or something! Everyone's doing their own thing. Even when we have time in the evening, we're too tired to chat and we have to get up early anyway, so we all go to bed early. It seems like this is the cycle...work hard when the weather is nice and then rest when the earth rests in the winter. It was nice to have a little social time today with Tricia and the kids though.

    I saw Meg again today and I don't know if it was because she was busy or distracted, but something seemed...off. We talked yesterday about her feeling weird around Luke and I told her she needs to trust her gut. I didn't trust mine with Jason and look where it got me! I told her it was okay to go slow and he should respect that (seriously...I kinda sounded like my parents...yikes!) I even made a joke about how I could have a talk with him and tell him to back off! We laughed, but she got quiet at the end. Maybe she's mad at me for saying to dump him??? I'll try to catch up with her again during lunchtime. I hope Luke doesn't hurt her...Stupid men. Always causing angst!

Fresh floral air and tired brain,
Ashleigh

May 18

Dear Mom,

Life is too complicated. And scary. I wish I weren't grown up—I want to be a little kid again, having other people to watch out for me. I told you I don't know what to do about Luke—that I wanted him to back off. But he found me alone at home yesterday and asked me <u>again</u> if I liked to get high. I told him <u>again</u> I didn't do that—never did. I felt like a <u>total</u> goody two-shoes cuz I've never even tried drugs and he made me feel like I was weird. He usually drops the drug conversation, but this time he kept on, trying to make me feel like I should at least try stuff cuz a lot of drugs that make you feel good are medicines—and they can't harm you if taken properly. He said even alcohol was good if used properly—not like Jason's doing, but a couple of glasses of wine or some beer isn't that big a deal. Doctors even tell patients that they should have a glass of red wine in the evening. He promised he'd be with me if I wanted to try anything and wouldn't let me get hurt or too high or anything. And then he brought up again that he knew I had the drugs for the community cuz Jason told him I did and he'd really like to have some. He'd be "cool with them" (his words) and wouldn't get all stupid or whatever. Besides, he said, now that Clarence is gone, there wouldn't be any problems. Clarence wouldn't have been able to handle access to all types of drugs, but he could. Then he made a joke about it's easier to make people do what you want after you slip 'em drugs! Seriously!!??

I told him I couldn't give him any. That we didn't have anything he wanted anyway. All the stuff he wanted had all been stolen before we gathered all the meds up. He got this angry look on his face and said he didn't believe me, that I could tell

339

that story all I wanted, but Jason had told him different--that he knew the truth. In fact Jason had told him where the drugs were hidden and they weren't there anymore, cuz he'd looked. I told him I had no idea what he was talking about and he said that I did. Then it was like he realized he was getting too angry so he laughed and said, "Hey, don't worry about it, Babe. I'll let you think about it and you'll see I'm right. But no big deal. If you don't want to, you don't want to." And he sauntered off.

I talked to Dad about it after supper and he said, "Don't worry about it. I think he was trying you out and you stayed firm on your "No" so you should be good. He's learned you can't be easily swayed. He seems to be okay and is working hard. But he's a young man and will try to see how far he can get. You <u>do</u> know you can stop him, don't you? Well...I know you can handle yourself and do what you need to do." And then he looked embarrassed and I was mortified and we stopped the conversation. Good grief! I didn't want to talk to Dad about sex!!! Just about the drugs!

I talked to Ashleigh about it too. She's waaay easier to talk to about boys. And she said the same thing Dad did about standing firm. And she agrees with me that it's weird he's pushing harder about drugs lately. But I guess it'd make sense. He wouldn't ask early in our friendship as he wouldn't know how I'd react. And now since we've been more than friends, it's easier for him. But I'm not going on walks with him anymore. I don't want him to keep asking and when he got angry yesterday, he looked scary. I don't want to be alone with him when he's angry. And it makes me mad that Jason told Luke where the meds were and that he went to find them. He knows our community rules!! I'm glad Dad and I moved them!

340

Well, I think I can handle this. I'm an adult now and have to handle this like one. I just have to stand my ground and not worry about looking like a total idiot.

Your favorite daughter

Meg

May 19

Dear Mandy,

What's up with Luke? He's been asking me all these random questions lately about our meeting minutes... I must've looked really confused because he said he knew I was the official record keeper for the town and he was wondering how things started here, where all the supplies went, stuff like that. He's asked weird stuff before, but today he just seemed more...I don't know...intense I guess. Meg says he keeps asking for drugs and now he's looking at the meeting minutes and asking me?! What the hell? The last thing we need is a junky in town! We already have a drunk! I kinda thought I should mention it to Mom or Dad, but they're so busy with everything and I really don't have any proof besides just awkward feelings and random questions....so I don't know.

I told Meg about it and she said the last time her and Luke were together they had a big fight and things ended awkward. She was really starting to like him and now it's like this other side of him is coming out...and it's ugly! I told her I was glad she stood up to him, but I was sorry he was being all weird. It's like he's got it in his head now that he needs drugs. First it was guns...now drugs. Why? And why all of a sudden?

I told her to protect herself and remember I'll always be here for her. We have to stick together. I may have been stupid about all the Jason stuff, but this community is bigger than that. We are strong together. Nobody better threaten that.

Puddles of mud, but fierce heart,
Ashleigh

May 21

Dear Mom,

Oh crap! I'm really tired of this whole thing—Luke wanting to be extra friendly to me, and everyone else thinking he's Mr. Wonderful!, and then him asking me for drugs every time he sees me. It's beyond awkward—it gotten to be unnerving and irritating and I don't know what to do. He gets more insistent every time we talk and he has less patience with me every time we're alone. Around Dad or anyone else, he's all friendly and smooth and you'd think he walked on water with the parents. He's so two-faced!!! And you know what? I HATE when he calls me Babe. I'm not his Babe. I'm no one's baby—except yours and Dad's. It's like he thinks if he calls me Babe then it'll make us closer. Well, it ain't workin cuz it's driving me crazy and makes me not like him at all. And I don't really know what he'll do when I keep saying no cuz he gets angrier each time I say no.

Yesterday evening he caught me in the kitchen making supper again. He props himself against the kitchen counter right where I'm working and I have to walk past him...yuck! He knows our schedule and what evening I'll be cooking so he shows up cuz he knows Dad and Mitchell are out. He asked me again and I told him <u>again</u> that we don't have any of the drugs he wants and Jason was wrong about us having more meds. He said in a quiet angry tone that Jason isn't wrong and he asked Jason again this morning what we had--that Jason didn't know exactly what was stashed but we did hide the "good stuff". I told Luke to ask Dad where the drugs were if he if wanted them that bad and he backed off a bit.

"Hey Babe. I'm not upset. I just don't like being lied to.

343

And you know I'm not going to ask the old fogies.... They'd just get the wrong idea. But with you, you're young, you should understand. You know, I just don't get it. You're a cool girl. I don't know why you're so hung up on sharing what you got. We wouldn't use all the dope and your Dad wouldn't even know it was missing. You could cover anyway. But maybe you just want it all for yourself, which isn't really fair. Is that what it is? You're not sharing? You want it all for yourself? You just want to be in control of the drugs because whoever controls those...controls everything.''

I just shook my head in disgust and walked out of the kitchen and down the street to make sure I wasn't alone with him. Really?! I'm shooting up in some old house somewhere getting high and not sharing!? How stupid it that?

I don't know. I've not told Ashleigh all this cuz I don't want her as depressed and anxious about this as I am. But she knows I'm upset and she knows Luke is asking for the drugs. But where is this going? I keep saying no and he keeps saying I'll give in to him eventually. To me this is a matter of keeping our community safe and drug free—protecting our extended family. We're supposed to protect each other. I must admit I'm disappointed in Dad, not taking me more seriously. I guess I should tell him all the times Luke's been bugging me, but part of me thinks I should be handling this on my own—that it's my problem, I'm a grown up now. The worried part of me that actually did tell Dad about all this didn't get the reaction I wanted—which should've been, "What! He's asking for drugs! Let's kick his butt out of our community and tell him he's not wanted! We'll make sure he leaves and we'll defend our honor and our homes with guns blazing!'' When I think things out like that, it seems rather silly to make a big deal about it cuz what can we do anyway...tell him to leave? What if he says no? Then what? How do we make someone leave? So I just keep hoping he'll give up and stop asking or go away and look for drugs in another town with some other people. That he'll disappear like Clarence did. That'd be the best thing—for him to just go away.

So it's turned into a standoff and one of us has to win. I plan on winning, but I don't know the rules of the game.

Your favorite daughter
Meg

May 22

Dear Mandy,

OMG. Luke needs to back off! He keeps asking Meg for drugs...even though she's said NO like a million times! What's his problem??!! Is he in withdrawal or something?? Did he take drugs before he got here? If he's so obsessed with getting high he should just move away, and LEAVE MY FRIEND ALONE!! I tried to talk to Mom and Dad about it, but of course they thought I was overreacting. "Really Ashleigh? Luke is not a drug addict. He works hard and is a good helper and honestly, we are not going to go around and start checking on people in their private time. Don't start spreading rumors about good people." Then they started saying how they couldn't believe I was so worried about Luke now, but apparently Jason's drinking didn't bother me. Grrr...Seriously??!!! Dad's just being selfish because he doesn't want to lose a worker! Once again, we're supposed to have equal say in community stuff, but when we bring up a really serious issue, they pull rank and we're just "little kids" making stuff up. Aaarrgg!! Ticks me off!

I hope Meg has better luck talking to Sam. Maybe he'll actually listen. We can't trust Luke anymore. He definitely has hidden motives...he's creeping me out AND totally pissing me off for bullying Meg. Isn't that what we always learned??? We're supposed to stand up to bullies??!! AAAAAND wasn't it my DAD that said it was SOOOO important for us to stick together and fight for our community now?? Wasn't HE the one that said if our house is threatened we have to protect it??!!! Because we can't afford to lose anyone so precious??!! HIS words! So why is he not listening to me when I am telling him someone is threatening our home? You know what? I don't care what they think. Luke IS dangerous! I'm keeping my eye on him and I'll be ready if I need to be.

Clouds brewing and angry,
Ashleigh

May 24

Mommy,

I am so scared. I have to give the drugs to Luke. I have to. I don't see how I can get out of it. He found me again making supper. Just came walking in. Dad and Mitchell were in the house, but in the living room playing a game. He was smiling so if Dad saw him it'd look like we were just talking, but in a low voice he told me I needed to show him where the drugs are. I said no. He turned so Dad couldn't see his face and his eyes got really cold. He said,

"Listen, we've played this game long enough. I don't like it when I'm told no. I don't tolerate that in anyone. Ever thought about where Clarence is? Ever wondered about that? Where he went? You should wonder. Just an fyi, he never made it to North Carolina. He's just a little ways out of town. You see, <u>he</u> didn't do as I asked, and now no one will find him. And what's sad is it was all his fault. All I asked him to do was to share the things we were collecting, and then I found out he was holding out on me. We had a deal. And he was supposed to share. He didn't and he suffered the consequences of his actions. And now you're not sharing with me. I don't like that.

"Look Babe, don't think you can get away from me or tell anyone about this conversation because I'll deny it and by the time you can convince anyone you're telling the truth, some of your little girls will be missing. And don't think I won't do it. Remember when your precious little Ava was missing? She didn't wander off alone you know. I helped her disappear just to prove that I could do it. It was easy. But I think I might find Tricia next time instead. She's a cute little thing and would be more fun. 14 isn't she?"
And he smiled.

He makes me shiver with fear and disgust. Mom, he's really scary.

I'm supposed to give him access to all the drugs, and he said he'd leave our community. But he smiled at me with this slimy smile and said, then again maybe he wouldn't leave—that there were pretty young girls here and he wouldn't know who'd be available in other towns. He said if I told anyone what he said, he'd kill as many people as he could before they got him. Did I want to be responsible for the "deaths of your sweet little family of survivors? Right now I could shoot your brother and father right where they sit." He showed me a pistol under his shirt. I stood there paralyzed.

"But," he said, "if you play nice, you and I can rule this town and do what we want and have all the power we want and all the money we want. How would you like to be my queen?" He smiled at me. "I think we'd make a pretty good couple, don't you?" A cold chill ran through my whole body.

Thank goodness Dad called from the other room about supper. Luke's expression changed, the coldness left his eyes, and he smiled at me, winked, and said in a quiet voice, "I'll see you later. Think about it. You'd be a pretty queen. But don't forget. I don't tolerate people not giving me what I ask for. And don't tell anyone what we've talked about. I know where Trish is. I'm keeping an eye on her. Well, Babe, what happens to all your people is up to you. Be sure to make the right choice." And then he left.

Now I know the rules of the game. I have to think of a plan. I can't let this go on. I have to think of a plan. I have to.

I miss you so much.

Meg

May 25

Dear Mandy,

     Meg has completely shut down. I have no idea what's going on with her, but she is refusing to talk to me!!! I keep asking her what's wrong and she keeps saying "I can't tell you!" When I went over the other night to drop off that extra lettuce we had, I saw Luke and her in a pretty intense conversation. Luke's eyes were narrowed and even though I couldn't hear what he was saying, he was leaning over her and I could tell he was mad. Meg looked angry and then terrified. Then Luke turned around and headed for the door, so I ducked behind the house before he saw me. He was laughing quietly to himself, but his face was hard and mean. I ran right in after he was out of sight and asked Meg what was going on, but she refused to tell me. She just made me promise to make sure me, the kids, and Tricia weren't going off by themselves. She looked so desperate! Something is wrong!!

     Luke is TOTALLY a two-faced liar and a thug. Why didn't KPox kill HIM??? What if HE'S the psychopath outsider we've always been afraid of and we just let him in? Way to go Jason! Idiot...

     The air feels funny...like something's coming or something's hanging over us....like when the sickness came. But it can't be that again. I feel like we need to prepare for battle, but I don't know why or how. Maybe Clarence is bringing people back to raid our town! We're all trained to defend ourselves so we could fight, but against what? War? Greed? Power? Evil?

     I think people have the ability to do anything they need to do, right? We have all shown that in surviving. But we just have to figure out what things to bring out...what things we want to define us, right? I know for me, I choose good. I choose this community and no matter what, I'm going to protect us and fight for what is right. We can't be afraid! We've already had too much fear. I'm scared, but determined! Even if I can't rely

349

on my parents for help, I am going to do something to protect our home. WE are the survivors!!!! We are the meek war horses that stand in the storm!!!

I'm not going to let Meg out of my sight. I'm going to help protect my friends and family. NO ONE is going to tear this community apart!!!

Determined,
Ashleigh

May 25

Mom,

He's given me til tomorrow. I have to meet him out at Noni and Kenneth's old house at 6 tomorrow morning. He doesn't want anyone to know I'm meeting him so he wants the meeting early. If I don't bring the first installment of drugs, he said he'll take Trish or Ava. He laughed when he said that. He's so horrible! It's quiet and isolated out there. He said not to tell anyone but I want to tell someone! But I'm so afraid that he'll hurt one of us if I do. We don't have jails or places to keep him locked up. So what do we do if he is caught? Keep him forever? Where? Chances are he could break out and then what?? And if I tell on him and one of the parents goes to get him so we can lock him up, he'll know something is wrong and would shoot them. He has at least 2 guns on him at all times—that I know of. And a knife. And he probably has more weapons now—just in case I tell Dad. Or he could take someone hostage and then hurt us and get the drugs anyway. I don't see how this is going to work. I really don't. I know that Dad would want me to tell him. But I'm afraid that Luke would kill him or Mitchell or anyone else. I can't have that on my conscience! I just can't!! Oh Mom! This is so scary. Maybe I just shouldn't go tomorrow and tell on him and see what happens. I don't know.

Later—Mom, I've been thinking and decided that I will meet him, but I have a plan to fix things. Well, maybe not fix things but will make them better for us. And I have alternatives in case things go wrong. I've tried to think of all worst-case scenarios and I know I can go through with all of them. I've played them all through in my mind over and over again, and

351

will have steady nerves and not show that I'm scared. I am scared though, but I know what I have to do. This is for our survival and we can't let someone evil take everything we have worked so hard for. I will defend our home. I love you Mom. I really do. And I love my whole big extended family. Please be proud of me. Please don't hate me.

Your favorite daughter
Meg

Mom,

We killed a man. Please forgive us.

I love you.
Your Meg

To Whom it May Concern:

On May 26th, we, the undersigned, Meg Shultz and Ashleigh Grace, do hereby confess to the death of Luke Boden. This necessary action was taken to protect and safeguard the lives of the people of Laurel. Below is an accurate description of the events as they took place.

Luke demanded our supply of medical drugs and threatened to kill members of the community if he didn't get what he asked for. He specifically targeted and threatened the lives of Tricia Kinsey, Ava Grace, and Mitchell and Sam Shultz. He said he would kill anyone who stood in the way of him getting what he wanted, which included drugs, guns, and ammo. He confessed to the murder of Clarence Dyer because he said Clarence was not sharing what they'd been gathering (stealing) from homes. He also kidnapped Ava during a community event by leading her away from her family and into the woods to show he could harm anyone at any time and no one would know. He threatened to harm her again if he wasn't given the drugs.

Luke told Meg to meet him at the old Oswald house to deliver the first installment. He said he wanted distance and privacy so there'd be no witnesses and he wanted to have a little fun before he let her go back to town. Meg arrived early, with rifle and silencer ready. Ashleigh had seen the strained conversation the night before and snuck out of her house in the middle of the night to stand guard over Meg. She waited outside Meg's house and followed her when she saw Meg leave, carrying her rifle. Ashleigh was carrying her hunting rifle for protection and hid in the side yard at Noni's house, behind the bushes to Meg's left, so she could hear everything and help Meg if Luke got violent.

Luke looked surprised to see Meg already standing on the porch with her rifle at her side when he sauntered through the front gate.

"Nice to see you here so early. Looking forward to seeing me? Where are the drugs, Meggie? You did bring them, right?"

"I didn't bring them. I never will. And you will <u>never</u> find them. You will also never hurt anyone in this community. I have a video camera set up and I'm recording everything. You are not welcome here anymore! Leave quietly and we'll tell everyone you left me a note saying you were going to find Clarence. But try and stay and I'll show the video to everyone so they will know what a snake you are. You can never come back. Leave now!!! Leave now and never come back!" Meg really hoped this would be enough to convince him to go. But she didn't think he would so she had her rifle, prepared for the worst.

Luke laughed. "Seriously?! You want to play this little game? Oh, I am SO heading right back to town to find Trish. You want that to happen? Guess you don't like little Trish too much. But I'll like her enough for both of us." He turned to his left as he moved back to the gate. Meg sighted her rifle. "I mean it! Leave and don't come back!" Her warning shot kicked up dust near his boots. His face contorted into this mask of rage and his eyes glittered with fury as he spun around on his heel. Ashleigh had never seen him look like that before. She crept closer to where Meg and Luke were standing.

"You'll never stop me you pathetic bitch," Luke's voice sounded like the growl the dogs made when they were getting ready to fight. "I'll poison whoever I want, kill whoever I want, and I'll still find the drugs and all the guns you stupid backwater rednecks have hidden. Then this town will be a nothing but a bunch of dead bodies rotting in the sun! All because you didn't want to share. All because you can't see the vision!!!" Spittle shot from his mouth as Luke snarled, "I'll rain down terror on this town that will make K-Pox look like a happy dream."

"I said LEAVE! I mean it!"

Luke took another step closer to the porch with an evil grin on his face.

"Don't make me shoot you! I WILL shoot you." Meg's voice was low and determined, but Ashleigh could see Meg's hands trembling as she pointed her rifle at Luke's heart.

Luke laughed again. "Go ahead Babe! I bet you won't!

355

You're afraid to kill anything. You won't even kill a deer! Or a little bunny! And I'm going to be much harder to shoot than a deer! So if you can't shoot an animal, how are you going to kill a man? And I shoot back! And I don't miss..." He slowly raised his pistol and pointed the barrel at Meg, laughter still in his eyes.

Ashleigh had been waiting to see if Luke would agree to leave, but when she saw Luke level his pistol at Meg, she jumped out of the bushes, raised her rifle and yelled, "Meg's not the only one who will shoot your ass!" Surprised, Luke jerked his head to his right and shot wildly in Ashleigh's direction multiple times. She and Meg both fired their guns once, the silencers deadening the sounds as the early morning sun crept up the pale blue sky. Luke fell and didn't get up. He choked once as the spread of crimson blood soaked his shirt...then he was silent and still.

Meg and Ashleigh hesitated for a moment, exchanging shocked glances over what they had done. Then they both moved slowly towards Luke.

"Wait!!" Ashleigh cried out. "Don't get too close! He might still be alive and try to shoot you!" But Meg drew closer to make sure he was dead. She could see Luke was not breathing and kicked Luke's pistol away from him. She knelt down slowly and took his pulse though the damage to his body and the huge amount of blood told them both he was dead. Ashleigh came closer with her rifle still raised. "I don't feel a pulse." Meg told Ashleigh. "He's dead."

Luke sustained gunshot wounds in the chest and neck, but since both Ashleigh and Meg used their hunting rifles, it was impossible to tell who hit him where. Both were fatal shots. There was so much blood.

There was nothing we could do to save him. We found Noni's shovel in her garden shed and we buried him in the woods, hiding his grave with fallen timber. We held hands and Ashleigh said a short prayer for his soul and asked for God's forgiveness.

Luke's death was not our intention. We only wanted to

make him leave us in peace. Yet after he refused and showed us he was capable of even more murders...We feel his death saved our lives and was necessary for the well-being of this community. We stand by our decision to fire our rifles with the intent of self-protection.

We have chosen to not divulge this death to our parents or other community members at this time. We feel it would cause undue stress and grief to parents with misunderstandings that we could never explain away. We write this document with heavy hearts and the understanding that one day we may be called upon to justify our actions. We stand together.

Meekly strong, passionately determined, and forever dedicated to the town of Laurel and its survivors,

Margaret Shultz   Ashleigh Grace

Discussion Questions

What would you miss the most if you lost your whole community? Would it be the people or the technology and why?

What would you enjoy about living without modern technology?

What job or role would you want to have if your community had to start again. Why?

After facing the challenges of the Covid pandemic of 2020, do you better understand why Jason acts the way he does or do you think he is overreacting?

How would you deal with people who deviated from the rules in your community? What would be your priorities if you had to set up a system of order? What types of consequences would there be for small infractions to behaviors that threaten others?

How did Ashleigh's and Meg's belief systems help them cope with the extreme circumstances they had to endure? How would your belief system help you deal with this situation?

At the end of the story, do you think that there was another option for Meg and Ashleigh? Should they have told their parents even though the consequences could have been deadly?

Acknowledgements

We could not have done this book without the help and support of our friends and family and we can't thank you enough. Rebecca Dussault has been unstinting of her time and patience throughout this process. She was our first beta reader and went through the initial rough draft of the book and made copious notes for us to review. We made huge amounts of changes at her suggestions, all of which made the book better. And at the end she helped us with formatting and editing. Also a great deal of thanks to Sandy Theile and her quick editing on our polished draft. We appreciate her keen eyes and attention to detail. We would also like to thank our other beta readers Amelia Rakestraw, Cassandra Weidman, and Richard Siira. Everyone helped get this book to the point where it was ready to publish.

Any mistakes belong to us and not to the people who graciously donated their time and effort to our project.

Thank you Julia. There aren't too many people who will jump on board and agree to coauthor a book just because a good idea was mentioned at lunch one day. Without your friendship, enthusiasm, ideas and determination to go on this journey with me this book would not have been written.

Thank you Cindy. I have enjoyed all the moments we sat together brainstorming and exclaiming, "Oooh! What about THIS?" My heart is full knowing our work will finally be shared with others to enjoy. We would not be in this moment without your dedication, energy, laughter, and incredible spirit. I am honored to write with you and delighted to call you my friend.

About the Authors

Cynthia Siira has always loved writing and has written numerous short stories, song parodies, and poetry. She also has several unpublished books including a memoir about growing up in Libya which she is planning to publish soon. She has book reviews published in The American School Board Journal and an article in The Virginia Journal of Education. Cynthia is a retired high school/middle school teacher with a Ph.D. in Special Education from the University of Virginia. A keen interest in art has Cynthia pursuing textile art design and exhibiting her work throughout the state.

Julia White, is a passionate storyteller and writer, and has a deep love of sharing the gift of words with others. She has published five Advent devotionals and enjoys embracing the world through a variety of imaginative lenses. Outside of writing, Julia enjoys creating art, cycling, and working with and supporting others. She is a Licensed Clinical Professional Counselor, a Certified Rehabilitative Counselor, and has a M.S. in Criminal Justice from Illinois State University.

Cindy and Julia both chose to counsel and support teens and young adults in their move towards adulthood, enjoying their varied personalities. Together, their work has given them an in-depth look at social and family interpersonal dynamics. Their experiences also gave them unique perspectives when creating these realistic and engaging characters and the world in which they live.

Check out our Facebook and author pages for exciting updates and events!

Julia Website:
https://sites.google.com/view/jcwhitewrites/home?authuser=0

Julia Facebook: https://www.facebook.com/jcwhitewrites

Julia Twitter and Instagram: jcwhitewrites

Cynthia Facebook: https://www.facebook.com/The-Meek-Shall-Inherit-117286506853251

Before you go we would love to receive your reviews on Amazon and Goodreads!

Coming December 2021!

The Meek Shall Inherit series continues in Book 2...

Battling the chaos of a world devastated by K-Pox, Theresa is desperately trying to get home to her family in Laurel. In her hunt for supplies, she meets Tim, an 18 year old whose parents disappeared while searching for his grandparents. Their journey across the country brings them face-to-face with other struggling survivors, but none as unexpected as Amber, a young, pregnant teen who is due almost any day.